ROGUE'S REGATTA

Also by Thomas Gately Briody

Rogue's Isles
Rogue's Justice
Rogue's Wager

ROGUE'S REGATTA

THOMAS GATELY BRIODY

THOMAS DUNNE BOOKS
ST. MARTIN'S MINOTAUR
New York

DISCLAIMER: As always, this is a work of fiction, and certain slight liberties have been taken with locations and events for the sake of dramatic presentation. As for characters, any resemblance to real people, living or dead, drunk or sober, blessed or damned, is entirely coincidental and, what's more, unintended.

THOMAS DUNNE BOOKS.
An imprint of St. Martin's Press.

Library of Congress Cataloging-in-Publication Data

Briody, Thomas Gately.
    Rogue's regatta : a Michael Carolina mystery / Thomas Gately Briody. – 1st ed.
        p.   cm.
    ISBN 0-312-24235-2
    I. Title.
    PS3552.R4886R646 1999
    813'.54–dc21   99-26654
                                                              CIP

First St. Martin's Minotaur Edition: November 1999

10 9 8 7 6 5 4 3 2 1

To Ernie, Doc, Shorty, and Karen,
my four best friends.
And to Tory and Alex,
my two best girls.

ACKNOWLEDGMENTS

My thanks to . . . Brenda and Charlie, two great proofreaders . . . Richard Feeny, Brown University's sailing coach, who shared invaluable knowledge about racing boats . . . Nik Arnegren, who is destined to achieve great things, and Tom Dunne, who already has.

ROGUE'S REGATTA

His name was Hunter Worthington, he was nineteen years old, and he didn't know it would be his last race.

Nor did he know if he would win, nor whether the wind would shift, nor, most important, whether the sonofabitch coming from the port side was going to yield right-of-way. What Hunter Worthington did know was that his legs were screaming from the pain of hiking out, as he tried to hold starboard tack for another fifty yards. And he knew that he would sooner collide and lose than tack and lose.

The Laser strained beneath him, the tiny sail fighting for release from the pressure of a wind that was gusting to twenty-five knots. But Hunter kept pushing it back, back, back down again, using all of his 180-pound frame to hold the slender white fiberglass hull flat against the rushing waves. His fist kept the mainsheet taut, enough to make his fingers white, then red, then purple, as he held the sail flat against the wind.

Hunter loved the Laser, with its tiny body and single sail marked with the red beam and splashing dot. His old man had told him that Solings and 470s were more "classic," that it would be easier to take a shot at the Olympics in one of the more established racing classes. That was the old man, all right: a total misfit, always looking for a way to fit in. Hell with him. Hunter stayed with the boat he loved, stayed with the tiny cockpit and the salty sting in his eyes and the cold wetness biting into his hands where the mainsheet sometimes nearly burned his skin raw. The Laser was as good as it got, as close to surfing as you could get without actually standing up on a board. And maybe he'd make the Olympics anyway, fuckin' A.

The guy coming up from port was twenty feet away now, with no sign of backing off.

"Starboard!" Hunter screamed, his voice hoarse from the salt. The boat kept coming.

By the rules, he should give way. When it looks like a collision, do everything possible to avoid one. So what if the guy didn't know what he was doing, if he had the wrong tack. Better to come about and avoid it all, better to bring a protest than have two broken boats and possibly two broken sailors.

But this was the last leg, and the winner would be champion. U.S. champion. With a path clear for the team that would compete in Sydney. So the rules could go down the shitter, as far as Hunter was concerned.

"Starboard!"

The sailor on the other boat was twenty-two, from a club on Long Island Sound. Westport. Mercer was his name, the son of a moneyman on Wall Street. He didn't like Hunter. Didn't like to lose. Fifteen feet.

"Staaarrboard, motherfucker!" Ten. Hunter held course. The other kid kept coming. Hunter shouted again. "Come on, I wanna feel the crunch!"

Eight feet. Five. Hunter wanted to close his eyes, but he could not. This was what it was all about. Playing chicken on the water, waiting to see who'd shake first.

And then the kid blinked. Jammed his tiller away and scrambled underneath the swinging boom on his own Laser while Hunter skated past, still holding course, maybe half a length higher on the leg, but that just might be enough.

"Thanks, baby," Hunter laughed.

Mercer glared, but said nothing.

He waited until they both were on the same tack, both starboard now. Then Hunter tacked again. He'd done it at least a thousand times in the past three years, and the moves came so naturally it was almost like climbing a set of stairs or down-shifting with a stick: slam the tiller away, feel the hull slide, yank the sheet line across as you duck under the boom and the nose of the little boat finds its way across the nose of the wind. Then straighten out the tiller and let the wind fill the sail once more, all in one fluid motion.

The move was perfect. It had to be, for one mistake would have again meant collision, only this time with Hunter at fault. That would have meant disqualification, and goodbye to a shot at Sydney. But there was no problem. The boats missed by inches yet again, with Hunter adding another precious second to his lead.

They had been dueling that way all afternoon. Now, with the wind picking up, they were less than a hundred yards from the final mark. Over his left shoulder Hunter could see the committee boat poised, filled with observers from the Ida Lewis, Newport, and even New York yacht clubs, all of them gathered to watch some of the best sailors in the country compete. Behind them was a press boat, filled with still and video cameras, and a few reporters trying not to be seasick.

And there, anchored perhaps fifty yards upwind of them all, was the Hinckley picnic boat named *Chardonnay*.

It was a magnificent little launch, made by one of the finest yacht builders in Maine and loaded with teak and polished brass. The boat was useful only for day trips, as it lacked overnight accommodations. Still, its price ran well into six figures, which made the boat hideously extravagant for all but the exceptionally wealthy. Which, of course, *Chardonnay*'s owner certainly was.

He was a middle-aged fellow, and he stood in the stern of the boat while three minions worked to give him food and drink and keep the boat in position. He wore a blazer and shorts and one of those captain's hats, ridiculous even by Newport standards. The white cap reminded Hunter of something Thurston Howell III wore on the old episodes of *Gilligan's Island*. He carried a bottle of something in one hand and a glass in the other. Champagne, had to be. As Hunter pushed the Laser toward the imaginary line that would mark the race's end, he saw the glass rise toward him in a silent toast.

The old man. Jesus, it was embarrassing.

The Laser shot between the triangular orange buoy and the committee boat, and Hunter heard the shriek of an air horn, signaling that the race officials had recognized his victory. On a loudspeaker came the garbled words of the timekeeper, announcing how long it had taken him to cover the course. But he didn't hear the words. Instead he focused on the people in the committee boat, who were pointing toward the elegant little Hinckley named *Chardonnay*. Toward the man in the white captain's hat.

And laughing.

The press boat rolled again, and the photographers all grabbed for the rail. The seas had been building for the last hour, until the waves had grown to four or five feet and the press crew had been knocked about like flies in a jar.

A rogue wave slammed into the stern of the boat and doused the bunch of them in spray.

"Hope this doesn't put salt in my lens," Earl Taylor groused.

Michael Carolina smiled. The boat's pitch and roll was oddly comforting, and he liked the cool feel of the salt water on his brow.

"Come on," he said. "It's what you live for."

Earl threw him a strange look. "What I live for is a glass of Alka-Seltzer."

Channel Three's senior videographer was sixty-two, slimly built, with hair closer to silver than gray. He pursed his lips and stared out at the Lasers flying past.

"Don't tell me," Carolina said. Earl nodded.

"You try looking through a viewfinder on a rolling boat for three hours," he replied.

"Another Nelson, that's what you are," Carolina smiled.

Earl blinked. "Another who?"

"Lord Nelson, the admiral. Father of the British navy."

"No shit? And he puked?"

"Used to carry a bucket next to him on deck."

"Staaarrboard, motherfucker!" The words of the skipper on the leading Laser carried well. One of the other photographers laughed as the boats nearly collided, one of them tacking just before impact.

The reporter next to Carolina wrote for one of the sailing magazines. The presence of all the local news photographers was obviously annoying him.

"That Worthington," he said, shaking his head in admiration.

"Who, the kid in the lead boat?" Carolina asked.

The sailing writer sniffed, doing nothing to mask his disdain. "You don't know him? He's a top contender. Kid's got balls big enough for the cannon at Fort Adams."

"Is that right?"

"Yes. You know, it wouldn't hurt for you TV types to do a little research on the people you cover," the sailing writer said. "Worthington sails like some guys play hockey. Tough as nails." He scribbled something in his notes, chuckling. " 'Starboard, motherfucker.' Sure as hell ain't like when the cup was here. You new to Rhode Island?"

"Fairly," Carolina said.

"My magazine is based here," the writer said. "But I travel a lot. Never seen you before. Don't watch much television," he sniffed. "And I never watch local news."

"That's all right," Carolina said. "I don't read too many sailing magazines."

"You ever tried it?" the writer asked, a snide look on his face. "Sailing, I mean."

"Oh, a little here and there." Carolina smiled again, and

made his way forward on the boat. "I'll see how long till we get in," he said to Earl. The photographer was now turning green, but he couldn't stop himself from smirking. The sailing writer noticed.

"I say something funny?"

"Oh, yes," Earl said. "What's the farthest you've ever sailed?"

The sailing writer swelled with pride. "Lots of club racing," he said. "And I did the Marion–Bermuda last year."

"And what's the biggest boat you've ever sailed by yourself?"

"Single-handed?" The writer sniffed again. "Nineteen feet."

"Yeah? Well, the guy you just insulted there, that's Michael Carolina. He used to be a charter boat captain. He sailed all over the Caribbean, and then up the coast before he gave it up. Then he sailed another boat all the way to Tahiti. Forty-footer. All alone. Or, uh, as you put it, single-handed."

The writer's face reddened, but he did not apologize.

"Am I supposed to be impressed? My point is that you people–" He pointed at the other local news crews. "You people don't cover this on a regular basis. It's just a feature story for you. And most of you know nothing about what you cover."

"Oh, I know something," said Earl, his face greener than ever. "I know about Nelson."

"Nelson?" The sailing writer wore a pained expression. "Who? Lord Nelson?"

"The one and only. He couldn't hold it, you know."

"Hold what?"

"His lunch."

The sound of the waves was masked then, by the sound of the sailing writer's shrieks and Earl retching enthusiastically on his docksiders.

The spectators gathered at the piers and pilings near Goat Island were oblivious to the stiffening breeze. Instead they pressed forward, a mass of photographers and sailors and relatives, friends and girlfriends, all straining for a glimpse of the Lasers as they glided along the channel.

The press boat had tied up moments earlier. Carolina and Earl scrambled off, ignoring the glares of the sailing writer as he doused his shoes in salt water.

"How you feeling?" Michael asked.

"Much better." Earl stifled a belch. "You know how when you puke, you feel so relieved?"

"Glad to hear it."

They picked their way through the crowd, anxious for a shot of the winner and a quick interview. It was already four-thirty and the station would expect the tape by six.

"Shirley need us live?" Earl wondered aloud.

"Absolutely," Carolina said. He pushed a hand through his hair, now thick and slightly damp from the salt and spray. "Live intro and then wrap around a package." This was the phrase describing the segment of a newscast that included a reporter "live" in the field, who introduced a pretaped report, and then returned live to finish the piece with a "tag," a few concluding remarks. At one time such a report was a luxury, reserved only for breaking news events. By the late nineties, however, such appearances had become commonplace, even when the news event had been over for hours.

Carolina was used to the pressure, the rhythm that accompanied gathering a television piece. He'd done it so many times—hundreds, even thousands of stories—that it was almost like riding a bike, or maybe even tacking a sloop. Together he and Earl watched as the boats began to appear at dockside. The crowd of people cheered and laughed, one or two of them falling into the water, victims of either celebration or inebriation.

"Where's that Worthington kid?" Carolina asked.

Earl shrugged, rolling off more video. "Haven't seen him since we got in. He isn't on the dock."

The other reporters had not yet noticed that the champion had failed to arrive. Carolina checked his watch again. Four thirty-five. Time was slipping by. Shirley Templeton, Channel Three's longtime news director, would be expecting a sound bite from the winner.

Apart from the crowd at the pier, the docks were fairly empty of people. It was a weekday in early September, which meant kids were back in school, and most parents were at work. All that remained were long lines of sail and powerboats, tethered to the pilings, bobbing gently as the sun began its slow fade.

It took a minute before Carolina spotted it, the Hinckley picnic boat that he'd seen anchored near the race's finish. The name, *Chardonnay,* seemed tacky, but was not as bad as many others he'd encountered. But the boat itself was beautiful, white and sleek, with a Laser tied up behind it, its sail fluttering freely. The two men standing on the pier did not notice, one of them dressed like a turn-of-the-century yachtsman, the other one in T-shirt, shorts, and deck shoes.

"Earl." The photographer immediately saw where Carolina was pointing.

"That the kid? Let's go," he said. If they moved quickly they could beat the crush of other reporters and well-wishers, if only by a few seconds.

They half-jogged down the pier, onto a concrete piling, and then another fifty yards until they reached the one where the Hinckley was berthed. The boat obscured their view of the two men for a moment. Which made it all the more surprising when they saw the older man in the yachting costume strike the young sailor.

"Whoa," Earl said. Instinctively he brought the camera to his shoulders and began to record.

The costumed yachtsman was cursing the younger sailor, but only snippets of speech could be heard. The young sailor remained defiant. And while he flinched, he did not back down: one, two, three more blows of the costumed yachtsman's open palm landed on his face.

* * *

The man in the ancient yachtsman's costume was Hunter Worthington, Jr., father of Hunter Worthington III. "Take it back." He raised his palm to strike again. His son only smirked.

"Why should I? You look like a jackass."

The older man flushed. "This is what is worn. I've seen it in the books."

"Maybe sixty years ago," Hunter Worthington III said. "But we're not in a fucking Lipton tea commercial."

Though it seemed impossible that he could turn a deeper shade of scarlet, Hunter Jr. somehow managed.

"Looks like all that booze is catching up, Dad-o. Maybe you should go sleep it off."

Hunter Jr.'s face did look as though he'd enjoyed too many while watching the races. But he did not stagger. It always amazed his son how well the old man held it. And how it never showed on his waistline. Must be the diet pills.

"I'm going to watch you celebrate your victory," Hunter Jr. said. "Then we are going out for dinner."

"The hell we are. I'll be out with my friends."

The father flushed again. "I can cut you off, you know. That boat—the cash it takes to race—I can take it all away."

"But you never will." The son smiled. "You wanted this more than I do. Something to brag about—to open the doors. That's why you're doing it—that's why you got rid of—"

The father's hand swept his son's face one more time, the blow nearly knocking his son down, and Michael Carolina cried, "That's enough!"

The son was the first to realize that a camera was rolling. It actually made him smile as he rubbed a hand across his cheek. His father turned just then.

"This is none of your business," he said.

"Maybe not," Carolina answered. "But if you hit him again, I'm going to make it mine anyway."

"Who the hell do you think you are?"

"I'm—we're—with Channel Three." Carolina shrugged. "Just looking to interview the winner. Who are you?"

"His father. And you're trespassing here."

Carolina shook his head and pointed to the press pass hanging from a chain around his neck. "For once, I'm afraid I'm not. We have the run of the docks."

Hunter III had recovered from the blows now, and stood behind his father. The look on the young man's face had changed from angry to quizzical.

"That's a pretty strange way of celebrating your son's victory, Mr. Worthington."

"It has nothing to do with the race," the older man sputtered. "Now leave."

"Does that mean your son doesn't want to talk about the race?"

The young man stepped out from behind his father. For a moment he showed no expression, not looking at anyone, instead staring at the wooden slats of the pier, while the breeze rearranged his sun-bleached hair yet again.

Finally he said, "I don't want to talk right now."

Carolina paused, then looked at Earl, who shrugged, as if to say, At least we *tried* to get an interview.

Carolina and Earl turned.

"Wait!" Hunter Worthington, Jr, took a step forward. "I want that tape."

"Sorry," Carolina said. "We can't do that."

"Goddammit," the man sputtered, "give me that tape!"

But reporter and photographer were already backing off the dock, pretending not to hear the shouts behind them.

Shirley's call came on the cell phone at quarter to six. Earl had finished editing Carolina's piece ten minutes before, then fed the "package" via microwave back to Channel Three's studio. The piece was short, just fifty-five seconds, consisting mostly of the sailing race, natural sound from the racers, and the committee boat horn as Hunter Worthington crossed the finish line. There were no interviews, but the video climaxed with the winner's father beating his son about the face.

"How's it going?" she asked.

"We're all set," Carolina said. "But this sure is a strange way to end a story."

"This is true," she said. "Though I must say that with you that's no surprise." She sounded a little strange, Carolina thought, as if she were—well, he wasn't sure.

Shirley Templeton had been his boss since the day he started working at Channel Three. She had recruited him right off the wooden sailboat he'd day-chartered off another Newport dock near Bowen's Wharf. Shirley was a pretty woman, in her early forties, a former television anchor who had enough brains to know when the time was right to start working behind the camera instead of in front. She was also a peculiar woman, with peculiar habits, like popping gobs of vitamins in between an almost endless chain of cigarettes. At times she also seemed lonely, and after a few drinks she was sometimes prone to conduct she later regretted. Mostly, however, she was a committed news executive. From time to time she screamed at him, chewed him out, or scolded him like a little boy. But all in all, Carolina was convinced she was the best boss he had ever had.

"Did you see the piece?"

"I watched while it was being fed in," Shirley answered. "So did the GM." The strange sound to her voice was there again.

"Is that right?" Carolina sat up in the vinyl chair bolted to the floor inside the editing console of the microwave van.

"Yes. Michael, he wants the last ten seconds of the piece killed."

"Why?"

"He says it's not relevant to the story. Has nothing to do with the race, or the Laser championships."

"To some degree that may be true," Carolina said. "But that

little fight says a lot about the kid who won the men's division. And about his father."

"Michael, he does have a point. We don't even know why the two of them were fighting, do we?"

Carolina said nothing. He'd been unable to hear the words exchanged. All that carried through the breeze was the angry tone, followed by the slaps.

"Shirley, I tried to talk to them. They told me to get lost. And they wanted the tape. You know damned well any other station in town would run this, and try to get some answers later on."

She didn't answer him.

"Shirley, how did the GM even know that this piece was coming in?"

"You can probably guess," she said.

"Someone called," Carolina mumbled into the phone.

"Two of the corporations sponsoring the racing series. And Mr. Worthington. The father, that is. And a lawyer who says he's representing Mr. Worthington."

Serious juice for a little scrap on the dock, Carolina thought. Who the hell was this guy?

"Shirley, we were invited to be there. We didn't intrude. Earl just recorded what we saw."

"I know," she said. "But that argument has been advanced and rejected."

So she had already fought with someone at the station for her crew in the field. And lost.

"I don't suppose you're going to offer your resignation if we don't air this?" Shirley asked.

Carolina chuckled. "I don't know. Are you?"

"Some battles are worth fighting, Michael. Do I really want to quit because the general manager doesn't want us showing a preppie getting slapped by his father? I don't think so."

"I see your point." But he didn't like it.

"Do you want me to tell Earl?"

"No," Carolina said. "I'll break the news. I'm sure he'll be devastated."

Shirley laughed. "I doubt it. Tell him that cheap beer is a good cure for petty censorship. Especially if his reporter pays."

The story came in the second block of the broadcast. The "lightweight section," as Earl liked to call it. "We really fit the bill tonight," he grumbled. "Lots of pretty boats, pretty pictures, but the best piece of video I shoot all day gets cut. Plus, we got no interviews."

"Relax," Carolina said. "No one else talked to Worthington, either."

"Yeah, but I'll bet they got that other kid. The one who lost. Pretty upset, I hear."

They were set up near the yachting center, just off Thames Street in the center of town. The background was a wharf loaded with row upon row of masts and rigging. Another crowd was gathering, gawking at the live truck and the TV crew. This was typical of anyplace where a story was being broadcast. Only here, the men were dressed mostly in shorts, boat shoes, and polo shirts. Some of the women wore the same, with a few exchanging shirts and shorts for sundresses. Their hair was clipped or pulled back, and, always, bleached from the sun.

A few of the younger people carried drinks, mostly beer, as if they had sauntered out of a Thames Street bar, or away from a dockside party. A few people joked, loudly, about who would be appearing on the news.

Earl and Carolina had seen it before. Crowds were to be expected, and could usually be handled, though the alcohol was often a wild card.

"What's yer story?" someone slurred as Carolina stepped in front of the camera and adjusted an earpiece.

"Sailing race," he said, smiling, trying not to make eye contact with anyone lest he encourage further conversation.

"He's cute," one of the women said. Earl grinned. Carolina pretended not to hear.

"Hey, bud," said a blond man in his early twenties. "Think you should interview me." His breath smelled of alcohol, and he swayed slightly.

Carolina turned and gave his best smile. "Right after we're done, okay? We can use you on the eleven."

In his earpiece the producer called, "We're a minute away, Mike. Everything okay?"

"Perfect," Carolina said. He looked at Earl. Who shrugged.

In the midst of the yachting crowd there emerged a woman. She stood out from those around her, in part because of the filthy stained khaki pants and denim blouse she wore, in part because of the broad straw hat that hung by a cord behind her back, sombrero-style. But the thing that set her farthest apart was the aroma. It was strong, and hard, proof that it had been some time since she had last met face to face with a bathtub. She parted the crowd like a scythe.

"Hey, TV man," she said.

"We're thirty back," the producer said in Carolina's ear. "You okay?"

Carolina did not respond. The woman's scent was making his eyes water. When she opened her mouth it revealed a set of teeth that were, strangely enough, white and even. He guessed her age at anywhere between forty and sixty; it was impossible to be more precise.

"TV man," she said again. "You ready to go?"

"All set," Carolina answered. Earl threw him a look that seemed to say, What do you want to do?

"Fifteen," the producer called in Carolina's ear.

He could hear the anchor introducing the piece, describing the race that afternoon.

"I'm ready for my close-up, Mr. DeMille," the woman said. She spit out a laugh. The crowd of sailors watched, fascinated.

Earl called out to them, "Someone want to give us a hand?" He nodded in the woman's direction.

No one in the crowd moved.

"Get as tight on me as you can," Carolina said. Earl leaned into the viewfinder and zoomed in on Carolina's face.

"You're hot," the producer said in the earpiece. Carolina looked into the camera, trying to concentrate.

"And Channel Three's Michael Carolina has been in Newport all day, following the races," the anchor called. "He joins us now with the latest."

"It's not exactly the America's Cup," Carolina began.

"Oh, come on," the woman said. "What's a girl have to do for a little attention?"

"But the competitors in today's Laser finals were just as serious—"

"I can show you serious, baby," the woman said.

"What the hell is going on?" the producer called. "Who is that woman?"

"We don't know," Earl said quietly. "But she just grabbed our reporter's crotch."

The crowd behind them was roaring. A couple of the younger, more inebriated women let out with a yell.

"Get out of it. Please, just dump it," the producer begged.

Carolina understood. But there was nothing to do but go on.

"Yes, today's finals were just as serious. And that led to some remarkable action."

"We're into tape," Earl said, fighting hard not to break up.

"Action? I love action," the woman sang.

"Get off me!" Carolina pushed her away.

"You mean I don't get the part?" The woman looked indignant.

"Michael, are you all right?" Earl's face was still merry, but he had sense enough to show at least a measure of concern.

"I'm fine," Michael said. The woman was strong, with a grip

like a block vise, but the only harm was to his pride. "Who the hell was that?"

Together, the two of them looked around for a moment. But the woman had melted away.

2

I t was getting close to dusk when Carolina started for home.

The ride from Newport took forty-five minutes, with Earl busting him all the way.

"I swear, Mike, this thing could work out between you."

"Shut up."

"I mean, people have met in stranger places."

"I'm not kidding, Earl."

"Maybe she's from one of those wealthy families, and she just wanted to be sure you don't love her for her money."

"Up yours."

The station was almost empty, save for a few technicians and editors and the evening producer, who cocked an eyebrow as he slipped into the newsroom.

"You really ought to leave your personal life at home, Michael."

He gave her a wan smile. "I'll try to do better next time."

He could hear her giggling with the assignment editor as he walked back to his desk.

Shirley had gone home for the night. So had the general manager. There was a message on his voice mail, from Carla.

"Oh, hon, I saw your piece. What happened? Listen, it really wasn't that bad, but—" Then she broke into laughter. "You looked like someone had just poked you with a cattle prod."

Carolina played the message back one more time. And allowed himself a little smile. Hell, if it had happened to anyone else, he'd be laughing, too.

He tucked his notepad in his desk and walked out the back

door, climbed into the blue Ford Explorer, and started the engine. The car belonged to Carla, but she hardly ever used it now, preferring a used Volkswagen that she claimed was more "inconspicuous." He rolled down the Explorer's windows and popped a Steely Dan CD into the player. Katy Lied.

Traffic was light on the way downtown, and he punched the buttons on the CD player until the piano and trumpet strains of "Doctor Wu" came out of the speakers. Only then did he pull the seatbelt across his chest, thinking absently that he should have done it sooner.

The strange interlude with that woman. What Shirley said still bothered him. Some battles are worth fighting. Maybe that was true, but he preferred to decide for himself which battle it would be. Instead the GM had made the decision, and that bothered him immensely.

His whole career had been marked by fights like this, by tangles with bosses and sources and anyone else who had crossed his path when he was pursuing a story. He knew it. His boss knew it, too.

"You, my friend," Shirley had said to him not long after they had met, "have one great gift and one great flaw."

He had smiled at her. "And they are?"

"You're relentless."

"And that's a gift?"

"That most certainly is a gift."

"What's the flaw?"

"You are relentless."

He smiled again, remembering the conversation, savoring the irony. What she said was true. It was what made him a great reporter, and it was why he was in his late thirties and still doing stories in a medium market. Most reporters his age had advanced to major cities, places like Boston, or Chicago, or New York, or off to the networks. That, or they'd move into news management, or into public relations, where the money was better and the hours more regular. As it stood, he was the oldest full-time reporter in the newsroom at Channel Three. There was no question he was valued, trusted to cover any kind of story. But there was also no question that he wasn't going anywhere else. At least not in news.

It hadn't always been that way. Providence was, in many ways, a redemption. Carolina's last job in television had been with a station in the Midwest, where he'd been on track for a spot in a major market, possibly Minneapolis or St. Louis, then maybe to CBS. Or NBC, or maybe one of the cable channels. But then he'd found that the station's lead anchor had a fondness for kids. A rather loathsome fondness. The message came down from the news director not to push too hard. Carolina pushed anyway. And while he finally broke a story that led to the anchor's being jailed, he was also out of a job.

Which led to the second reason he wasn't covering the President or a war or something else that journalists considered to be "important." As good as he was as a reporter, he wasn't that crazy about it anymore. In many ways the business was very different from the one he'd started in after college. And that was the point: it was a business, and he hated that. What mattered was the story. Unwrapping it, breaking it down, smoothing it out. The story. The goddam story. That was what made his blood run. What made him get up early in the morning and fall asleep, exhausted and happy, late at night.

There was only one other thing in the world that made him feel so good, and that was catching a piece of breeze in a sail. So when he was invited to leave the station in the Midwest, knowing he was probably blackballed, he didn't even try for a new job in another town.

The plan was to put the boat into charter, to try to last a season in the Caribbean. But the season stretched into two. In the summers he would sail north, to Martha's Vineyard or Nantucket, looking for business among the tourists. Finally he found his way to Newport, which was where Shirley had spotted him, and asked him to give the business another try.

It seemed so long ago, though in fact it had only been a few years. Carolina had thought about leaving, had even bought a new boat and gone sailing for a time. But Rhode Island drew him back again. He liked Providence, its streets and its architecture, its bars and its restaurants. Especially the restaurants. How he loved the food, from the fine French cuisine of Pot au Feu to the chowder at Hemenways, from the Indian and Thai restaurants on Thayer Street to the northern and southern delicacies served at Walter's or L'Epicureo or ten other Italian places on Federal Hill. For a city dwarfed in size by Boston and New York, Providence more than held its own at the dinner table. Carolina knew he'd gained fifteen pounds since he started working at Channel Three. The extra weight was a reminder of more pleasant meals than he could count.

But it was not just food. Rhode Island had a pace, an attitude, a culture all its own. The politicians, so many of them, had grown up together, often attending the same schools, playing the same sports, attending the same churches. The same was true of the doctors and lawyers, the bankers and merchants, the teachers and the firemen and police. It was almost impossible, Carolina had concluded, for two native Rhode Islanders to meet for the first time and not share a mutual acquaintance or friend. He tried to imagine another state where this could happen, but could not think of one. It was part of what gave "the biggest little state in America" its charm. It also permitted the sort of cozy relationships and associations that easily slipped over the edge from loyalty and friendship to secret deals and corruption.

And then there was the water. More than half of the state's thirty-nine cities and towns bordered on the Atlantic Ocean or Narragansett Bay. No other place in America, with the exception of Hawaii, could boast such a ratio. Salt water swirled around Rhode Island like wind across a Nebraska wheat field. When he was stuck on a story, at the State House or a few miles north in Woonsocket or off to the west in Coventry or the "backwoods" of Glocester, Carolina still found the nearness of the water comforting. Yes, Rhode Island had taken hold. Its cities and towns, its people, its lands and its waters held him close, warmed his insides, and for the first time since he was a boy, made him feel he had a home.

Driving into Edgewood, he felt himself starting to relax a bit. He could not forget about the events of the day, but at least they seemed to slip into perspective. Steely Dan continued to flow out of the speakers, washing over him with the sounds of "Rose Darling" and "Bad Sneakers." Carolina loved the touch Donald Fagen had with keyboards, the mournful vocals that permeated so much of the music. He slowed down and turned into the side street off Narragansett, looking for the little house he shared with Carla, wondering how her day had gone and what they would make for dinner.

There she was, on the little lawn in front of the tiny white Cape with the cedar shingles, the image of the contented home-owner. Except for the angry look on her face. And the nine-millimeter making a lump in the back of her pants. That and the neighbor from next door, hurling expletives as he reined in a very anxious-looking pit bull.

Dinner, he realized, would have to wait.

"I'm tellin' youse, it wuddn't the Chief."

The man's name was Santoro. Eddie Santoro. He worked for the Cranston fire department, and his squat body was layered with muscle. Santoro was in his mid-twenties, Carolina guessed, and he still suffered from an acne problem. He yanked roughly on a leather strap that was wrapped around his straining dog's neck. The action appeared to make the dog gag, which in turn made Santoro's face turn red. No, not red, Carolina decided. Actually, it was more of an orange tone. Indeed, the color extended past his face, up and across his clean-shaven skull. Eddie Santoro's head looked like a gigantic piece of Florida fruit.

Carla appeared not to notice. She ran a hand through

a hank of raven hair and pointed at something on the ground.

"And I'm telling you, Mr. Santoro, that you own the only dog on the block. And since he is your dog, I would appreciate it if you could—uh, clean up after him."

Santoro's eyes narrowed. "Youse didn't see him do nuh-inh."

Carla did not answer. She stood there, one hand on the left hip of a faded pair of jeans, the other hidden beneath an old button-down shirt with the tails untucked. It was Carla Tattaglia's favorite leisure wear.

It was true, Michael assumed, that she had not caught Chief in the act. But she had been complaining for a week. Santoro's dog was transforming the front yard into his own personal outhouse.

"Mr. Santoro, I don't want to argue with you. But there is a leash law—"

"Youse ain't even a real cop," Eddie said, enjoying the confrontation. "G-head, call the real cops, see what they do. I got friends, you know."

"How nice for you. Do they walk on four legs or two?"

"Hello, darling," Carolina said. "Anything I can help with?"

Carla smiled wearily at him. "We're fine," she said. "Just having a little chat about natural fertilizers and local ordinances."

"This your new boy toy?" Santoro's eyes were slits now. Chief strained again at the leash, and Eddie yanked the dog into submission.

"That would be me," Carolina said. "And that's Mr. Boy Toy to you."

Santoro frowned, unsure how to respond. Michael turned to Carla.

"Did you hear the Cranston police are investigating the sale of illegal steroids?"

"Is that right?" Carla smiled.

"Yeah, they called the station tonight. Said something about bringing a crew along when they go out with a warrant. A little later tonight."

"No, I hadn't heard about that. Did you hear anything about it, Eddie?"

Santoro's eyes were wider now, shifting from Carolina to Carla and back again.

"Where—where youse t'ink they're goin'?"

Carolina shrugged.

"Never know, pal. The cops, they love to take down people in power."

"I gotta go." Eddie hauled again on the dog leash. Chief gave a yip, then followed his master as he returned to his own house at a trot.

"He'll be flushing his toilet for the next two hours," Carla said. She kissed Michael on the cheek. "My hero."

"I have a question," Carolina said. "What were you going to do if he let the dog go?"

Carla smiled again, and patted the gun, still tucked in the back of her jeans. "I would have been prepared," she said.

"That's good to know," Carolina said. "You need to defend yourself."

They walked back inside. "And if I had to shoot that animal, it wouldn't be so bad."

Michael raised one brow. "Why not?"

"Because after, I'd feed his dog the meatloaf left over from dinner."

Carla turned just as they reached the front door.

"Before we go in, I have something to tell you."

"Why don't we sit down first," Michael said. The late summer air was very comfortable just then, and the street was quiet. He leaned back on his elbows, stretched his legs down the steps. Carla sat next to him, her elbows on her knees.

"I had the craziest day," he said.

Carla smiled. "I saw the broadcast, remember?"

"Not the woman. Let me tell you what you *didn't* see."

He told her about the race, and the crowd, and the problem between Hunter Worthington and his father.

"I'm telling you, this kid's old man is such an asshole. Imagine doing that to your son on a day when he wins a big event. And the kid just took it. Didn't say anything. Just stood there."

"Michael," Carla said. "We should talk about this later."

"I know, I'm sorry. It just bothers me. I mean, this old man was a total jerk. You've never seen anything like him."

"Michael—"

"Just don't get me started on the subject of bad fathers—"

"Michael." Her tone was more strident now.

"What?"

"We have a guest."

"We do?"

"Yes." She rose, and Carolina followed as she opened the screen door.

"Mr. Carolina?" she called.

"I'm right here," Michael said.

"I'm right here," a voice echoed, over the sound of a television. They walked back into the tiny living room in the back of the house. A man in his mid-fifties sat in an easy chair, staring at the TV screen, watching a baseball game. He raised his eyes slowly.

"Hello." The voice was deep, rich, and smooth.

Michael Carolina swallowed.

"Hi, Dad."

Paul Carolina had graying hair and a seamy face that made him look every bit of his fifty-three years. But he also had a smile that could charm the hardest policeman, the meanest schoolteacher, the toughest nun. He used it then, springing out of the easy chair and wrapping his son in his arms.

"Look at him," he said, again and again. "I mean, look at him. It's been too long. Far too long, eh?"

Michael said nothing. He stared at the man in front of him. They were roughly the same height and build, but Paul Carolina had the olive skin of a full-blooded southern Italian. His hair was thick and dark, just like his son's, but it now carried sharp lines of salt and pepper at the temples. His face sagged slightly, heavy from years of drinking. He wore a dark green polo shirt, a pair of cotton dockers, and tasseled loafers. Carolina noticed that the shirt seemed well worn, and one of the loafers was missing a tassel.

"He can't say anything, Carla. Not a thing. He's in shock." Paul Carolina laughed in a rich, deep baritone. "Who ever would have thought he'd be at such a loss?"

"How did you find me?" Michael asked.

"What, you think your old man doesn't keep up with the exploits of his famous son? You're a big newsman these days. I've seen you on the tube. They run your stories on the morning news or CNN every once in a while. You're gonna make it to New York or one of the networks soon."

"I like it here just fine," Michael said. "And what I meant was, how did you find this house?"

Paul Carolina stepped back and his grin faded a little. "I called your station. Told them who I was."

Michael looked at Carla. "They're not supposed to give out my address," he said.

Paul Carolina's grin faded further. "What, my son isn't happy to see me? Is this how it's gonna be? Carla, what do you think of this? I ain't seen this kid in what, three, four years?"

"Seven," Michael said.

"Whatever. This is how you act? Carla, would you have ever bet that your boyfriend would treat his own father this way?"

"Betting is one thing you know about, Dad. And why don't you leave her out of this?"

"Michael," Carla said softly, her discomfort obvious. "I invited Paul when he called this afternoon." Her dark eyes shifted between the two men. "I thought you wouldn't mind."

The conversation was interrupted then by the sound of a New York Yankee broadcaster, hysterical because a rookie had homered to tie it up with the Red Sox in the eighth inning. The crowd roared, and both men looked down at the screen as the lanky outfielder did a slow, comfortable jog around the base path.

"Who's pitching?" Michael asked, just loud enough to be heard.

"That Japanese kid," his father answered. "He's having a better season this year. But I think they're gonna pull him for the Spanish guy."

It was still awkward in the tiny room, but the tension eased, if only a little bit. A breeze, the one the locals loved to talk about, slipped in through an open window and made a pair of light blue curtains flutter.

"Can I get anyone a beer?" Carla asked.

"I don't drink," Paul Carolina said, too quickly.

"I'll have one," Michael said. He sat down on a couch to the left of where his father was sitting. Paul Carolina watched him, and took his own seat again. Carla came in, carrying two Coronas, still in the bottle, and a glass of water. She handed one to Michael, set the other beer down, and offered the glass to Paul.

"It's warm," she said. "I thought you might like this."

"You're so sweet," Paul said, and smiled his charming smile again. "She's such a sweet girl, Michael. I can't believe she's a police officer."

"Ex–police officer, Mr. Carolina." Carla threw Michael a knowing look, which he returned. If Paul noticed, he did not let on.

"It's Paul. I told you to call me Paul. Why'd you, ah, leave the force?"

"She's starting a business, Dad," Michael said. "Private investigations."

"Oh yeah? Hey, that's great. And you, Michael, how you been?"

Michael took a long pull at the Corona and watched the glass on the bottle fog up in the warm air. "I'm fine, Dad. Been just fine."

"That's great, just great."

There was a dearth of conversation then. Both father and son stared intently at the game, keeping their eyes trained on the television even when the inning ended and a car commercial came on.

"You never told me what brings you to Rhode Island," Carla asked.

"Well, Carla, I've been down South for a few years, and I missed the seasons. Thought I'd head north and try some more temperate climes, you know? So I may be looking for a new job, new start, I guess, and what better place than where I can see my boy? What do you think, Michael?"

Michael grinned, and took a pull at his Corona. The look on his face came out more as a grimace. Paul appeared not to notice. He looked once again at Carla. "And look at you. Such a beautiful woman. Michael is a very lucky man. Lucky man indeed. He have any plans to make an honest woman of you?"

Carla laughed, but not comfortably.

"How long do you plan on staying?" Michael asked.

"Michael," Carla said.

Paul Carolina looked at his son with hurt in his eyes, as if he had been severely wounded. He glanced up at Carla once more, as if to ask, Do you see how I suffer? But Michael did not blink.

"I'm making a change, Michael," Paul finally said, very quietly. "Taking some new steps in my life."

"And what steps would those be?" Michael asked. "Gonna hit the dogs now instead of the ponies? Or do you have plans for one of the casinos in Connecticut? Craps is your game, isn't it?"

"Michael!" Carla looked horrified.

"It's all right, Carla. It's all right." Paul Carolina hung his head. "I figured this was coming. And the truth is, I deserve it. I deserve the reputation I have with my son." He paused for a moment, and the three of them listened as the Yankees' new Latin closer got another strikeout. The game was almost over.

"It's just that this time, Michael, I really want things to be different. I know how much I've hurt you. How much I hurt your mother. But the years have slipped by, and I'm not getting any younger. It's time I kicked myself in the ass and started acting like a man. And part of being a man is being there for my son. For you. That's why I'm here."

Michael still said nothing. But inside, there was a small part of him that melted. He wanted to believe the man sitting in front of him, who looked as if he was ready to fall to his knees and beg.

"You go to Gamblers Anonymous?" Michael asked.

Paul nodded. "I went to a meeting down South. Atlantic City."

"I'm sure they have chapters there," Michael said grimly.

"It was a start, Michael. They helped. Look, I'm here, right? I'm not there anymore."

"Well, you need to go here. And AA, too."

Paul looked at him. "I'm okay with that, son. See that hand? Like a rock."

"Mr. Carolina," Carla said, "I can help you get hooked up with some of those things. The meetings, I mean. And if you need a place to stay for a while, there's the extra bedroom down the hall."

Paul's smile returned. His eyes grew wet. "I'm so embarrassed."

"Don't be," Carla said.

"You don't know how grateful I am. I—I can't even begin to describe it to you."

Carolina looked at this father. "And you need a job, Dad."

"I know. I know. There any machine shops around? I was pretty good with metal. Michael, you know that."

"Why don't you worry about that in the morning, Mr. Carolina." Carla smiled at him. "Tonight, we can all relax." She threw Michael another look. He understood: Leave your father alone. If you only knew, Michael thought.

Paul was wearing a worn polo shirt, and he used a sleeve then to wipe his eyes. "Bless you, Carla. Bless you. And call me Paul. Please. My friends call me Paul."

Paul Carolina went to bed an hour later, after the game ended and he'd consumed a half hour of *SportsCenter*. Carla made up the extra bed in the Cape's guest room, and Michael heard her wish him good night.

He stayed in the living room, watching a few more sports highlights. ESPN was not carrying anything about the sailing events in Newport that day, which was not surprising. Television rarely covered competitive sailing, except for the America's Cup and briefly during the Olympics.

He hoped Carla would come downstairs. She did not. He walked to the staircase and looked up. The light was still on in the room where they shared a queen-size bed. Still awake.

He did not go upstairs right away. Instead he went to the kitchen. In the tumult of seeing his father, he'd forgotten to eat, and realized now that he was hungry. Carla was not lying about the meatloaf. There was a cold plate wrapped in foil. Carla made wonderful meatloaf.

He found a plate and some bread and built a thick sandwich with lettuce and mayonnaise, no ketchup. Then he drew a glass of water and climbed the stairs. The light was still on.

Carla lay on top of the bed, reading a magazine, dressed in an oversized T-shirt that just barely covered her hips and left a pair of long, brown legs exposed on top of the bedcovers.

"Hungry?"

She cocked an eyebrow at him but said nothing.

"What are you reading?"

She lifted the cover. It was a magazine about saltwater fishing. Fly-fishing.

"I didn't know you fished."

"Well, I haven't lately. Starting a new career, it kind of interferes with your hobbies. But I enjoy it."

Michael sat down on the bed and laid the plate on the nightstand. He took a decent bite of the sandwich. Carla was ignoring him again.

"Sure you don't want a bite?" She shook her head.

"You make great meatloaf, you know."

Carla put the magazine down and rolled over on her side, facing him. He noticed the curve of her breasts filling out the shirt.

"I'm mad at you, you know," she said.

"I know."

"You were so cruel to him."

"You think so?"

"Yes, I do."

"Okay."

She stared at him for a moment. Then she said, "That's it? You haven't seen your father in seven years and you treat him like something the Chief left in my yard. And all you're going to say is okay?"

"No," Michael answered, smacking his lips, "but I'd like to finish this sandwich first."

She wanted to smile then, Michael could tell. But she didn't. She waited for him to finish, which only took two more bites.

"That was great," he said, with an exaggerated groan of pleasure.

"I'm waiting, Michael." She did not laugh.

He took a long look at the dark eyes in front of him. So beautiful, and so sad.

"How could you be so, so mean?"

"I don't have an excuse," he said.

"You don't?"

"No. But then, I don't think I need one."

She sat up on the bed, gathering her legs underneath her. "Do you think you could elaborate?"

Michael Carolina sighed. Seeing his father had been enough of a shock, but calling up the memories . . . the broken promises . . . the embarrassment . . . produced a strange sensation inside. It was as if a gate were opening to a place he did not wish to go.

"Do you remember what I told you about my father?"

She nodded. "I know he has a gambling problem, Michael. That seems obvious. But he wants to deal with it, don't you think?"

Once, not long after they had first met, he had tried to explain to Carla. About his father's gambling problems, how it had affected him, and his mother. It didn't matter whether it was a team sport or a race or game in a cheesy casino; there was no bet Paul Carolina would not make, and usually at terrible odds. But that really only scratched the surface. Michael never told Carla about the awful conclusion he'd reached about his father long ago. That the odds, good or bad, were beside the point. What mattered was the gamble, the chance, the opportunity to win, or even to lose. That was what mattered to his father, even if it meant the ruin of those he loved.

Once Paul Carolina had held a decent job, machining parts in a tractor plant. It was union work, and the pay was good. His father was a master at crafting the proper tools and parts used to construct the combines and tractors that tilled the fields of Iowa, Nebraska, and the Dakotas. They'd lived in a decent house growing up, in a friendly working-class section of Dubuque. But eventually everything had slipped away. On top of that was the drink. Carolina couldn't think of a time growing up when his father didn't have a beer in his hand, or a bottle of whiskey in a kitchen cabinet. Always smiling, always with a happy look or thought. Paul was a happy drunk, a man who lived for the joys of the cards and the dice and the horses and the bottle.

One day, Paul Carolina had simply disappeared. He'd left no note, no warning of what he was doing or where he was going. He just left. By then, Michael was seventeen, old enough not to need a father, perhaps, or numb enough not to care.

Paul Carolina had drifted in and out of his son's life ever since, appearing once on the campus where his son went to college, and later where he worked at television stations in the South and the Midwest. He talked about wanting to settle down, to get some stability in his life. He always borrowed money, and then borrowed more. Then, sooner or later, he disappeared again.

Michael wanted to explain this to her, sitting there in the half-light from the bed lamp. But he did not. Instead, he asked, "Did your father ever disappoint you?"

She thought for a moment. "Of course," she said. "All parents disappoint their children, don't they? But that doesn't mean you shouldn't love him."

She reached out and touched him lightly on the forehead. It was a simple, almost motherly act, one he had not expected.

"It's not loving him that's hard," he said. "It's trusting him."

He placed a hand on her side, slid it down to her hip. "Funny," he said. "You don't act like a cop. Or even a PI."

She smiled. "I'm off duty, pal."

"That explains the costume."

He got up.

"Where are you going?"

"Thought I'd brush my teeth, comb my hair, maybe go out on a date."

Carla's smile turned into a leer. "Oh? Where to?"

"Not too far. Thought I might take an off-duty PI for a little ride."

She stood up, pulled the shirt over her head, and dropped it on the floor.

"Clothing optional?"

"Definitely," he said.

They were sleeping soundly when the phone rang underneath the bed. Carla reached down and grabbed it, listened briefly, then shoved the receiver in Carolina's direction. It hit him on the nose.

"Ow." Carla mumbled something that sounded close to "I'm sorry" and rolled over, pulling a pillow over her head.

Michael listened for a minute, and hung up. Five minutes later he was showered and dressed. Carla rolled over again.

"I really was sorry," she said.

"It's all right."

"Where are you going?"

"Newport."

"What for? I thought the regatta was over."

"It is."

"Then why the hell are they calling you at—" She looked at the clock, which read 6:18 a.m.

"Murder."

3

He was hanging from the yardarm.

In this case, the "yardarm" was a spreader jutting out from the mast of a sixty-foot Little Harbor yawl, an absolutely gorgeous yacht with a deep-sea-green hull and enough varnish on the rails to fill a swimming pool. Not that it much mattered to the dead man, who twisted slowly as the boat rolled ever so slightly in a gray mist that covered Newport like a shroud.

A decent crowd was gathered, despite the early hour. They lined the waterfront, eyes glued to the gruesome sight. Many appeared to be revelers from the night before, still drunk or contending with the onset of serious hangovers. A few merchants peered out from storefronts along Thames Street, straining for a glimpse of the corpse suspended in midair. Two or three had cameras.

"Can you believe these vultures," Earl snarled, "getting their kicks off other people's misery?" He set the Sony Beta on a tripod and trained the lens for the body. Michael Carolina stared at him for a moment. The irony was inescapable, but it was better to ignore it, he decided. Get the pictures now. Debate the ethics later.

More television news crews appeared, along with print and radio reporters. They all found places along the piers and walkways that lined the waterfront.

The yacht swung at anchor, cutting a slow arc, in time with the boats that surrounded her. It would have looked like a ballet, were it not for the lifeless body. That and the police boat that had finally arrived alongside the Little Harbor, which bore the name *Stream* on the stern. Two officers threw fenders off the police boat's side, careful not to damage *Stream's* glossy hull. Strange, Carolina thought, that they would take that sort of care at such a moment. But then, it was Newport. The two officers scrambled aboard the yacht, and then stood for a moment staring upward, unsure of what to do next.

"God, the face. Michael, did you see the face?" Earl's camera was zoomed in on the body, and his voice contained that strange blend of emotions often found in reporters who covered crime scenes: sadness, even pity, for what he was observing, but also a weird sort of exhilaration, an excitement known only by those who spend careers observing the tragedy of others.

"I see it," Carolina said. He had seen the face, and the ugly, misshapen hangman's knot poking out beside the dead man's head. He did not want to look again, and did not need to. The face was one he would not soon forget, for it was the same one that had shown such joy the day before, after a victory in a sailboat race that now seemed meaningless. The same face that had stoically endured a ringing slap on a nearby pier.

Michael Carolina turned his back on the body and scribbled the name "Hunter Worthington III" three times on the notepad in his hand. He didn't need to write the name. It was just something to fill the time, to take his eyes off the awful sight before them.

Earl asked, "When the hell is someone going to cut him down?"

It took another half hour before the police did.

One of the officers on board finally located the halyard, the line that held Hunter's corpse so high above the deck. With two other officers waiting below, he lowered the body to the deck. Carolina was struck by how gentle the men were, as if they were helping a wounded animal, or a small child.

Carolina noticed another officer, wearing rubber gloves, in

the cockpit of the yacht. Slowly he bent down to pick something up, taking care to use only two fingers.

"Shoot that," he said to Earl. The photographer complied.

"What is it?"

"A winch handle," Carolina said. Winches on a yacht helped to maintain the trim of the sails. On a yacht the size of *Stream* the handles would be made of steel, and probably weighed at least a pound. "Can you zoom?" Michael asked.

Earl let out a long, low whistle. "Sharp eyes, Mike. There's something on the grip. Looks like blood to me."

"Then the betting money is he got conked on the head before he got hanged."

The fog was beginning to burn off. A van from the Rhode Island medical examiner's office had pulled up to the pier, waiting for the body. Carolina had excellent sources inside the ME's office, but he did not recognize the men assigned to this job, as they pulled the customary gurney and black body bag from their white vehicle. Judging from the appearance of the corpse, cause of death did not appear to be an immediate issue, though he made a note to check with the office later.

But Michael did recognize the man who emerged from a gold Mercedes. It was a late-model four-door, and it pulled up just behind the ME van. The driver was dressed in pale gray slacks, a pair of soft Italian loafers, and a cotton sweater. He walked in front of his car and stared at the boat. The body was still on the deck. One officer stood guard over it as another took pictures. A third cop disappeared belowdecks, presumably to conduct a search.

The man in the gray slacks said nothing, showed nothing, did nothing. He merely stood on the pier and watched the commotion on the yacht.

"That the kid's old man?" Earl asked.

"Looks that way."

"What's his name?"

"Hunter Worthington, Jr."

The man continued to observe the activity aboard the yacht. The only movement he made was to fold his arms.

"He seems so broken up," Earl said. He quietly turned his camera. "We need a shot of the grieving father."

"Take it easy, Earl." Worthington's odd behavior was not lost on Carolina, but he reminded himself not to judge too quickly. It was obvious that the relationship between father and son was less than perfect, and might well be totally dysfunctional. But grief, Carolina knew, did strange things to people. Sometimes it made them explode with anger and tears. And sometimes it drove every emotion deep inside, to places that could be neither seen nor heard nor easily understood.

Earl rolled off fifteen, perhaps twenty seconds of tape before Worthington turned to scan the people strewn across the waterfront. He seemed to be looking for someone, but it was impossible to tell who. When his eyes lit on Earl and Michael, he offered a withering stare before turning away.

"Guess he doesn't want to be interviewed," Earl sniffed.

Carolina looked at the photographer. "You're cold today, aren't you?"

Earl shrugged. "What can I say? I don't like rich guys. And I don't like guys who hit their kids. So he's got two strikes starting out."

At that moment, Carolina noticed two uniformed Newport police officers walking quickly along the pier. They stopped Worthington in his tracks. Worthington and the officers engaged in brief conversation. Then one of the officers reached out and touched Worthington's arm.

Worthington, older than the officer by perhaps ten years, pulled away as if stung. His voice carried across the water.

"I said I would meet you there."

The officer looked at his partner, who, eyebrows raised, subtly shook his head. Both officers nodded politely then, and backed away.

"See that?" Carolina asked.

"I'm rolling on it," Earl murmured.

The officers walked back toward a patrol cruiser in the distance. Worthington turned back to the yacht. The police boat had brought the two men from the ME's office alongside *Stream*. They quickly went to the body and began unfolding their long black bag.

Carolina looked again to Hunter Worthington, Jr. His face remained devoid of any expression as he watched the men attend to his son. He made no move to get closer, to approach the officers; showed no sign that he cared about what they were doing. Finally, he turned and walked back to his car.

Carolina turned to Earl. "You know your way to Newport PD?"

The station wasn't far, just a few blocks from the waterfront. Carolina expected to see the gold Mercedes, but it had not arrived. Earl pulled his camera from the car and took a post near the police station entrance. Carolina went inside, where a uniformed sergeant behind a desk glumly took his name and said he would advise his superiors. Carolina smiled and stepped outside again.

Earl looked at him. "Anything?"

"Not yet." It was early to be looking for any kind of meaningful comment from the police, but it never hurt to say hello.

Earl lowered the camera from his shoulder. "What do you think? The old man a suspect?"

"I suppose," Carolina said. "Or it could just be routine." This he truly doubted. The hanging could not have been an accident. The son's body was too high off the deck; there was no way that he could have pulled himself to such a height. At the same time, it was still far below the spreader. If Hunter III had tried suicide he would have decapitated himself. Or was there something he was missing?

And then there was Hunter Jr. It was strange enough to see the father of a dead man behave in such a cold way on the dock. Stranger still for uniformed police to approach him even before his son's body had been removed from the yacht. The whole thing appeared to be so . . . casual. As if the father had expected the police would question him.

Yet Worthington had actually gotten away with dictating to the police how he would arrive at the station. What the hell was going on?

Another fifteen minutes went by before the Mercedes arrived in the station parking lot. Hunter Worthington emerged once again. He wore the same slacks and shoes, but the cotton sweater had been replaced by a navy blazer, a button-down shirt, and a maroon tie. Worthington looked like a middle-aged preppie.

He noticed Carolina and Earl, and quickly ignored them again as he leaned against the car and glanced at his watch. Within another minute, a blue Lexus pulled into the lot. A tanned, slightly paunched man in a double-breasted suit got out. He had a cell phone glued to his left ear, which he dropped and slipped into a pocket only as he approached Worthington. The two men embraced.

"I'll be damned," Carolina said.

Earl chuckled. "So you remember him, huh?" Without being asked, he slung the camera on his shoulder and began rolling off more tape.

The two men started walking toward the station entrance. Worthington continued to ignore Carolina, but the man in the suit made eye contact.

"Hello, Rico," Carolina said.

The man scowled. "I know you? Oh, that's right. You're from Channel Three. I never watch you."

Americo Balboni was a defense attorney, known as Sleeko Rico and considered by some to be among the slickest defense lawyers in Rhode Island. Carolina was not among Rico's admirers.

"Nice to see you too. Like to tell us why your client is here?"

Worthington either pretended not to hear the question or truly did not. He continued into the station, not bothering to hold the door for his attorney. Rico hesitated, then stopped. Unable to resist a chance for a few seconds of television glory, he waited for Michael to bring a microphone into range.

"We're here to assist with a police investigation into the tragic death"—he pronounced the word "det"—"of Mr. Worthington's son. I would hope that in this time of terrible grief, you and the other media would have a little respect. Give the fam'ly some room."

Balboni turned and walked inside. Earl set his camera down.

"If that guy's representing him he's gotta be guilty."

Carolina smiled and looked at his notepad again. At the name Hunter Worthington, scribbled three times. If only it were that easy.

They packed the camera and were talking about a run for some breakfast when a uniformed officer came out the door of the station at a trot. He was the same officer who'd approached Worthington by the pier.

"You guys from Channel Three?"

Carolina nodded. "What can we do for you?"

"Captain wants to speak with you."

The uniformed officer led them inside the station, and glanced at the camera as he held the door. "You can leave that here," he said, pointing at the sergeant's desk.

"Where I go, it goes," Earl said.

The officer frowned. "Captain may not like that."

"It's not on," Carolina said.

The cop said nothing more, just took them down a hallway to a cramped office. Rico Balboni and his client were nowhere in sight.

Inside the office, behind a small desk, sat a silver-haired man in his early fifties. He was dressed in a brown sports jacket and blue chinos, and a knit tie hung loosely from the open collar of his shirt. The man's face was red from the sun, and heavily lined. He stood when Michael and Earl entered the room and dwarfed both men by at least six inches.

"Jack Cicero," he said. "I'm chief of detectives here." Cicero pointed at the uniformed officer, who'd closed the door behind them. "This is Detective Belton." The younger officer nodded.

Earl and Carolina shook hands with the policemen.

"Understand you're covering the death of that young sailor this morning," Cicero said.

"That's right," Carolina said. "We were wondering if we could ask a few questions."

"Actually, we want some information from you." Cicero smiled, showing a set of teeth that bore signs of heavy tobacco use. Carolina raised his eyebrows.

"Tell you what," Michael said. "I need some confirmation that you're looking at a winch handle as a murder weapon."

Cicero tried to hide his surprise, realized he could not, and shrugged. "Where did you hear that?"

"Didn't," Michael said, pointing at Earl's camera. "We saw it. Will you confirm that?"

Cicero thought for a moment. "Not for attribution," he said quietly.

"I'll call you a source close to the investigation."

"Deal. Now then, I understand you saw the young man and his father yesterday," Cicero went on. "That you saw them in a fight, maybe even put the whole thing on tape with your camera there."

"Is that right?" Carolina looked at Earl, who'd suddenly found the pattern in the office carpeting to be extremely interesting.

"We want to see the tape," Cicero said.

"Don't have it," Earl mumbled.

"Excuse me?" Cicero looked at Earl.

"Sorry." Earl offered a lame grin. "I have indigestion."

"Where do you keep your video?" Cicero asked. His tone was urgent now.

"At the station," Carolina answered. "I'm not saying we have a tape like that, but if we did, I'd have to check with my boss before it could be released. And I doubt it would be."

Cicero turned toward him, a look of contempt coming over his face. "Well, you were on the docks yesterday, right?"

"That's right," Carolina said.

"And you saw Hunter Worthington and his father?"

"We did."

"Then we're going to need statements about what you both saw."

"Like I said, Captain"–Carolina kept his tone as respectful as he could–"I need to speak with my boss."

Cicero looked at his subordinate. "Get them a phone," he said.

It took Shirley Templeton, Channel Three's news director, less than five seconds to make up her mind when Carolina explained.

"You tell them nothing."

"Kind of what I figured you'd say," Carolina said. "I was going to tell them they could have whatever we air or whatever they can get through a court order."

"Sounds about right," Shirley said. "Now what are you getting?"

"Well, that's the flip side, I'd say."

"What do you mean?"

"They just confirmed that a winch handle from the boat is the probable murder weapon. If we don't give them something, I expect they'll freeze us out."

Shirley did not speak for a moment. Carolina knew she was mulling over what he'd said. He also knew she wouldn't change her mind.

"The price we pay for independence," she said finally, "is we have to stay neutral. We don't hinder the police, but we don't help them either. We report. That's it. And you ought to know better than to try and make a deal."

"Yes, and if we'd run the tape last night, I wouldn't have this problem."

Both having scored points, Michael and Shirley both shut up for a moment. It was stupid to fight, Michael thought.

"I guess it won't matter much," he said to his boss. "After we run the tape, the police will have what they want anyway."

Michael glanced around. Earl was still in the office with the two policemen, but the door was open. Every few seconds Cicero would throw a baleful look Carolina's way. "Can you have someone bring it down to us," he said into the phone. "Or do you want to drop it in back in Providence?"

Shirley did not respond.

"We'll have to run it tonight," Carolina said.

Shirley still said nothing.

"I mean, we are going to run that tape tonight, right?"

"Michael," Shirley said quietly, "I have to get to a meeting. Call me later and we'll figure out our plan for tonight." She hung up.

Without an opportunity to review the station's tape of Junior—as Earl now called him—slapping his son, Cicero had little use for a reporter from Channel Three.

"I'd like a written statement," the officer said.

"Can't do it," Michael responded.

"I'll get the attorney general to subpoena you before a grand jury."

Michael shrugged. "Maybe that will do the trick."

Cicero glared. "Get out."

"Gee," Earl said as they walked out the station house door, "and we were getting to be such good friends."

Earl and Michael ate breakfast at a hole-in-the-wall diner near the courthouse on Eisenhower Square, where a perky waitress kept their coffee cups filled and smiled happily.

"It's nice to have celebrities in here."

"Where?" Carolina looked around.

"Oh, don't tease me," she giggled. "I see you on TV all the time."

"You do?"

"Sure. I love it when you do backyard weather. Channel Nine is my favorite station."

The waitress hurried off as Earl nearly fell out of his chair laughing.

"Isn't it great to be famous?"

"I try not to let it go to my head," Carolina replied.

They returned to the police station, where a few more reporters had appeared. The gold Mercedes, along with Balboni's Lexus, were still parked in the lot.

"Guess Junior's still inside," Earl said.

Within ten minutes Balboni and Worthington walked out, however, spurning any more questions, Balboni saying "No comment" every third or fourth step. The two men climbed into their cars and drove off.

Earl looked at Michael. "What now?"

"I guess we find out where he was last night."

Which did not prove to be easy.

They started at the downtown yachting center, with the officials at the Laser Association, who uniformly declined any comment regarding the death of the new champion except to say that it was tragic.

"He was a tough competitor," one older gentleman said, shaking his head. "Great loss to the sport."

They tried the hotels, near Thames Street and on Goat Island, where several of the out-of-town racers had been staying. And on Goat Island they were lucky.

"Remember that kid?" Earl asked. He was looking at a young man, perhaps twenty or twenty-one, checking out of the hotel.

Carolina did. He walked toward the young man, with Earl hanging back.

"Excuse me, I'm from Channel Three. Weren't you in the Laser finals yesterday?"

The young man nodded warily.

"I'd like to talk to you about one of the other racers. Hunter Worthington."

The sailor's expression did not warm up. "What about him?"

"You heard the news this morning?"

"No."

"That he was found dead. Hanged."

The young man's jaw dropped.

"No shit," he said. "No shit."

"What's your name?"

"Mercer. Jim Mercer."

"Where you from?"

"Westport, Connecticut."

"How long had you known Hunter?"

The young man sat down in a chair next to the checkout desk. "I don't know. Couple years, I guess. I raced the dude a lot, you know what I'm saying?" Mercer dropped his head and stared at the floor. "And they found him hanging, huh? Whoa. That's totally strange. What boat was he on? When they found him?"

Carolina looked at Earl and gave the barest nod. Earl caught the look. He turned back to Mercer.

"Big green yacht. *Stream,* it's called."

"Whoa. The Little Harbor, huh. It belongs to his old man. Outrageous piece of boat."

Earl shuffled up with his camera.

"My friend and I were wondering if we could ask you a couple of quick questions. About Hunter."

Mercer looked up. "I don't know."

"I'm not trying to pry," Carolina said. "But a lot of people are going to want to know about who Hunter was. His family is pretty torn up, and you knew him."

Mercer hesitated. He kept bouncing one knee up and down. Almost like a nervous tic, Carolina thought.

"Okay. Just a few."

Earl started rolling. With his left hand he passed a microphone to Michael, who slipped closer to Mercer.

"Tell me what's running through your mind right now, Jim."

Mercer offered a deep sigh.

"Just, like, shock, you know what I'm saying? I mean, the guy was a racer. He ran with the wind. It's kind of a loss to the sport, know what I'm saying?"

"I know what you're saying," Earl mumbled.

"Were you close with him?" Carolina asked.

Mercer paused. "I guess you could say we were friends. Yeah, I'd say that. We raced all the time. I saw him a lot. It's gonna be weird not having him around."

"He won yesterday, right?"

Mercer nodded agreement. "And where did you place?"

"I was second." Mercer's eyes flicked briefly toward the camera and back again to Carolina. Michael wanted to ask another question. What would Worthington's death mean to Mercer's chances for the Olympics? But it was not the right time.

Instead he tried another approach.

"You mentioned that the yacht belongs to Hunter's father. What was their relationship like?"

Jim Mercer looked around briefly, as if he wanted to see who was around. Which seemed strange to Carolina, because the camera was still rolling. The hotel lobby was a busy place, and the camera was not attracting much attention from other guests. Mercer apparently decided it was safe to speak.

"They were like, intense, you know what I'm saying? His dad wanted him to win, and had the money to help him do it. I mean, the guy must love the son to do that, right? And, like, Hunter Three was into it. Way into it. Even so, you could feel how intense it was between them, kind of the love-hate thing, know what I'm talking about?"

His words hung in the air for a minute before Carolina said, "Thanks, Jim. Earl, could we get a little setup?"

Earl threw him a strange look, as if to say, That's it? But he pulled back to reveal a "two-shot," a picture of reporter and subject chatting. After ten seconds he reversed the shot, to catch a glimpse of Carolina's face. The extra video would help to edit the evening's piece. Carolina kept talking with Mercer.

"So when's this gonna be on?"

"Probably tonight at six. We might do something at noon, too."

"Sounds like a plan," Mercer said. Carolina stifled a grimace and smiled. "So where are your folks, Jim?"

Mercer almost snorted. "The father's in the city, making money. Mom's down with the garden club in Westport. I'm at this one on my own, know what I'm saying?"

"The city. You mean New York?"

"Is there any other?" Mercer grinned.

"What's your father do?"

"Wall Street, man. Big-time finance. Stocks, bonds, and market cons." Mercer laughed at his own rhyme.

"So when did you see Hunter last?"

Jim Mercer shrugged and thought for a moment, then licked a set of windburned lips.

"Guess it was just after the race yesterday, at the docks. I mean, it was kind of a mess. I was sorta pis—mad at the guy 'cause we had gone nose to nose tacking yesterday. But I didn't get to talk to him after. Hey, you weren't taping that, were you?"

"Don't worry, I'm not using it in the piece." Carolina looked at Earl again. "You all set?"

"Think so," Earl said.

"How about one more question," Carolina said, taking the microphone again. Mercer stood there.

Earl focused. "We're rolling."

"How did you know Hunter was on a boat?"

Mercer stared at him, not understanding the question. Then it hit him, all at once. "I—you told me."

"I told you that he was found, hanged. I didn't say where. And you asked which boat."

Mercer tried to smile again, easy and friendly. It was the kind of look that had probably carried him many places and helped him obtain many things. But when Carolina remained silent, the smile faded, and then dissolved into a look appropriate for a funeral.

"Look, this whole thing is tragic. My friend is dead. You just came in here and dropped it on me. I tried to accommodate you, but if this is supposed to be some sort of investigation, I think you're way out of line."

"I still don't understand how you knew it was a boat, Jim."

Mercer looked around again. But there was no one to help him. "I have to get going. What station are you from?"

"Channel Three, Providence. So how did you know it was a boat, Jim?"

"You better go, man. This is some kind of weirdness, and I don't let other people's weirdness make me crazy."

With that Mercer turned. Earl kept rolling, but the camera angle didn't quite catch the shove Mercer gave to Michael's chest. It was enough to push Michael off balance. Mercer grabbed a canvas bag he'd been holding in one hand and headed off toward a hotel elevator at a fast walk. Earl kept rolling until he got into a car and disappeared.

"Nice kid. Must have been a real good friend."

Carolina nodded. "Did you notice how much his speech improved there at the end?"

Earl's brow furrowed. "That's right. He actually sounded like he studied English once. I guess he's a little smarter than he first appeared."

Carolina nodded, and handed the microphone back to Earl. "But maybe not quite as smart as he thinks."

* * *

Shirley called on the van's cell phone and asked for a live shot at noon.

"Use one of the bites from Mercer," she said, "and the video of the father arriving at the police station."

"What about the pictures of Junior and Hunter Three from last night?"

"I don't know what we ought to do with that," Shirley said. "It's not clear that the dad is a suspect, is it?"

"The Newport police have removed me from their list of people to advise," Carolina said.

"I hear you," Shirley said. "But there are two problems with that tape. The first is that we don't know what the father and—what did you call him? Hunter Three?"

"That's what Mercer called him," Michael said. "It's easier than Hunter Worthington the Third."

"Okay. We still don't know what the father and Hunter Three were fighting about."

"That's true. But isn't that for them to answer?"

"Well, ordinarily it would be." There was a catch in her voice.

"I'm not following you," Michael said.

Shirley paused for a second. "We, uh, don't have the tape anymore."

"What?"

"The general manager took the tape last night. He erased it."

"You're shitting me."

"No. I'm not."

It was one thing to decide not to air video gathered during a news story. Stations did it frequently when they were not sure of what they had and were attempting to be fair. But intentionally erasing video . . .

"I don't believe this," Michael said.

"Neither do I," Shirley agreed. "I didn't know about it until after the fact."

He hung up the phone. Earl pulled the wagon in at a lot just off Thames Street. A live van from Channel Three had set up across the street, with the harbor in the background.

"What's wrong?"

"Nothing," Carolina said. There was no point in telling the photographer just then about what had happened. They had work to do.

But as Michael sat in the car writing his piece for noon, his thoughts kept drifting back to the lost video. What sort of pressure had been brought to bear on the station? Had the GM just made a mistake? Or was something else going on?

A few years back, I would have quit over something like this, he thought to himself. But as angry as he was, it was difficult to imagine quitting. What else can I do for a living? he thought. And where am I going to do it? He thought about Carla, and the life they were starting to build together. About Rhode Island, and how comfortable it had become. Even about his father, telling Michael he wanted to start over.

They edited the video from the morning, careful to keep the shots of the body wide and from a distance. Carolina made a note to warn that some of the pictures would be graphic. No sense frightening some toddler watching the noon news with her mother.

He looked carefully at the interview with Mercer. The segment where Mercer had blown up was terrific; the microphone picked up the young sailor's under-his-breath remarks, and it was obvious he had pushed Michael backward. Still, the scene was troubling, Michael thought. The kid was young, and perhaps still under the shock of what he had heard. Or was he? Was it all an act for a television crew? Am I suffering from the same disease as the GM, he wondered, or am I just trying to be cautious?

He looked at the tape again. It was powerful stuff, he was sure. But there had not been enough time, enough opportunity to report. The confrontation with Mercer would have to wait until he had more information.

They fed Carolina's taped story from the microwave van at

eleven forty-five, leaving Carolina with plenty of time to get in front of the camera set up once again on the waterfront. There were fewer people gathered to watch, owing perhaps to the time of day.

Michael plugged in his earpiece and listened to the broadcast of a soap opera. Someone, presumably a doctor, was telling a woman she had cancer that could be treated only by heavy doses of chemotherapy. The woman sobbed as music swelled in the background.

"The plots on these shows never change," he said to Earl. But Earl wasn't listening. He pointed to his left.

"Don't look now, Michael, but your girlfriend is here again."

Michael looked around, wondering why Carla might be in Newport. Then he saw her: not Carla, but the woman who had grabbed him on camera the night before. Staggering toward him. The reek of vodka preceded her.

"How's my favorite reporter today?"

God, not again, he thought.

Earl stepped from behind his tripod and camera.

"Listen, lady, we're trying to do a little work. Think you could wait until we finish?"

The woman stared at Earl as if he were vermin.

"I'm talking to my friend here. Back off, picture boy. I've dealt with plenty like you. You're just jealous you can't have a taste."

Earl stopped moving. He looked at Michael, his expression made up of equal parts of mirth and revulsion.

Desperately, Carolina looked around. There were no police, and once again, no one who appeared willing to lend a hand.

"I like the men who work on camera," the woman said happily. "They're what it's all about."

Michael swallowed. "My friend here's right, ma'am. We're about to go on the air, but we'll be finished in a minute or two. Can I talk to you then?"

The woman kept smiling, her eyes glassy and unfocused. She

rolled them to the sky, and swayed slightly. Carolina noticed she was wearing the same clothes she had worn the night before. Probably the same clothes she'd worn for weeks.

"Oh sure," she said at last. "I know. Got a big story, don'tcha. Got to get the news out about the Billy Budd and his father. Yeah." She brought her gaze back to him. "The sins of the fathers, honey, they get visited, now, don't they?"

"We're about a minute away," Earl warned.

Carolina strained to smile. "Yes, they do. They certainly do. I promise I'll talk to you when we're all clear, all right?" He kept watching the woman, who was now perhaps five or six feet away. What was she talking about? Billy Budd? Was she going to stay there? He dreaded the thought of doing another live shot while he waited for this woman to grab him.

Then the woman turned around.

"Sins of the fathers, honey." She took a step, tripped, then righted herself and kept walking.

Relieved, Carolina did a clean report, free of flubs, glitches, and uninvited guests. When it was over, he turned to look for the woman. Billy Budd. Melville's tale of the good-natured sailor who hanged when he stood up to pure evil. The lady was rude, crude, and inebriated. And she smelled bad. But she had education. And wit. Hard, black wit.

The waterfront near the yachting center had swallowed her up.

The tourists and sailors swelled until they nearly overflowed the footpaths and sidewalks that crisscrossed the wharves and surrounded the harbor. There was no sign now of the grim fog that had started the day. In the distance, Michael Carolina saw *Stream,* still anchored, twisting around her mooring, without a soul on board.

4

The first call came just before twelve.

Carla willed herself not to get excited, to let it ring at least twice. She'd had the phone for only three days, one line installed up in her bedroom, the other down in the kitchen, both just for business. But so far the only time it had rung was when the phone company called to see if it worked. There had not even been a wrong number, though she realized she should be thankful for that. Still, it would have to ring, and soon, if she was going to afford to keep it.

She picked up as soon as the second ring came to an end. "Tag Investigations," she said, in her best business voice. She liked the way the name sounded: short, snappy, but professional. Besides, it was easier than saying Tattaglia. One syllable instead of four. The name would be easy to remember.

"Carla Tattaglia, please." The voice sounded strangely familiar to her, though she could not quite place it.

"Speaking," she said.

"This is Rico Balboni."

She placed the voice instantly. He must know a dozen investigators, she thought. What the hell is he doing calling me? "What can I do for you, Counselor?"

"I have a client who requires investigative s'vices. You were, ah, highly recommended."

Carla wanted to laugh.

"Can you be in Newport this afternoon? Say, by one-fifteen?"

"Where?"

"Do you know Château du Printemps?"

Carla did not, but the name certainly sounded interesting. "I think I can find it."

"One-fifteen." Balboni hung up.

She came downstairs to find Paul Carolina building himself a sandwich. Roast beef and cold cuts. He ladled a generous helping of mustard on a knife and smeared it across two pieces of rye.

"Hey, there she is," he said. "What have you been up to?"

"Just taking care of some business," she said with a smile. "You comfortable?"

"Thanks to you." He smiled back, then sliced the sandwich in two. "Want half? Or I can make you one."

"No thanks," she said. "See any jobs in the classifieds?"

"I looked," Paul said, sounding distracted now. Carla glanced into the den. A copy of the *Providence Herald* was spread across the sofa, the pages split open in the sports section.

"I'm gonna make a few calls this afternoon," he said. "Hey, you wanna watch Michael on the noon news?"

Carla thought for a moment. Michael was in Newport, wasn't he? He'd left in a hurry, mumbling the word "murder" and not much else. But he was often like that, and it had never bothered her. That was the nature of reporting. Just like investigating. Secrets had to be kept.

Something inside, she didn't quite know what, told her it was better not to know just what Michael was doing right now.

"I have to rush," she said. "I have an appointment. Good luck with the job search."

He bit into his sandwich, and smiled again, this time with his mouth closed. He was cute, Carla decided, though a bit lazy. She thought about it for a moment, and then kissed him on his forehead before grabbing a set of car keys and walking out the door.

She drove to Newport in her new car, a used Volkswagen convertible, purchased with some of the compensation money from the shooting. The car was tan, with a white top, which she gladly folded down. The sun was still high, it was warm, and the day was full of promise.

She pulled onto Route 138 and passed three cars as she approached the Jamestown Bridge. It felt good to be moving fast, on the way to a meeting with a client, even if it was a referral from someone like Rico. The decision to open a private investigation business had not been easy. But after nearly eight years with the Department of Environmental Management's enforcement division she had concluded that a lifetime of chasing poachers and polluters was not what she wanted.

Leaving was difficult. Despite the long hours and the relatively low pay, working as a conservation officer was oddly satisfying. So while she was restless, Carla knew it would take something significant to get her to pick up and leave.

The something turned out to be a shootout involving a crazed clam digger and two overanxious wise guys. That made up her mind. She told her boss when he came to visit her in the hospital, after a surgeon had removed a bullet from her right hip. When he asked why, she smiled and said, "If I'm going to get shot, it's going to be over something more important than clams."

She'd filed a claim for victim's compensation with the state. The settlement was $25,000, though she'd waited nearly a year. But Michael had moved in, and he helped with expenses. Michael was definitely a keeper, she'd decided.

She was in Jamestown now, and she slowed for the series of curves that would lead to the Pell Bridge. There was almost no traffic on the road. She paid the toll, then soared up the bridge and looked off to the right. The water below was dotted with white streaks from the wakes of powerboats, and the sails of a few yachts. Beyond them the city of Newport beckoned. Thirty-five minutes, all told. She'd made very good time.

In ten minutes more she was through the city and making her way along the graceful streets that led to the mansions, the outrageous structures that had made Newport a playground for the filthy rich in the latter part of the nineteenth century. The names of the places sounded like something from a gothic fairy tale: the Breakers, Clarendon Court. And now a place called Château du Printemps. Castle of the Spring. Some would say the name had the ring of class, or gentility. Nearly all would agree it had the ring of money.

She pulled the Volkswagen down a narrow lane, past two massive granite pillars and a heavy iron gate covered with chipping black paint. The lane had hedges to both sides, and these were kept in better shape. Perhaps the landscapers are paid more, she mused to herself.

The main building reminded Carla of a dormitory on a college campus. It was made of white brick, and Carla guessed that the front of the structure was nearly two hundred feet in length. She counted two dozen windows. Fifteen steps, nearly thirty feet in length, led up to a broad porch. Six stone pillars rose up from the porch. Peeking out from behind the third and fourth pillars was a set of lacquered mahogany doors, the brass handles and hinges showing slight tarnish.

I hate this place, she decided.

Carla climbed the steps and saw what looked like a bell to the right, and a pair of brass door knockers. She chose the bell, and was surprised that she could hear no sound. When fifteen seconds had passed she reached for the door, but just before she touched it the door opened. A reed-thin man of indeterminate age stood before her, dressed in a butler's suit that would have comfortably fit a man thirty pounds heavier. He wore his dark hair slick and split down the middle of his head. Carla thought he looked like something from a grade B horror movie from the sixties, except for the beach sandals that exposed a set of blue-veined, corn-covered feet.

"You are," he said, in a tone that should have been but lacked the inflection of a question.

Carla held out a card. "I received a call from Mr. Balboni."

The butler, if that was what he was, looked at but did not take the card. "Yes," he said. "Yes you did. Come."

The entrance hall was marble, black and white squares, like a giant checkerboard. Without another word the butler closed the heavy door and started off toward the back of the house, his sandals making a slapping noise with each step. Carla followed, trying to keep a smile off her face.

They passed through a dark, wood-paneled study, past a kitchen that looked antiseptically clean and unused, and out onto a terrace laid with more of the hideous white brick. There was Rico Balboni, his jacket tossed over a lounge chair, standing with a man in his early fifties. On a glass table between them was a pitcher of what appeared, judging from the green olives impaled on swizzle sticks inside it, to be martinis. Rico and his host both held glasses in their hands.

Carla studied Rico's client for a moment. His thick hair was dirty blond, cut short in the front, but long enough to touch his collar in back. There were hints of gray at both temples, and he looked to be in decent physical shape. His jaw was close to square, and a small mole was apparent on the right side of his neck. Overall, Carla decided, he was good-looking. But his face bore signs of hard living: slight touches of red on the cheekbones and nose, crow's-feet and bags under his eyes.

"Miz Tattaglia," the flip-flopped butler said.

"T'anks, uh–" Balboni looked toward the other man.

"Boz," his client said.

"Boz?" Rico looked perplexed.

"Bosworth."

"Had to be." The words were out before Carla realized she had uttered them. All three men turned toward her. Carla smiled sweetly. Bosworth nodded, then disappeared back into the house.

"Don't t'ink we've ever met before." Rico extended a hand

covered with rings, and wet from the condensation on his glass. "Americo Balboni. This is my client, Hunter Worthington, Jr."

Worthington bowed slightly. He did not offer to shake hands.

"Would you like a drink?"

"Thanks, maybe later." Carla had no intention of drinking, not on her first serious job. "I understand you need an investigator."

"Right." Rico took another sip. He wasn't bothered in the least by Carla's decision not to join them. "You know about the body found in Newport this morning?"

She remembered Michael's leaving so early, and wondered whether it would have been smarter to watch the news. "I heard something about it."

Rico was watching her. "Yes. Well, it's my client's son who died. Hunter Worthington the Third."

"I'm sorry," Carla said, almost by reflex. Hunter Jr. gave a slight nod, and sipped from his drink. He showed no emotion.

She turned back to Balboni. "How are the police treating it?"

"As a homicide." It was as she expected, but she wanted to hear him say it, to watch him. Balboni's face was totally blank, as if they were conversing about the day's weather.

"Do they have a suspect?"

"They interviewed my client this morning. I cut things off when I saw where they were going."

"And where was that?"

Rico took another sip.

"The cops are interested in a dispute Hunter had with his son yesterday, after the Laser races in Newport. His son won that race. My client had a minor disagreement with him when the race ended."

"And what was that about?"

Hunter Jr. turned in the direction of a swimming pool that lay beneath the terrace. Beyond the pool was a magnificent view of the coastline.

"It was a personal matter," Balboni said. "The whole t'ing was blown way out of proportion. When they kept tryin' to press my client, we walked out."

Carla marveled at Rico's speech pattern. At times it was cultivated, even refined. And then, every so often, he slipped back into the hard accent native to so many Rhode Islanders. Carla knew that accent. She'd worked hard to get rid of her own. Rico, it seemed, was still trying.

"Did the son live here?" she asked.

"Yes," Rico said. "Mr. Worthington and his wife live here with the children."

"There are other children?"

"A daughter. They are both inside, grieving."

Carla glanced back toward the house. There was no sign of other life, but the place was huge. Mother and daughter could be anywhere.

"I'm going to tell youse—you—" Rico said, "that Mr. Worthington had absolutely nothing to do with the death of his son. The problem is we don't t'ink the police are willing to accept that."

He paused. Carla did not respond. Hunter Worthington took another drink.

"That's why we need to hire you."

"Is it?" Carla said mildly. She'd already decided she did not like the case. But work was work.

"As I said, Mr. Worthington is innocent of any involvement in his son's death. It's not clear to me that this is even a murder, but since the p'lice are treating it that way, we need someone to start looking around. To gather enough evidence about Hunter the Third's death that we can convince the p'lice to do their job."

"Why me?"

Rico stared at her. " 'Scuse me?"

"I said, why me? You've been a lawyer in this state for many years, and I'm sure you know a dozen investigators, all of them with a little–" Hell, why varnish it, she thought. "No, with a lot more experience than I have. So why me?"

From his expression, Rico had not anticipated the question. Still, he was quick with a response. "You really want to know? Because you're not well known. I t'ink that will help. Besides, I've seen worse-looking investigators in my time." He said the last line with a smile that was so patronizing she thought about slapping him. Carla did not believe the lawyer was telling her the whole truth, but his answer was hard to argue with.

"About my fee," she said.

Rico looked to his client, who nodded. "What's your rate?" Rico asked.

The fact was she had been trying to decide from the moment she'd left Edgewood. She took the figure she had in mind and doubled it.

"I'll need ten thousand as a retainer against a thousand a day. Plus expenses."

"That's robbery," Rico said.

"From what you just said, Mr. Balboni, I'm a unique commodity. And frankly"–she looked at Hunter–"I think you can afford it."

Worthington actually smiled then.

"Pay her," he said.

"There is a condition," Balboni said. "This arrangement is confidential. You do not tell anyone who you are working for. Understood?"

"Of course." Carla hesitated. "I have a condition as well. Two, actually."

"What are they?" Rico looked annoyed.

"One, I want to interview everyone who lives here. Mother, daughter, Boz." She looked at Worthington. "And you, sir."

"It will have to be tomorrow," Rico said. "As I told youse . . . these people are bereaved."

"Fine. Tomorrow. But I do have one question for Mr. Worthington right now. Did you have anything to do with the death of your son?"

"I've already told you—"

"I want to hear it from him, Mr. Balboni."

Hunter Worthington put his glass to his mouth once again. Carla watched as he took a good-sized swallow. The brick deck where they stood grew very still. In the distance, Carla could hear waves. She had not thought about how close Château du Printemps was to the ocean. But then, most of the Newport mansions were.

"I expect you're going to hear a lot of bad things about me, Miss Tattaglia. Things that'll skeer most people."

It was a strange accent he had. Some of the vowels were long and drawn out. Was it Canadian? Carla could not place it.

"The truth is," Worthington said, "I loved my son. I did not kill him. And I need to know who did."

After yet another silence, Rico said, "That satisfy you?"

"Yes," Carla said. "For now."

"Good," Balboni said. "I need to be kept advised of your findings. Every few days should be good enough. You don't need to put it in writing until I ask."

Curious, Carla thought. Nothing on paper. Something told her that the payments would be coming in cash, that no receipt would be requested.

Worthington sipped again from his drink. When it was empty, he refilled it from the pitcher. He was oblivious again, as if he were not connected to the conversation, nor even to the events that had brought the conversation about.

The sound of flip-flops announced Bosworth's return. He seemed to have sensed that she was about to leave.

"I'll be calling tomorrow about that meeting."

"Check with me," Balboni said. "I'll take care of the arrangements."

Neither Worthington nor Balboni said goodbye. They simply turned their backs on her and began some private conversation.

Carla followed Boz through the study, down the hall, and back to the marbled foyer.

"Very friendly place, this," she said to him.

Bosworth yanked the door open, then stopped to look at her. He started with her shoes, a pair of beat-up loafers, then slowly worked his way up her jeans, belt, and blouse, until he was peering into her eyes. Carla had the uneasy feeling of being appraised in the same fashion as a fine car, or a bottle of wine.

"Ever do any acting?"

"Excuse me?"

"Acting. Films."

"Uh, no."

Bosworth offered a grin that made one side of his mouth droop.

"Too bad. You might have been good."

She drove all the way back to Edgewood wondering about who Hunter Worthington was. And what a Newport old-money type could possibly be doing with a Providence lawyer who primarily represented defendants who were one step away from the gutter. And why in the world Americo Balboni had called her, because she did not believe for one minute that he'd told her everything.

But mostly, she wondered what the hell Bosworth was talking about.

Carolina spent the early afternoon digging. He started at the yachting center, which had a set of programs from the Laser championships of the day before. Hunter Worthington III was described as "one of the brightest new additions to Rhode Island's long and honored tradition of great sailors," along with rather standard blather about his potential as an Olympian.

There was also a glossy reproduction of a news clipping. "THE HUNT" LEADS ST. IVES TO REGATTA CHAMPIONSHIP was the headline. Beneath it was a photograph of five young sailors, presumably members of the winning team, all of them smiling.

Hunter Worthington stood in the middle of them, his wind-blown hair a mess, but his face radiant.

Earl sat nearby, paging through a sailing magazine.

"Interesting reading?"

"I consider it research," Earl said. "I could learn something from these still guys."

"Ever hear of a school called St. Ives?"

"Sure. St. Ives Academy. Private school at the other end of the island, up in Portsmouth. For what I make a year I could send my kid there for a semester."

"I guess our dead sailor was big man on campus up there." He showed Earl the headline.

"Figures," Earl sniffed. "Where I went to high school, we didn't even have a tennis team, let alone a sailing team."

"Where'd you grow up?"

"Fall River."

"Well, that explains it."

"Hey, don't be knocking Fall Reev, babe."

"My apologies. Just giving you a hard time."

"Okay, then." Earl handed the clipping back. "So. We taking a ride to Portsmouth?"

"You read my mind."

St. Ives Academy was located on a sloping hillside rolling down to a rocky shoreline. The school buildings were uniformly constructed of rust-red brick, and most were laced with ivy. The lawns were immaculate, as were the hedges and trees. The narrow asphalt paths that ran between the buildings were filled with young men and women carrying schoolbooks. The males wore dark slacks, white shirts, and ties striped in blue and red. The females wore pleated skirts. Everyone had a blazer with a gold seal.

They pulled in front of a small, neat little building, built of brick like all the others, but also dressed with thick white rose bushes. The roses were in bloom. A sign in front of the building announced that it housed St. Ives Academy's administration.

"If Martha Stewart had children," Carolina said, "I bet she'd send them here."

"If she has kids," Earl said, "I feel sorry for them."

The lobby of the building was painted off-white and covered with black-and-white photographs of severe-looking men and women, most dressed in academic garb. A pleasant-looking young woman in a school uniform occupied a wooden desk in the center of the room. Carolina guessed she was no more than sixteen.

"Can I help you?"

"We're from Channel Three," Carolina said. "Do you have a public affairs officer we could speak to?"

"The news, huh?" The young woman smiled, and for a moment Carolina thought he saw a flash of metal. The girl picked up the phone and dialed.

"Yes, Mr. DeLaurent. Two gentlemen here from Channel Three. They want to speak to a public affairs officer. I didn't ask, but I bet it's about Hunter." She listened for a moment and hung up.

"The head will be out in a minute."

"That would be the headmaster?"

"Yeah. You know, I always wanted to be on TV. Looks fun." The professional tone she had on the phone had evaporated, and she sounded once again like a teenager. The girl smiled again. Again Carolina noticed the flash. Must be a gold tooth, he thought.

"Why aren't you in class?" Earl asked.

"Triple D's," the girl said. She was pretty, with brown hair and a hint of freckles on her nose. "Demerits. Got to sit for the head as a work crew."

"What got you in trouble?"

"Just a guy," the girl said coyly. "I like older guys."

"You mean college students?" Carolina asked.

"For a start."

"Can I help you?"

The man's voice was deep, and matched his frame. He stood well over six feet, Carolina guessed.

"I'm Michael Carolina, from Channel Three in Providence." He introduced Earl.

"Charles DeLaurent. I'm the headmaster here. It's too bad you didn't make an appointment."

Michael smiled. "Yes, I'm sorry. We didn't know we'd be coming by until a few minutes ago."

DeLaurent grunted. "Yes. Well. Come into the office. Jennifer, I'm sure you have some work to do while you're waiting for the phone." Jennifer did not reply, but a pouting look came over her face as DeLaurent turned his back on her and walked down a hall. Carolina and Earl looked at each other, then back to the young woman at the desk. She shrugged and flashed a grin again.

"Did you see something metal in her mouth?" Carolina whispered as they followed DeLaurent. Earl shook his head.

DeLaurent's office was filled with athletic memorabilia, including ancient lacrosse and hockey sticks, and an old soccer ball on a shelf. Behind him in a gilt frame was a diploma: Charles DeLaurent, St. Ives Academy, 1958.

"How can I help you gentlemen?" DeLaurent said. He leaned forward on his desk, showing two large, red-knuckled hands.

"We're covering the death of Hunter Worthington the Third," Carolina said.

"Yes, we heard about the accident this morning. Sad indeed."

"I understand he graduated from this school."

"That's true," DeLaurent answered. "Fine young man. Won the sailing prize."

Carolina nodded agreement. "I wonder if I could look at the school yearbook."

"I don't think so," DeLaurent said.

"And I'd like to interview some students."

"That's impossible."

"And perhaps some teachers."

"Absolutely not."

"Well," Earl said, "how about you?"

"Sure," Carolina said. "Isn't someone from this school going to speak about the death of a recent graduate?"

"Mr. Carolina." DeLaurent lifted his hands off the desk, and drew himself up to his full size. "This is a private school. We train young minds and we train young bodies. And we do it in a private setting. My students, their parents, and the alumni would not appreciate having our school being dragged into some vignette on the evening news."

"Vignette?" Earl frowned. "Is that what we do? Vignettes?"

DeLaurent did not react.

"Perhaps you wouldn't mind if we took a couple of pictures before we left," Michael said. "So the people who watch our vignette know where their betters are educated."

"As long as you do it from a public road."

"I'm not just wounded now," Earl said. "I'm dying inside."

DeLaurent looked down at his desk. "I apologize if I offended you. I know you have a job to do. I hope you can appreciate that I also have obligations."

"No problem," Carolina said. He looked down at the headmaster's desk. It was exceptionally neat, with a short stack of papers, a fountain pen, and a message slip. Michael turned his head, and thought he could make out the words "Hunter Worthington" and above them "Balboni."

"By any chance have you heard from anyone in Mr. Worthington's family today?"

DeLaurent looked up and met Carolina's gaze. With his right hand he picked up the message slip and placed it into the desk's center drawer.

"At this school," he said, "we teach our students about honor. And manners."

"I'm pleased to hear that," Carolina said. "In this business honor only counts when you get the story."

DeLaurent glared at Michael. Then he stepped around the desk and opened the office door. "You'll have to excuse me."

Earl and Carolina walked down the hall.

"Guy was a jerk," Earl said.

"He's under pressure," Carolina told him. "Balboni already called."

They reached the lobby. The young woman at the desk had disappeared. Outside, most of the students had disappeared. It was early afternoon, and Carolina guessed that classes were back in session.

"Where do you want to take a shot of the school?" Earl asked.

"I saw a pretty nice bronze plaque up near the entrance," Michael said.

"So you wanna know about the Hunt?"

They both turned. The girl from the lobby was standing under a tree. She held a cigarette in her left hand, in a manner that suggested she was well on the way to acquiring the habit.

"Jennifer, right?"

"My friends call me Jen," the girl said. She took a drag and flicked her ash, though there was almost no ash to flick.

"Aren't you supposed to be in class?" Carolina said.

"Work crew, remember? I'm taking a butt break."

"You ought to stay away from those things," Carolina said.

"You sound like my mother." The girl looked annoyed. "You wanna know about the Hunt or not?"

"What I want to know," Michael said, "is why your mouth keeps flashing."

"This?" The girl giggled and opened her mouth, revealing a solid gold post, at least an inch long and a quarter inch thick, piercing the middle of her tongue.

Earl smirked. "Does St. Ives know about this?"

"Isn't it the balls?" the girl laughed. She flicked her tongue so that the gold post clicked against her teeth.

"That wasn't quite the word I had in mind," Carolina said.

"Guys like the Hunt loved it. They hang out down at the Porcelain God. You should see what I can do with it."

Carolina decided he did not want to see. "Where is the Porcelain God?"

"In Newport. I went once, with a fake ID. It's way cool. They talk about it in here." She held out a large black book with silver lettering on the spine. *The Ivy,* it was called.

"Is this the yearbook?" Carolina asked.

"That's what you wanted, right?" The girl gave another smile, and the gold post flashed again. "You can take it with you. There's lots of them left in the office. Now, how about an interview?"

Carolina looked at her for a moment. Then he slid into the car. Earl climbed behind the wheel.

"So aren't you going to interview me? I'll meet you off campus if you want."

Earl started the engine. Carolina closed his door but rolled down the window. "You know, you're pretty, and I'll bet you're smart if you're in a school like this. Why don't you finish your work crew and go back to class?"

The girl got the pouting look on her face, the same one she had displayed for the headmaster. "I'm not a kid, you know."

"In my limited experience, if you have to say something like that, you probably still are." He did not mean it unkindly, but there was no way that the girl would take it well. She turned around and stalked away.

"After we get a shot of the campus or that plaque," Carolina said, running his hand along the yearbook, "I need to take a look at this."

Earl slipped the news van into gear. "Why didn't you just talk to her? She probably has a lot of background on this place, and she was dying to tell you."

Michael gave a small sigh. "She probably doesn't know anything."

"That's not the reason," Earl said. "You laid off because she's young, and she might get into trouble."

Michael did not respond. But Earl did not give up.

"I thought honor only counts when you get the story."

Carolina flipped through the yearbook. "So maybe I lied a little."

The Ivy was a glossy, handsome book, loaded with photographs of St. Ives Academy students and their teachers. There were pictures of boys playing lacrosse, of girls in field hockey uniforms, of a high school production of *Macbeth,* and dozens of candid photos of well-heeled young people smiling and laughing, clearly enjoying the process of attending an expensive and exclusive private school, one that prepared them to attend expensive and exclusive colleges and universities.

In the midst of them all was Hunter Worthington.

There was a color photo of him in front of a sailboat, his hair streaked in shades of brown and gold. His eyes were the color of water in the tropics, and they were intense, staring at a slender halyard he held in his hands. "The Hunt checks his rig," the caption beneath the picture said.

His graduation picture showed him in the standard school blazer, his hair combed, his tie straight. He seemed to be looking somewhere past the camera lens, Carolina thought, perhaps to a sight that remained invisible to mere mortals. Beneath the photo was a string of words:

> HUNTER WORTHINGTON III, Varsity sailing, 3, 4, 5, 6. Honors, English, History. "The Hunt." Amicus brewski, Life of the Porcelain God. I'm a Newport moke, mate. Ali, you're the one. Starboard, baby. I got starboard. "Youth to itself rebels, though none else is near." Billy S.

"Learning anything?" Earl said. They had grabbed video of the front entrance to St. Ives Academy and were driving back toward Newport for a six-o'clock live shot.

"Hard to tell," Carolina said. "The kid likes to sail, I'll say that."

"Sounds like sailing is all the kid did."

Carolina grinned. "No, he liked to party, too."

"Anything else?"

"Apparently he was a decent student, at least in some subjects. Other than that . . ."

"Yeah?"

"You remember the name of that place our friend Jennifer was talking about?"

"The Porcelain something."

"God. The Porcelain God. Hunter mentions it in his yearbook quote."

"I hate to think what that means."

"It means," Michael said, "that we need to pay a visit."

It came as no shock that the Porcelain God was a dive nightclub, located in an alley off Thames Street. The front was painted a glossy white, and the door had a stainless-steel handle in the shape of a toilet flusher. Two bouncers, both crew-cut, and both looking freshly imported from Gold's Gym, stood outside. They wore white painter's pants and T-shirts with the words "American Standard" in pale blue letters on the back.

Carolina stood in front. "Kind of a theme bar, wouldn't you say?"

Rather than agree, Earl remained silent. The bouncers, who were within earshot, did not smile.

They started to walk inside, but the bouncers stepped in front of them.

"Three bucks," one of the bouncers said.

"Is there a place to wash your hands?" Earl asked.

"Three bucks."

Earl looked at Carolina. "Pay the man—it's your story." Michael did.

The interior of the Porcelain God was decorated in a toilet motif. The bar was a glossy white, and shined to a mirror finish. A bartender poured drinks and served them on swatches of bathroom tissue. The pale gray walls were decorated with photographs of what appeared to be outhouses and old commodes. Between the pictures were various items of graffiti. The place seemed to be doing quite a solid business. Despite the relatively early hour there were at least a dozen people at the bar, and a band was setting up on a small stage in the back.

The bartender was a mean-looking skinhead, maybe thirty years old, with a brass ring in one ear and arms roughly the size of small fire hydrants. A name badge read "Mr. Clean."

"Whatayadrinkin', dirtballs?"

Michael turned to Earl. "This must be one of those attitude bars. You know, where the insults are part of the ambiance?"

Earl gave Mr. Clean a withering look. "Got any house specials, Hercules?"

"Let's not go there," Carolina said. Mr. Clean grimaced. Earl thought for a moment and nodded.

"Just a Coke."

"Two-drink minimum," Mr. Clean said. "Three for pussy soft drinks."

"Make it three pussy soft drinks, then," Earl responded. Mr. Clean looked at Michael.

"I'll have the same. Who's the band tonight?"

Mr. Clean shrugged. "Some skanks out of Providence. Billy and the Scuzzbuckets." He swaggered off to get their Cokes.

Earl called after him, "I like pussy soft drinks."

"Billy and the Scuzzbuckets?" Carolina said.

"You had to ask," Earl said.

"Just getting the lay of the territory," Carolina answered.

Michael glanced around the bar. The patrons all appeared to be in their early twenties, and most were drinking beer. A few were dressed in shorts and polo-type shirts, while others wore torn clothing and sported tattoos. Some of the men, and one woman, had their heads shaved. The confluence of preppies, grunge, skinheads, trenchcoats, tattoos, and pierced flesh was beyond surreal.

"Do you get the feeling," he said to Earl, "that we just walked onto the set of one of those old Mel Gibson films?"

Earl frowned. "Well, it sure as hell ain't *The Wizard of Oz.*"

Mr. Clean returned, three Cokes splayed between the fingers of each hand.

"Nice place you have here," Carolina said.

"I pissed in your drinks," Mr. Clean said.

Neither Carolina nor Earl knew whether to believe him. "That's ten bucks," Mr. Clean said.

"Very reasonable for pussy soft drinks with a urine spritzer," Carolina said, smiling. Mr. Clean did not smile back.

"I wasn't thirsty anyway," Earl mumbled.

"We're from Channel Three," Carolina said.

"I know." Mr. Clean stared at them.

"Yep, definitely not thirsty," Earl said.

"We were covering the death of a sailor."

"I heard," Mr. Clean said.

"Then you're very well informed."

"And you're a piece of shit." Just then Mr. Clean glanced down toward the end of the bar. Carolina followed his gaze.

And saw Jimmy Mercer.

"Yeah, those are the fuckers," Mercer said in a loud, slurred voice.

Carolina grimaced.

Mercer got up, swaying slightly. "He's looking to hang somebody for Worthington."

Mr. Clean threw Mercer a quizzical look. "That asswipe that was in here last night?"

"Shut up." Mercer snapped the words off at the bartender, who actually looked startled.

"Hey, I was just—"

"I said shut up."

Mr. Clean did. His bald skull, however, flushed red.

"Jimmy seems to have recovered from his grief," Carolina said.

"We ought to beat it," Earl said.

Mercer was moving toward them now. Carolina looked over his shoulder. Mr. Clean remained behind the bar, his biceps flaring out from his white T-shirt as he cracked the knuckles on both hands.

"Just trying to find out about your friend," Carolina said.

"Screw you, he ain't my friend," Mercer said.

"You said so this morning."

Mercer swayed again, but got closer to Carolina, until Michael could smell the sweet stench of vodka.

"You think I killed him, newsboy? That what you think?"

Carolina couldn't help pulling away. "What do you think, Jimmy?"

"I think—I think Worthington was an asshole, and I won't miss him. And I think I ought to—" Mercer swung wildly with his left hand, and Michael ducked. The blow caught him on the shoulder and slid off. Off balance, Mercer grabbed for the bar, then slid to his knees. Michael did not back up.

In one clean move, Mr. Clean was over the bar, helping Mercer to his feet.

"You ought to get him out of here," Carolina said.

"And you ought to be trying to stay alive." Mr. Clean said the words calmly, as if he were discussing the proper method of watering flowers.

"I quite agree," Earl said, tugging at Carolina's arm.

Carolina threw a ten-dollar bill on the bar and walked toward the door, with Earl close behind. The two of them stopped and turned back toward the bar in time to see Mr. Clean swilling one of the Cokes and trying to get Jimmy Mercer to drink another. Jimmy Mercer watched, laughing.

"So long, newsboy," Mercer called.

Earl looked at Michael. "I guess he was kidding when he said he pissed in them."

"I wouldn't be too sure," Carolina answered.

As they pushed the doors open to get outside, one of the bouncers stopped them.

"Y'ain't gettin' in again without a new cover."

"That won't be a problem," Carolina said.

Paul Carolina was gone when Michael returned home that night. Carla had made bowls of pasta, bowties with pink vodka sauce. They sat down on the steps to her back porch and split a bottle of red wine.

"Where'd he go?"

"He didn't say," Carla said. "I asked him about looking for a job earlier, but he was watching soaps when I left."

Michael sighed and shook his head. Carla put her bowl down and placed a brown hand on his arm.

"He may need a little room, Mike."

"He's probably trying to find his way to the dog track right now."

She sipped her wine. "Understanding your relatives isn't easy."

Her words triggered thoughts of that morning. He put his own bowl down.

"Try to picture a dead body hanging off a boat. There's a man on a pier, watching. Do you see it?"

"I do," Carla said quietly.

"Now. Imagine that the body is a young man. That the guy on the pier is the young man's father. And he says nothing. He shows nothing. He doesn't even blink. What kind of person would act like that?"

Carla sipped again. She did not look at Michael. "That's what you saw this morning?"

"That's it. I didn't want to be too hard on the guy. The

father, I mean. But I can't figure out for the life of me why he'd act that way."

Carla did not respond. Michael waited for a moment, then shrugged.

"So. Let's change the subject to something less morbid. What did you do today?"

"Not a lot," Carla said. She picked up the pasta again. "Just trying to get some clients."

"Any luck?"

Carla smiled. "A little."

"That's great." He kissed her then, lightly, on her lips.

"A pink vodka kiss," she giggled.

"What could be better," he said. "So who's the client?"

"I need to be discreet about that." She had finished the pasta by then, and held out a hand for his bowl. Michael looked at her, puzzled, then gave it to her.

"What's the big deal?"

"No big deal," she said. "My client just insisted on discretion." She walked into the house. He followed, and turned on the television.

She called from the kitchen. "Yanks playing?"

"Yeah," he answered. But the television showed a picture of a rainswept Yankee stadium, the mound covered by a tarp. "Looks like a delay," he said.

She finished the dishes quickly, and joined him.

"You mad at me?" she asked.

He shook his head.

She put her arms around him and whispered, "If you come upstairs, you can show me your best pitch."

They left the light on for Michael's father. They left the television on, too, because Carla worried he might hear them upstairs. But they were asleep when he staggered in, and passed out on the couch in front of a screen showing nothing but a test pattern.

5

There was no fog the next morning. But it was still cool, and Carla kept the top up on the convertible for the drive to Newport. She punched several radio buttons looking for something to hear, but found nothing except the usual smart-assed announcers and music that was programmed according to market research. Classic rock. Heavy metal. "Lite" music. "Soft" jazz.

"Charlie Parker," she said aloud. But there was none to be had. She turned the radio off.

Carla thought about Michael, and the night before. The questions he'd asked were innocent enough, and he did not press when she refused to answer. She wanted to tell him what had happened, about the strange meeting with Balboni and Worthington, and the meeting she expected to have when she visited the mansion once again. But the client insisted on confidentiality. Besides, Michael was working the story. She could not think of a quicker way to harm her own reputation than to share pillow talk about the case with a reporter. If I were still a cop, she thought, I wouldn't be able to tell him anything.

Her reasoning, she knew, was sound. Still, it did not make her feel better. She paid the toll in Jamestown and her car hummed its way up the Pell Bridge. Off to the right she could already see a few yachts raising their sails, heading out for a cruise to Block Island or Cuttyhunk somewhere beyond the horizon. The appeal of a long voyage was not lost on her, and Carla wondered whether she would ever make such a trip. I should ask Michael about that, she thought to herself, and day-dreamed about the two of them cruising to Europe or the South Seas.

Then she realized if she mentioned she had been to Newport, he would want to know why she was there, whether her new clients were there. It would not take Michael long to figure out who her new employer was. I've got to be careful, she told herself. I don't want to lie to him.

Carla hoped that the mansion would look better on a second look. It did not. The architect who had designed the place, she decided, should be flayed. She pulled into the same spot as the day before. There were no other cars parked in front. Balboni had called her at eight-thirty and said she would be expected by the family at ten.

The man in the tails and flip-flops greeted her silently.

"Morning, Borsalino."

"Bosworth."

"Right. Sorry." He sounded mildly annoyed, which Carla found amusing.

They moved from the foyer through the study and past the kitchen again. But Bosworth did not take her out to the pool. Instead he took a left turn down another hall and into a room roughly the size of a tennis court. There were fireplaces on each end, and the walls were dressed in black-and-white Italian marble. There were dozens of paintings, some of them vaguely familiar, as if they were reproductions. The furniture was a blend of classic and modern styles: Georgian, Swedish, Early American. Nothing matched, Carla thought. She had never seen a room before where everything looked so out of place.

"Miss Tattaglia," Bosworth announced. He did not leave immediately, but stood staring from the far end of the room.

There were two people. Hunter Worthington, Jr., wore a pair of tennis shorts and a pale green polo shirt. He leaned against a fireplace mantel, hands shoved in his pockets. A woman, probably in her forties, was next to him. Her hair had once been blond, Carla suspected, and it was swept back with a scarf. Her face was smooth, too smooth, the likely product of a scalpel and a series of skin peels. The woman was curled up on a gilt-edged love seat. She wore blue slacks and a white designer sweatshirt. Hunter and his lady friend held glasses in their hands. Judging from the olives, it appeared they were having breakfast martinis.

"Good morning," Carla said.

Junior nodded. "This is my wife. Pippa, this is the investigator." From the flatness in his voice it was as if he were introducing a sewer repairman.

The woman identified as Pippa smiled serenely, as if she were lost in a cloud.

Carla said, "I thought Mr. Balboni was going to be here."

"He can't make it," Junior said.

"And he mentioned your daughter."

"She'll be right down." Junior appeared to be doing all the talking. Pippa paid neither of them any attention. "Do you want a drink?" Junior lifted his glass toward Carla. "Or is it too early for you?" The questions sounded almost snide, a faint jab to determine whether she disapproved.

"I'm not thirsty, thank you."

Pippa giggled at this, and sipped her drink. They all looked at each other, as if wondering who should speak first.

Hunter Jr. evidently decided to take the plunge. "What do you think of Château du Printemps, Miss Tattaglia?"

"It's quite a place." That's good, she told herself. Nice. Neutral. No argument with it.

"This is one of the later Bellevue mansions, you know. Built by Richard Morse Hunt. He did all the better homes."

Carla smiled politely. She doubted Worthington's statement was true. Even if it were, she remembered reading somewhere that Hunt was famous for ripping off wealthy Newporters by building with shoddy materials. It was probably best not to bring the subject up.

"Did you know the place was almost in the movies?" Worthington seemed impressed with his own question.

"Really?"

"The Great Gatsby," Pippa said. "With Redford. During my first marriage. But they used another cottage instead."

"That's too bad," Carla said.

There was an uncomfortable pause before Worthington jumped in. "Yes, Pippa, but you are far more beautiful than Daisy Buchanan."

Pippa giggled at this, and drank again. Isn't this delightful, Carla thought. Their son is dead, Dad's a murder suspect, and we're chatting about films and expatriate literature.

"Perhaps while we're waiting for your daughter, you could tell me a little more about your son," she said.

"He's not." Pippa Worthington's words were sufficiently slurred to indicate that the drink in her hand was not her first of the day.

Carla raised an eyebrow. "Excuse me? Not what?"

Pippa took another sip before answering. "Not my son."

There was a pause before Junior said, "This is my second marriage. My first wife died seventeen years ago when Hunter was a little boy."

Pippa seemed oblivious once again, resolutely sipping her martini.

Carla was not sure what to make of her, though it seemed clear that she was doing a fine job of hiding any grief over the loss of her stepson. Carla turned back to Junior.

"How long have you been married?"

Junior hesitated a moment. "It will be ten years in November."

"I understand that Hunter just finished prep school?"

"That's right." For the first time, Junior showed some hint of a smile, and his voice betrayed his pride. "Captain of the sailing team, top ten percent of his class."

"Did he plan to go to college?"

"Oh, uh, of course." He said it quickly, and he made a point of looking her in the eye. "That's what must be done. But not right away. He was taking time off from school. Sailing. Lasers. He was the champion, you know."

"Yes. I've heard."

"He was going to be an Olympian."

"That's what the news reports said." Carla watched him. The only times Hunter Worthington, Jr., seemed to show animation was when he mentioned sailing. And then there was that accent. Was it Canadian? She could not be sure.

"Do you sail?" she asked.

"Me? For years. But I don't race. That's for younger men. And frankly, racing hasn't been the same here since the Cup left Newport."

"You mean the America's Cup?"

"Of course." Worthington smiled with such an air of condescencion that she almost wanted to laugh.

"But you do have a boat?"

Junior's smile faded. "You know where my son was found."

Carla knew. She also knew there was little chance of seeing it, at least while the police were looking at it. It would be like a waving flag that the Worthingtons had hired an investigator.

"Did Hunter have many friends?"

"Sure, lots of friends," Junior said. At this, Carla thought she heard Pippa giggle. But when she glanced down, Pippa was sipping once again.

"I'm done. Need another," Pippa said. Her face was turning pink.

"You have to excuse her," Junior said. "This is all shocking and hurtful to both of us."

Carla looked at Pippa again. She did not look shocked. She did not look hurt. She looked smashed.

"I'd like a list of his friends. People he went to school with. Kids he brought home. People I can call. Interview."

Pippa giggled again. "It won't be a long list," she said.

Junior glared at her, but did not respond. He turned back to Carla. "I'll speak to Mr. Balboni. We'll get something to you."

"Fine," Carla said. "As I understand it, your son was in town on the night he died?"

"That's what the police have told us."

It was a strange answer. "Well, he wasn't here, was he?"

"No." Junior seemed startled. "No, not at all."

"Okay. Where were you that night?"

Junior looked at her again. "I was here. I came back right after the race."

"You watched the race?"

"Yes." Now Junior sipped his own drink. "I wanted to see my son finish. We spoke afterward."

"What did you say to him?"

"I congratulated him."

"And how was he?" Michael had told her of the confrontation between father and son on the dock. And how quickly the tape had been suppressed. Carla waited to see what Junior would say.

"He was fine. Happy as could be. I told him I was very proud. He said he wanted to celebrate with his friends. And I said goodbye to him." There was a tear, just then, in Junior's right eye. He waited a moment too long to brush it away, and it fell, making a small spot on the green polo shirt.

There was no mention of a fight, of striking his son on the dock. Carla considered telling her client what she knew. She decided against it.

"How about you, Mrs. Worthington?"

Pippa looked up, her eyes as glassy as a pool of water in a dead calm.

Hunter Worthington, Jr., said, "She was here, too."

She dropped her head and stared at her empty glass. Her hands were beautifully manicured, Carla noticed. The nails were long, hard, and real, not the press-on kind from beauty salons. They were perfect hands, not used for any kind of hard work. Carla wondered whether holding a drink was the hardest labor Pippa Worthington did.

"I assume," Carla said, "that you have someone who can verify that you were both here?"

Junior hesitated only a moment. "Bosworth."

A paid servant in a monkey suit and beach sandals. Perfect, Carla thought. One hell of an alibi.

As if he were reading her mind, Junior said, "I thought that Mr. Balboni made it clear that you are to look for suspects. I do not expect to be interrogated by someone I'm paying."

Carla glanced once more around the room. The Worthington mansion demonstrated beyond any doubt that money did not necessarily translate into good taste. Still, there was enough cash invested in this one room to pay off the mortgage on her house. What would be accomplished by pissing the client off on the first day?

"Mr. Worthington." She was amazed at how calm she sounded. "You want me to find out what happened to your son, and you've told me the police are treating you like a suspect. You've also told me that you are innocent. If the police are focusing on you unfairly, then the best way to get them to stop is to eliminate you as a suspect."

Junior listened, his eyes slightly narrowed.

"And the best way to eliminate you as a suspect," she said, "is to lock down where you were so the police can verify it."

Just then she noticed how much the pictures she had seen of the dead sailor on the news resembled the man who stood in front of her. Hunter Worthington III had been a handsome young man. At one time, his father must have been, too. And yet, there were some peculiarities that she could not quite place. Something strange about this man. He was hard. Tough. Carla sensed that even with all the alcohol, and the knowledge that his son was dead, Hunter Jr. was in control.

"All right," he said abruptly. "At least you've cleared that up."

"Let me know when I can pick up that list of friends. If there are any enemies, people who hold grudges against your son, I need to know that as well. And I still need to see your daughter."

"Stepdaughter. She's right here," a female voice said.

Carla turned in time to see a young woman, in her late teens or early twenties, coming into the room. She was dressed in black canvas pants and heavy black boots. There was a ratty gray cardigan hanging from her shoulders, covering a T-shirt that matched the pants and boots. Her spiked hair was dyed, probably with Kool-Aid, Carla thought, in alternating strips of hot pink and lime green.

"This is Morgan," Junior said, with the same enthusiasm one might have when introducing a small rodent. "Morgan Scott."

Carla made mental notes. Not the same last name. Not adopted. And evidently not terribly close to the stepfather. Carla extended a hand. Morgan stared at it a moment, then extended her own, revealing chipped robin's-egg-blue polish on the nails. Carla looked at Pippa, who was still staring at her empty glass. Mother and daughter definitely did not share the same manicurist. Stranger still was the tattoo across her fingers: SARAH.

"Another drink," Pippa said.

Carla asked, "You both have children from previous marriages?"

"That's right," Junior said. He had finished his own drink, and Bosworth appeared without being called.

"More martinis," Junior told him. He looked at Carla again. "Sure you won't join us?"

"Still not thirsty." Carla smiled weakly.

Junior held up two fingers for Bosworth. He offered nothing to Morgan, who did not seem to mind.

Ordinarily, Carla would have felt the need to express sympathy. The three people before her had, after all, just lost a family member, related either by blood or merely by the force of habit that comes with living together. But the—the only word she could think of was "dynamics"—of the meeting were such that Carla knew any expression of sympathy would seem out of place. No, it would seem downright bizarre.

What was it that Fitzgerald wrote? The rich are very different from you and me. And if so, Carla thought, all us poor people are better off.

She looked again at Morgan. "Were you close to your step-brother?"

Morgan peered at her from behind two strands of green-dyed hair. Carla realized that the young woman's eyes were the palest blue she had ever seen.

"Sure," she said. "He was cute. Nice butt. He could, uh, shiver my timbers, as the sailors say."

"Morgan!" Pippa's distress did not cause her to look at her daughter. Junior's face was like stone.

"Don't lecture me on morality, Moms. He was cute. But he wasn't my brother." She turned and looked again at Carla. "Really, I'm all torn up."

Carla asked, "Did you see him two nights ago? The night he died?"

"Yes and no."

Junior's eyebrows arched, but he said nothing. Evidently it was not the answer he was expecting.

"You were here, weren't you?" he said. "I'm sure your mother saw you."

Morgan shook her head slowly. She was not going to be taking any hints. "No, Steps. I was out. Way out. Didn't see you or Moms at all that night."

"Think you could elaborate on that a bit?" Carla asked.

Morgan had a half-smile on her face, apparently enjoying all the ambiguity.

"Steps knows I don't do the sailing thing," she said. "Too prep. Too white. Too clean. You could say that Hunt and I run in different crowds."

She kept the half-smile going. Carla decided it was probably something genetic. "So where did you see him?"

"At the God, off Thames. You know it? A band was playing. Hunt likes it there. Oops. Liked it. So did his little sailor friends. Just happens I like it, too."

Carla remembered Michael briefly describing the bar he had visited the afternoon before. "Would that be the Porcelain God?"

Morgan half-smiled again. "There's only one God, and you have to kiss it."

Now Carla half-smiled. The two women seemed to understand each other.

"What was Hunter doing?"

"Drinking. Hanging. Oops." She stopped. "Sorry. I meant, being with people, you know. Those sailor boys and their wenches, or whatever they call them."

"Did you talk to him?"

"Not a lot. Hello. Congrats. Gave him a kiss. For the race and all that. Like I said, he was cute for a preppie. But we don't hang—ummm, sorry. It just keeps coming out that way." The half-smile again. No one laughed. Carla glanced at Junior. He was staring hard at a painting. Probably dreaming about tearing it off the wall, Carla thought, and breaking it over his step-daughter's head.

"When did you last see him that night?"

"Late. When they closed down. After one, I guess. He was still with that group. I left and came home. Crashed."

"Did you see who he was with?"

"I don't know." Morgan looked away then. "He was with his pals from that school he went to." The way she said it rang false. It was as if Morgan wanted to put distance between herself and her stepbrother.

Carla asked, "Where did you go to school?"

"Farmington," she said. "Miss Porter's. All girls."

"Are you going to college?"

"That's undecided," Junior cut in. "And it's not really relevant."

Morgan laughed, and it sounded bitter. "Steps and Pips say I have to make certain, uh, lifestyle changes before any funding comes through."

There was a sob then, and Carla turned and saw Pippa Worthington curling tighter on the couch. "I said this wasn't relevant." Junior's voice was stronger now, closer to anger.

Bosworth appeared, with two glasses on a tray. Pippa grabbed hers, and the sobbing stopped.

The answers she'd heard raised at least a dozen new questions in Carla's mind. But Hunter Worthington, Jr., and his stepdaughter were clearly on edge. Besides, Pippa was too polluted to be of any further use, at least that day.

"I think I'm all set for now. Morgan, would you know any of the kids your stepbrother was with if you saw them again?"

Morgan shrugged, and another wisp of dyed hair fell across her face. She did not attempt to brush it away.

"Depends. Maybe. I'd have to see."

Not an encouraging response. Carla tried to think of anything she'd missed. Her eyes fell on Morgan's hands, the fingers laced across one knee.

"One more question, then. Why the Sarah tattoo?"

Morgan's half-smile erupted then into a full-blown grin. "It's my band. I sing."

"Oh please," Junior said. He turned back toward the painting. Carla ignored him.

"Do you play at the God?"

"Couple times." Now Morgan's voice showed some sign of pride. "Mostly we do clubs up in Providence. You should check it out."

Carla said, "I'll have to do that."

"It's hardly music," Junior said. "Morgan could do much better."

A flash of anger crossed Morgan's face. "Yes, I could be more like you, Steps." She turned to Carla, her gray cardigan sliding slightly off her shoulders.

"Steps has always said I could do better. Make a better impression. Keep up appearances, you know? That's why I was late coming down. I was supposed to be here, but—"

"Don't," Junior warned. But Morgan did not look at him.

"Steps here," she said, "didn't think I was dressed properly to greet company."

She let the cardigan fall completely off her shoulders, into a heap around her ankles. It revealed the black T-shirt Morgan wore. Carla did not care much for the color, but otherwise the shirt was normal. Except for the holes exposing her nipples. And the silver hoop earring that pierced each one. The rings looked like silver eyes peering out of the young woman's chest.

"Ever hear of pasties?" Carla asked.

Morgan's smile twisted into a look that blended pride and arrogance. "Don't worry, it only hurts a little," she said. "And it's worth it to see the look on people's faces."

Junior flushed. Then flushed again. He was almost shaking. In a split second, his right hand shot out from his side.

"Go ahead, Steps," Morgan cried. "Show me what you showed Hunter."

Just as quickly, Hunter Worthington, Jr., stopped. His hand dropped. He turned toward the fireplace, fighting to keep the rage off his face.

Pippa quietly sobbed again.

"I think I'll be going," Carla said. "Thanks for your time." She handed out business cards. *Carla Tattaglia, Investigations.* The cards bore a telephone number, the one that rang the new phone in her house. There was no address.

"Call me, please, if you come up with anything you think I can use."

Morgan gave a nod, her silver earrings bouncing slightly.

Pippa concentrated on her new martini. Junior shoved his card in the back pocket of his tennis shorts. He seemed fully recovered from the anger displayed only moments before.

"I'll show you out," he said.

"What about Boz?" Carla asked.

"He's gardening," Junior said. Carla wondered how he knew this.

"I didn't mean for him to wait on me," she said. "I want to ask him some questions."

Junior looked at her, once again appraising what she had said. Once again, Carla felt like a piece of cattle.

"Bosworth does not give interviews," Junior said. "You will have to accept my word on this."

He turned and walked toward the far side of the room, not bothering to see whether Carla would follow. She did, barely having time to bid goodbye to the drunken mother and angry daughter behind her. Junior walked swiftly through the mansion, all the way to Carla's car.

"If Bosworth changes his mind," she said, "have him call me."

"He won't change his mind." Junior gazed at her Volkswagen, again with that odd appraising look. Carla could not tell whether the car got a passing grade.

"Tell me," Junior said, "what qualifies you as a private investigator?"

"I was a police officer," Carla answered. Junior showed no reaction.

"Federal? State? Providence?"

"State," she said.

"A trooper? Were you a detective?"

"I was not a state trooper," Carla said.

"But you said state—"

"I was with the Department of Environmental Management."

Junior seemed amused by this. "And why did you leave the Department of Environmental Management police?"

"I got shot." Carla smiled slightly. Junior's look of amusement disappeared.

"Who shot you? A poacher?"

"She was what the movies like to call a hit man."

"She?" Junior's eyes narrowed. He was clearly intrigued by the turn in the conversation. "And what did you do to her?"

"I shot back."

To this, Junior offered no immediate response. Carla looked up. The sun was high now, and it made her squint.

"If I were you, Mr. Worthington, I'd be very careful how you treat your stepdaughter."

Junior looked down for a moment, and when he looked up, any sign of amusement was gone. "I don't see how that is any of your business, Miss Tattaglia."

"Maybe not. But then, you never know what a woman can do." She winked at him. He might have replied, had it not been for the strange cackling that interrupted them.

The woman wore khaki pants and a denim blouse and had a broad straw hat perched on her head. They were the same clothes she had worn the day before on Thames Street and the wharves. And the day before that. And so on. Her laughter was low and guttural. The sound bounced off the monstrous building and back at Carla and her client.

"That's right, you never know! You never know!"

Carla could not guess the woman's age. Her skin around her mouth and cheeks was laced with seams. Even from a distance Carla could smell the unwashed aroma the woman carried with her.

For the barest moment, Junior seemed flustered. Then the moment was gone, and he regained not only poise, but arrogance.

"Boz!" he called.

And Boz came flip-flopping up from behind them. Along with the tails he now held a pair of dirty gardening gloves and some pruning shears. The old woman saw him and laughed again. "Hi, Boz! How's the weeding going? You never know, do you, Boz?"

Boz stared at her but did not reply. "I called the police," he told Junior in a dull voice.

Carla watched the woman. In addition to the dirty pants and blouse she wore a pair of torn canvas tennis shoes. She seemed to be enjoying herself thoroughly.

"So this is the new girl, Hunter?" The woman's eyes danced beneath her straw hat. "Going to show her the ropes? Or is Boz going to handle this one? Are you ready for your close-up, little girl?"

"Just ignore her," Hunter said to Carla. As the woman continued to rant, a Newport police cruiser slowly rolled down the driveway. It came to a stop and two officers climbed out. One went immediately to Hunter and Bosworth, with a weary look that suggested he had been to the mansion before, and for the same reason. The other officer walked toward the ranting woman.

"Don't touch me!" she warned. "I live here, you know."

The officer who had approached Hunter and his butler raised his eyebrows.

"The usual?" he asked.

Hunter nodded. "Trespassing." His voice was practically a whisper.

On some unseen signal the officer next to the woman took her arm. She screamed, and for a moment she flinched, as if fearing the officer would strike her. And then the woman relaxed. Calmly, almost serenely, she permitted the officer to escort her to her car.

"That's a relief," the officer next to Hunter said.

"How's that?" Carla asked.

The officer looked at her quizzically for a moment. Then he inclined his head toward the woman, now sitting in the backseat of the squad car.

"When she gets her fire up," he said, "she's mean as hell. And strong. She threw me once. Had to charge her with resisting. Hell, I'm lucky she didn't break my arm."

"Thanks very much, Officer," Junior said abruptly. "I'll be happy to sign any complaint. If you'll excuse us now."

The officer pursed his lips and stared at Junior. "Yes, sir. Sure. I'll be going now. I'm sure if we have any questions, our captain will get in touch." The officer walked back to the cruiser.

"You're not exactly winning the police over," Carla said.

Junior turned to her again. "What the police think is of little concern to me."

"That's funny," Carla said. "I thought I was hired because you *were* concerned."

Junior paused then. Bosworth, still holding his gloves and clippers, broke the silence.

"I'll be getting back to work."

"I wish you wouldn't, Boz," Carla said. "I'd like to ask you a few questions."

Junior now sounded genuinely annoyed. "Must I remind you again, Miss Tattaglia, that my servant does not give interviews?"

Bosworth exchanged a glance with his employer and fiddled with the lapels on his tux. "That's correct. I don't," he said. Bosworth flip-flopped off toward some unseen garden.

"I'll expect you to keep Mr. Balboni up to date," Junior said.

"Why don't you want me to talk to him?" Carla asked.

"Because nothing he can say will help you."

"Do you realize it makes me wonder what you're hiding?"

Junior smiled again, his eyes as dark and dull as day-old coffee. "As with the police, Miss Tattaglia, I do not care what you wonder, or what you suspect. I only care that you gather the necessary information to demonstrate my innocence. If you do not want the job, we will find someone else. But if you do, then you will have to accept my rules."

I don't want the job, Carla thought as she climbed into her car, watching Hunter Worthington, Jr., walk back into his hideous home. If I had a decent alternative, I'd have nothing to do with you. But I need the money.

6

Despite the fact that its campus was located on prime waterfront property, the St. Ives Academy boathouse was located in a marina two miles from the school. This fact was not lost on Michael as he walked toward the cedar-shingled building that was home to the St. Ives sailing team. Access to people who knew the school's late star sailor might, he hoped, prove easier here than on the campus proper.

Shirley had asked him to keep up with the story, which did not surprise him. She was intrigued by his experience with Earl at the Porcelain God, and by the attention the Newport police had paid the dead man's father. Still, he couldn't resist giving her a hard time.

"The way you've shut me down on that video, I can't believe you want me to follow this."

Shirley did not blush. Instead, she tapped a finger on a pack of cigarettes sitting on her desktop.

"You know full well I would have let you use the tape if word had not come down from the GM."

"There was a time you would have ignored him."

"Yes, and there was a time you would have ignored *me*, Michael. You didn't do that either."

She was right. Some stories were not worth fighting about. At the time Earl's camera caught Hunter Jr. striking his son, it certainly did not appear that the Worthingtons of Newport were about to become embroiled in a murder investigation. Still, it was galling that the video had been erased once it was returned to the station.

He tried to push the thought from his mind as he approached the boathouse. He was working alone; Shirley needed Earl for other projects, but promised to make him available if Michael needed a camera. And Michael knew there were benefits to not having a photographer around, especially on sensitive stories. That was an advantage he'd always believed that print reporters enjoyed over their television colleagues.

The shingled building was silvered from the weather, like so many homes on the New England shore. The sides were taken up by large sliding white doors, through which the boats would pass for races at some distant school or regatta. The doors were open now, and Michael walked in. The inside was a blend of smells: cedar, like some giant closet; salt, drenching a floor built of crushed seashells over hard-packed dirt; and the odd scent of paints and solvents, used to mark or clean the hulls. Carolina liked the smells. They were comforting, in a way that only a sailor could understand.

He could hear a radio playing rock and roll in a corner, along with the sound of someone whistling, though it wasn't clear that both were playing the same tune. He came around the side of a boat hull perched on a set of rollers and found a man repairing a sail with a needle and thread. He looked up at Michael and stopped what he was doing.

"Can I help you?"

The man was probably forty, his hair tousled and his face bearded in the same color as the shingles outside. He wore shorts, a torn cotton jersey, and a pair of boat shoes. He seemed friendly.

"I was hoping to find someone who can talk to me about the St. Ives sailing team."

"That would be me," he said. "And you are?"

"Michael Carolina."

A light of recognition appeared in the man's eyes. "Channel Three?"

"That's right."

"I'm Charles Nathan. Sailing coach and biology instructor." He held out a callused palm, which Carolina shook. "You must be here about Hunter."

"You're right."

"I'm not doing any on-camera interviews," Nathan said. He was still polite. Calm. He did not break eye contact. He did not ask Michael to leave. Best of all, he had not ruled out all interviews, just those that involved a camera.

"I was more interested in finding out about your program here," Michael said. "I'm doing some background." This was in fact true, though Michael planned to use the information to learn more about Hunter.

"Does the school know you're here? The headmaster, I mean."

"Only if you tell them, Mr. Nathan."

Nathan's eyes danced. "Call me Charley."

Michael looked around. There were sixteen boats, all of them fiberglass, all on rollers.

"What do your kids race? 470s?"

"420s. They're kind of the younger cousin to the 470s. Tabor, Moses Brown, St. George's, most of the schools around here sail 420s." Nathan ran his hand over a white hull. "They're really pretty sweet."

"What about Lasers?" Carolina asked.

Nathan nodded, warming to the subject. "They all like the Lasers. I think they're made by the same company that builds 420s now. But the Lasers, they're the hot boats. They separate the sailors from the kids that just want to go for a ride."

There was a breeze stiffening then, and Carolina could see boats starting to heel out on the silver-and-blue waters on the bay. There was a chop that appeared now and again on the water. Carolina glanced at a set of brass instruments bolted to the shed's wall. The barometer was high, and a wind indicator hummed steadily at eleven knots.

Nathan caught him looking. "You sound like you know something about this. I noticed it on the tube the other night. You sail?"

"Some," Carolina answered.

This made Charley Nathan chuckle, as if he'd known the answer before it came.

"I was kind of a wood boat guy," Michael said. "I did a little offshore work, and I had a charter in Newport a while back."

"Wait—" Nathan said, the recognition sliding into place in his sea-green eyes. "Are you the guy who trussed the mayor of Providence on your foredeck and then had to quit the business?"

"Something like that," Michael said, giving a little smile of his own.

Nathan nearly doubled over in laughter. "That story's made the rounds in half the bars in town. You're sort of a legend."

"I certainly hope not," Michael said.

"Why did you do that? To the mayor, I mean."

Carolina sighed. "He was drunk, and he took a swing at me." He would have stopped there, but Nathan would not let him.

"I remember something about the guy having a weapon. Broken bottle?"

"You probably did hear that," Carolina said.

"So it's true?"

Michael did not answer, which Nathan properly took as affirmation. "Takes some big brass ones to do that on rough water."

"Like I said, it was a while back."

Nathan stood up then. "Well, I suppose I can spare a few minutes for you. Then I have to take out one of the boats. We broke a mast in the last regatta, and I have to retune the rig."

"Need any help?"

Nathan smiled, and stroked the whiskers on the left side of his face. "I hoped you'd ask. But if we talk about Hunter, it isn't for the record."

This was not a surprise, though it was frustrating. But then so was the experience with the St. Ives headmaster. And the friendly staff at the Porcelain God. On balance, it would be better to know more than less.

"Deal."

The 420 was true to Charley Nathan's description. She fairly skimmed across the water, easily riding through the gray chop. The sailing coach took the tiller and kept a hand free for the main, while Carolina worked the jib sheets. They tacked the boat hard, hauling the sails in tight, until the telltales lay straight back, parallel to the surface of the sea. Then they both hiked over the rail, forcing the boat's hull down, the spray soaking the backs of their shirts.

"Told you she was sweet," Charley Nathan called, shaking a few drops of water from his beard. "Just need to tighten down the forestay a little more and she'll be fine."

"How'd you get into sailing?" Carolina asked.

"College, or my excuse for college." Nathan pulled on the mainsheet and brought the sail in a little tighter. A puff lifted the boat off the water for a moment, and they hiked farther to make it balance.

"My old man was a fisherman," Nathan went on. "But he said he wanted more for me. Scraped together every penny to send me to Mass Maritime. Four years there, and I finished near the top of the class. Got on the sailing team, too. Day I graduated, my father put every penny he could into getting me an old boat. A Lightning."

"That old one at the dock? She's beautiful," Carolina said.

Charley Nathan nodded, the pride in his voice unmistakable. "I've tried to keep her up."

"So you got a third mate's ticket from the Maritime Academy?"

"That's right."

"How'd you end up here?

Nathan looked at him, bemused. "Ever hear of the Moonstone Beach spill?"

The name brought bad memories. A winter storm, battering the coast, destroying beach dunes on the Cape and the southern Rhode Island beaches. And driving a barge aground, her hull gutted, spilling tens of thousands of gallons of crude black oil onto the rocks and sand. The losses had run into the millions. The press had been voracious, the public had screamed, and the government had been eager to blame the owners of the ships and the crew that had let it happen. . . .

"I had a second mate's ticket," Nathan said. "I wasn't even on watch that night. But the only thing people remember is where I had my last berth." He stared at the mainsail again, checking the trim, then gazed at the line of houses across the bay in Jamestown. A trio of clouds moved across the sky, each tinged with a dull shade of silver, cutting in front of the sun and making Nathan's face go pale.

"This job," he said, "this is what I have left. Hunter's old man made it worthwhile."

Michael looked at him quizzically.

"Was Hunter's father a big donor?"

"He paid for the fleet of boats. And the boathouse they're kept in."

Carolina wondered to himself what a fleet of sailboats would cost. Whatever it was, it would be more than a year's salary. Maybe two years, given the wages at Channel Three. And a boathouse. Clearly, Hunter Worthington, Jr., was not shy about financing his son's sporting endeavors.

After an hour they turned the boat back toward the marina. Carolina wiped an arm across his brow and his mouth and tasted the salt. He couldn't tell if it was spray or sweat. Nathan set the sails on a broad reach, the wind now pushing the little boat in gentle gusts so it felt as if they were surfing.

"This was what Hunter loved," Nathan said. "He loved the tacking duels, and the chaos at the start, but this was the part he loved best, just sliding along on the way back." The look on his face was wistful, as if he were thinking about a younger brother.

"How long did you know him?" Carolina asked.

"All four years of school," Nathan said. "He was the first kid out here nearly every day, and the last to leave. I think this was an escape."

"From what?"

"School. He wasn't much of a student."

Michael's eyebrows raised. "No? I thought St. Ives set high standards."

Nathan looked up and checked the trim on the mainsail. "Of course it does. All these schools do. But money has a way of lowering the bar."

"Did the other kids know who paid the tab for the boats?"

Charley Nathan gave a helpless shrug. "They weren't supposed to. But the old man was down here a lot. Watching the kids get ready to practice. For every regatta. He tended to be a little heavy-handed. Eventually the word got around."

"Did Hunter catch hell?"

"Surprisingly, no. But then, Hunter wasn't your average kid."

Nathan's meaning was not immediately apparent. And he did not explain right away, instead watching as a powerboat slowly rolled past. Nathan adjusted the sails to allow for the wake displaced by the bigger boat. When the 420 had resumed its reach, he tossed a leg over its tiller.

"The fact is," he said, "Hunter was the most ferocious competitor I've ever seen. It was like war when he went into a race. He was tough as hell. He sailed like he was a fullback who gained five or ten yards on every carry. Most kids like that, they make enemies. And Hunter did. But only with the people he competed against. I swear to you, he was the best teammate I've ever seen. Kind. Friendly. Even gentle. And he had this ability to get the best out of whoever was on his crew. It was amazing to me, because he never complained if I paired him with a new sailor. And they always did well."

"What was his father like?"

Nathan shrugged. "Other than spending a lot of money, he kept to himself. Didn't talk to me, didn't try to tell me how to run the team. I had to respect that. But he was always here. Always watching, usually with one of his other boats."

Michael remembered the Hinckley picnic boat. The father had money to burn. Or, in sailing vernacular, to pour down the drain.

"What about other family? He have a brother?"

Nathan once again adjusted sail trim. He had a habit of caring for the boat before answering questions. "I've heard he had a sister, or half sister. She didn't go to St. Ives, though."

"What did you hear about her?"

"That she's part of a band. You know, one of those grunge-type outfits? I heard Hunter talking once. Said the band played a lot of dates in Providence."

"You know the band's name?"

Charley Nathan shook his head. Michael made a mental note to check around for the sister.

"You know anything about a guy named Mercer?"

"Jimmy?" Charley Nathan's face screwed up as if he had just been exposed to a piece of rotting food. "He's Eddie Haskell in a pair of docksiders. Personally, I think he's just a punk."

"I'm not surprised," Carolina said. "I met him yesterday morning, and then again yesterday afternoon. He doesn't seem too upset that Hunter is out of the racing business."

"Makes some sense," Nathan said reflectively. "He used to race for one of the other schools. Tabor, I think, but he graduated a few years back. He's been screwing around ever since, spending summers in Newport, sailing, raising hell. Then he goes off to the regattas. I don't think he ever went to college. He's a boat bum, hoping to catch on with one of the bigger boats. But then, Jimmy's never had enough of the killer instinct on the water. That's why he always tends to come up short in the big races. If he's the guy we send to compete in Sydney, the U.S. can kiss a medal goodbye."

"Do you know if Mercer ever partied with Hunter?"

Nathan thought for a moment. "These kids, the ones who go to the bigger regattas, they tend to run in the same circles. So I'm pretty sure they would run into each other. But Hunter and Jimmy? Definitely not close friends."

The 420 was closing in on the marina again, and the wind dropped as they neared the docks. Carolina helped the sailing coach to drop the sails and tie up. They pulled the running rigging down and pushed the 420 on a pair of rollers until it was tucked away inside the shed.

"I appreciate your time," Carolina said.

"I doubt that I was much help," Nathan answered.

"I wonder, do you know if Hunter had a girlfriend?"

Nathan thought for a moment, then shook his head. And then stopped.

"Damn."

Carolina could see the sailing coach thinking, and decided not to speak. It was better to just wait and see what Nathan shared.

"I remember Hunter got into it once. With Jimmy Mercer. It was at a race last year, one of those open regattas, just outside the harbor. Solings, I think it was, those big heavy boats with three people for crew?"

Carolina nodded. The boats were monsters, classic Olympic boats.

"I remember there was some yelling on the docks." Nathan was watching him now, as if he wanted to make sure that Carolina understood. "It was about a girl."

"Really?"

"Yes. What was her name? I can't remember. Wait. It was Ali."

"Ali?"

"That's it. I don't know the last name, but the first one was Ali. Alison. Ali."

Michael extended a hand. "Good luck with the sailing team."

Nathan shook, his grip made strong by years of hauling lines. "We'll see how it goes. The headmaster said they may have to scale back the sailing program now if Hunter's father stops giving money."

Michael considered what the man had said as he returned to his car. When he looked back he saw Nathan standing, hands on hips, surrounded by the upturned hulls of small boats. He seemed forlorn, like an old mariner, powerless to stop a gale from descending upon him.

Michael watched the six-o'clock broadcast in Shirley's office, his head just below a cloud of cigarette smoke. His boss's ashtray was loaded with butts, some Kools, mostly Merits, and blue-gray strands trailed from each nostril as she watched the monitors of all three Providence stations.

"Nobody has shit tonight," she said.

Shirley wore a skin-tight green sweat suit that revealed decent legs and a body that might have been envied by women in their twenties, much less Shirley's peers, who'd all lived two decades longer. Her blondish hair bore traces of the bleaching method hairdressers called "highlights," and it was split across the middle of her forehead by a sweatband that matched her outfit.

Carolina knew better than to tell her she looked good for her age.

"Exercising tonight?"

"What gave me away? I'm trying to do an hour on one of those stair things every night. Between that and these"—she flicked ash into the loaded tray—"I can keep the pounds off. Besides, I might meet a nice boy out there."

Carolina smiled. Shirley was easily the best news director he'd ever worked for. She was also a woman who kept passion tethered by the lightest of bridles.

"What happened to the vitamins?" Michael asked. For most of the time he'd known her, Shirley was notorious for popping vitamins instead of eating.

"I still do that," she said. "But my doctor's convinced I'm going to get ulcers."

Michael nodded weakly. In the TV business, it wasn't outside the realm of possibility. She pressed MUTE on the trio of remote controls in front of her. "So what do you think? Is it worth staying on this Worthington story or do we wait until the cops make an arrest?"

He did not have a ready answer. He flipped through a set of notes he'd written that afternoon. They took up more than a dozen pages, all of them detailing Hunter III's education, his whereabouts, and the people seen with him near the time of his death. Carolina had reviewed and logged what was left of the raw video from the last day of the Laser regatta and the tape from the morning Hunter's body was found. But if there were answers to be found, he had yet to find them.

"If I had to guess," he said, "the police haven't strayed from looking at the kid's father. But Balboni isn't going to let them near his client, and there'll be a fight if they want to get any forensic evidence. Besides, Dad doesn't seem quite right to me."

Shirley stamped out the cigarette in her hand and crossed her arms. "Why not?"

"Because the kid was his pride. I mean, he sends him to an expensive school. Pays for a fleet of boats. Buys him his own Laser. He wants the kid to succeed, right?"

"Then why does he slap him that night?"

They stared at each other, both trying to figure out an answer, but coming up with nothing.

"I agree with you," Michael said finally. "The guy's father isn't Ward Cleaver. But not many parents are." He tried not to think just then about his own father, and failed.

"Is there something I'm missing here?" Shirley asked.

"Weren't you the guy who was all hot to pin this on his old man?"

"I'm not saying Dad didn't do it, just wondering about other possibilities. Like this punk Mercer, who lied about how close he was to Hunter and pretended he didn't know where Hunter was before he died. I've got the sailing coach basically confirming that they weren't friends, plus Mercer was a drunken asshole at that bar yesterday."

"So Mercer's a possibility," Shirley said. "What are the chances you can convince this coach—Nathan—to go on the record?"

That, of course, was always the problem with sources who refused to be quoted: they usually provided good information, but it was often next to impossible to get them to stand behind their stories. Nathan was a teacher and a coach at a school that had made it clear it would not cooperate with reporters. One way of looking at the matter was to conclude that Nathan had done more than his share.

Or had he?

The sailing coach had been awfully friendly awfully fast. And he was quick to share his views about Worthington's relationship—or lack of one—with Mercer. Almost too quick. Nathan had been so helpful, as long as nothing would be attributed to him. And for a man employed by a wealthy prep school, Charles Nathan had difficulty hiding a certain degree of bitterness toward the wealthy. There was a veiled contempt, Carolina thought, in Nathan's offhand remarks about the man who purchased the school's sailboats. Was Charley Nathan trying to point me in another direction? he wondered. Or am I just being paranoid?

"You're being paranoid," Shirley said.

"What?"

"You asked. So I answered." She smiled mischievously and grabbed another cigarette.

"Sorry," Carolina said, embarrassed. "I was thinking out

loud. Can you spare me for a while longer? There are a few more things I need to check out."

Shirley punched a button on the computer and kicked up a schedule. "We're okay for the next couple of days," she said. "But I want you available if something breaks."

"Deal."

"Good." She stood up and switched the televisions off. They walked out of the building together. The evening was cool and the sky was turning from blue to a pale orange glow.

"Want some advice?" she asked before climbing into her car.

"Go ahead."

"Don't be trying to explain this whole thing yourself. Bits and pieces, enough to move the story along, that's all we need. We're not the cops."

"I know that."

"I know you do. And I know it's easy to forget. Now that's enough. I'm going to work out and check the scenery." She started her car. "I never knew that a men's locker room was such a pretty view." Shirley roared out of the parking lot, leaving Michael to think of sailboats called 420s and Hunter Worthington.

And who was it again? A name. A girl's name.

Ali.

That night Carla sautéed four chicken breasts in butter, pepper, and white wine and served them with rough greens and angel hair tossed in olive oil and garlic. Michael found a bottle of '95 chardonnay, and they each had a glass. Paul Carolina drank from a bottle of ginger ale and helped himself to extra pasta.

"This girl here," Paul said, "she can cook."

"Thank you." Carla kept her eyes on the plate. Paul Carolina was beginning to bother her.

"How's the job search?" Michael asked, trying to keep his voice even.

Paul Carolina chewed slowly, looking out the window. "Got a few possibilities," he said. "Few possibilities. Don't ask me where, I don't want to jinx anything. You know how superstitious I am."

Michael did not know. He could, however, sense the kiss-off. "When do you think you'll hear something?"

"Couple days," his father said. "Maybe a week. Hey, how come you didn't have a story on tonight?"

"I was working," Michael said. He looked at Carla. Her face was blank, and she kept concentrating on her food.

"This guy," Paul said, "Carla, this guy should be at the network, don't you think? He's smart enough. He's got the right looks." Paul Carolina gave a small chuckle. "Just like his old man."

"I like it where I am," Michael said.

"Anyone going to have that last piece of chicken?" Paul looked from Michael to Carla and back.

"Go ahead," Carla said quietly.

Paul Carolina forked the breast onto his plate and cut into the meat. "Well, it's okay with me, son. Some people, they just don't have the drive, I guess. Takes a special kind of guy to make it big."

The remark stung. Which, Michael figured, was what had been intended.

"You ought to know, Pop," he said.

Paul Carolina set his knife and fork down.

"Now what's that supposed to mean?"

"What was your remark supposed to mean?"

They stared at each other, each one waiting to see who would make the next move, and what it would be.

"Isn't there a game on tonight?" Carla asked.

Paul slipped the last piece of chicken into his mouth. When he spoke, there were traces of sadness in his voice, mixed with wounded pride. "You know, you don't have much respect."

Michael glared at his father. "I have plenty of respect," he said, "for people who deserve it." Paul Carolina threw his napkin down, not bothering to pick it up when it fell to the floor. He stood, and walked out of the kitchen.

Michael put his own fork down.

"I suppose you're going to tell me I shouldn't have said that."

Carla ran the tap water and rinsed her plate. She walked behind Michael and picked up Paul's napkin. When she did, her hand brushed Michael's neck.

"Not going to tell you anything." I don't have to, she thought. It's eating you up all on its own.

Michael stood up and helped her with the rest of the dishes. Just as they finished, the front door to the house opened and closed. Michael walked down the hall and looked out a front window.

"I guess he's gone out," he said quietly.

Carla came up next to him. "Do you have a few minutes for me?"

"Sure."

He wondered whether she wanted to go upstairs, to use the time alone to make love, or to talk. Instead she disappeared into a closet for a moment, and came out with a long tube, perhaps five feet in length, wrapped in canvas, with a large hump at the end.

"What's that?"

Carla smiled. "Come see."

They went out into the backyard, where she unzipped the tube and carefully removed two slender, tapered pieces of graphite, one thick, one thin. The end of the thicker piece was wrapped in cork, and at the bottom of the piece was a gleaming reel made of polished aluminum.

"A fishing rod?" Michael looked at her quizzically. Carla fitted the rod pieces together, then slowly stripped out line from the reel and began feeding it through the rod guides.

"This is a Redington," she said. "Two-piece, nine-foot, ten-weight, with an intermediate sinking line."

Michael watched her. "Would you mind translating for those of us in the gallery?"

"It's a saltwater fly rod," she said. "For stripers. You ever try casting?"

"Not with a fly rod," he said. He was afraid to tell her he wasn't sure he'd even seen it done.

Carla finished stringing the rod, then stripped out ten or fifteen yards of thick green line. She flicked a wrist, and the line snaked out in front of her on the lawn. Carla lowered the tip of the rod to the ground with her right hand, and took hold of extra line with her left.

"It's all in the arm and the wrist," she said. Then she raised the rod and the line jumped off the ground as if by magic. It rolled behind her in a long graceful curve before straightening out, parallel to the ground. Then Carla brought her arm forward, hauling on the line with her left hand. The fly line was alive now, dancing back and forth in front of her and behind, a living creature that seemed to grow with each back-and-forward cast. Michael watched, mesmerized.

"It's so beautiful," he said. And it was, as each cast grew by a few feet more, as Carla rocked the rod back and forth, back and forth, the slight movement of her forearm and wrist moving the line fifty and sixty feet in each direction.

"When you're casting," Carla said, "you have to be able to land the fly on a piece of water the size of a pie plate. Some of the older guys can cast a hundred feet." Suddenly she brought her arm to a stop, and the line hung suspended in front of her for what seemed like several seconds before it withered and fell to the grassy lawn. "Want to try it?"

She made him stand next to her and showed him how to hold the rod, how to grip the extra line with his free hand.

"Start slow, but be firm. Bring it straight back, and then snap your wrist. Then come forward again."

He tried, but the line refused to obey him. It made a fat, wobbling arc before landing behind him in a tangled heap. He threw his arm forward, trying to straighten the line out again, but with the same result.

"You did some spin fishing, didn't you?"

Michael nodded. Carla took his arm again and slowly worked him through a cast.

"Spinning rods are designed to throw the bait or the lure," she said. "With a fly rod, you're actually throwing line. The line is thick, and firm. And it's the rod that does the work, see?"

He tried again. The line bunched up and dropped into a pile in front of him.

She stood behind him, her hips nuzzling up against his back, and she reached around once more. "You're forcing it," she whispered in his ear. "You're pushing too hard. You just have to let the rod tip move. See?"

"You smell good," Michael said.

Carla gave a soft laugh. "Try it one more time," she whispered. "A little movement can go a long way."

He didn't feel like casting just then. But Michael knew she wanted him to try. He raised his arm once more, and the line lifted, quickly, and straightened behind him. He watched until the line was flat, and the rod strained. Then he shifted his arm slightly, and the rod snapped forward. The fly line rolled into a tight, controlled loop, and shot forward like a bullet until it extended fifty feet in front of him, and fluttered to the grass in a long, even path.

"Beautiful," Carla said. "That was beautiful. You have a wonderful stroke."

The light was fading then, and she stepped in front of him. The breeze produced a flutter in her hair as she took the rod from his hand and turned the reel. The line jumped across the grass, while shadows danced across Carla's brown arms and legs.

"I was just thinking of something."

"Go ahead." His voice sounded hoarse, he thought. And he

could not take his eyes off her. She turned and smiled at him.

"Casting a fly line is like dealing with difficult people, especially people that you love. You can't force it. You can't push. Or it turns into a mess."

She replaced the rod inside its case and looked up at him, her eyes as dark as her hair. "Do you hear what I'm saying, Michael?"

He did hear, and he told her so. But he would not understand what she was trying to tell him until much later on. He put a hand on her hip and pulled gently until their lips touched.

"Let's go inside." he said. And they did.

Later, when it was dark, he looked out the window at the moon. It was nearly full, and the pale light made sharp outlines of the trees against the sky. It is so good here, he said to himself. It felt peaceful in this room, with this woman next to him.

Carla traced pictures on his back with her finger, using long, light strokes.

Michael asked, "How was work today?"

"Kind of boring," Carla said. "Frustrating." She stopped tracing and lay back on the bed.

"Have any new clients?"

Carla sat up and wrapped her arms around her knees. "A few. But nothing earth-shattering."

She offered nothing more, just rocked a little bit on the bed, her face moving in and out of the light shadow from the moon. Her answer didn't surprise Michael. He knew that investigators needed to be discreet. It would be best to leave her alone. Besides, it was probably some divorce case, or a phony worker's comp claim. Small cases, important mostly to the parties involved.

"Want some ice cream?" he asked.

"I think I just want to sleep," she said quietly. In a few minutes she was breathing deeply. Michael went down and grabbed a bowl of mint chip from the carton in the refrigerator, then switched on the cable. He watched a movie on one of the pay channels and a late-night comedy show. The star comic specialized in raunchy humor, and the audience ate it up. At eleven he caught the news, flipping between the channels. Three had nothing new to offer on any of the stories of the day, and breaking news on the other stations was equally spare. He hit the mute button and watched the images cut from weather to anchor to sports to tape to anchor and commercial, until it all began to blend together, and then drifted into images of Carla with the long, heavy saltwater rod again. He could hear her saying over and over that the rod should do the work, that he must not force the cast, and the line would travel back over his head again, almost like one of the serpents come to life in the first plague scene of *The Ten Commandments*. Then his father appeared, smiling that magnificent smile, the one that could charm the hardest of hearts. I want a little respect, son. I need a little respect.

A banging sound woke him at one thirty-five, according to the clock on the cable box. There was another movie playing now, some low-budget martial arts feature that looked as though it had been shot in a warehouse in Oxnard. Michael shut the television off and stood up as his father shuffled into the room. Paul Carolina's movements were slow and less than fully coordinated. He peered at his son through heavy-lidded eyes. His pants and shirt needed pressing, and his shoes were scuffed. The faint smell of beer, stale beer, carried across the room. Michael decided not to ask where his father had been.

"You wait up for me?"

"I was thinking about you," Michael said. It was better not to answer directly. "I'm sorry about what I said before. At dinner."

Father looked at son, and smiled slowly, sadly. He clearly enjoyed hearing the attempt to make amends. Michael ignored it. When he was my age, he thought, he was working full-time paying the mortgage, keeping it all together for us. And then one day he just walked out for good. Gone. Is that why I came down here tonight, without even realizing? Was I afraid that he was going to leave again?

And then he heard himself talking. "Dad, if you need some help, I can check around and see about finding you a job. Maybe with some people at work, or with one of the advertisers at the station—"

"I don't need help," Paul said, in a tone that was strong enough to discourage his son. He sat down, hard, on the couch. Michael remained standing.

"What, am I wearing out my welcome here already?" His speech was slurred now.

"It's not that," Michael said. "I just thought you might want some help."

"I can take care of myself. Maybe I didn't do so well with you, but I can take care of myself." Paul Carolina ran a hand through his hair and leaned back into the couch. "I take care of me, you take care of you. And your girl, she takes care, too. Got that big client now, she takes care just fine."

Michael looked at his father. "What are you talking about?"

Paul chuckled. "You don't know? Your old man is going to break a story."

Michael said nothing. In the half-light, he could see the amusement in his father's eyes.

"Carla got a call from a big lawyer yesterday. That guy, what's his name, Rambon—no, Balboni. The guy you interviewed on the news. Asked her to come to Newport for an interview at some mansion. Must be that rich guy whose son got killed, right?"

Carla's reluctance to discuss her new business came rushing back then. This was no small case. Michael remembered her saying she had nothing "earth-shattering." He understood why she would not want to tell him what she was doing. At the same time, he could not help feeling that he had somehow been deceived. He realized his father was watching him then.

"How do you know this, Dad?"

"I was here when the phone rang. I guess we both picked up at the same time."

Michael stared at his father. "And you didn't hang up?"

"Well, no, not right away. I guess I should have, but I'd just seen the guy on the news, and it sounded kind of interesting. I figured Carla would talk about it later. At least with you." Paul shifted on the couch. "Guess I was wrong."

"You shouldn't do that," Michael said. It was next to impossible to separate feelings just then: envy that Carla had access to an important news subject; betrayal that she would not tell him of her new client; anger at his father for prying.

But Paul Carolina's words penetrated like a knife slicing a loaf of warm bread.

"Come on, son. Did I do anything that a reporter wouldn't do? That you wouldn't do in the same situation?"

The words hung in the air. Michael wanted to dispute them. Wanted to tell his father that he was wrong, that there was a difference between chasing a story and prying into the business affairs of his son's girlfriend.

But he did not. And Paul Carolina's suggestion—no, his accusation—bounced around in Michael's thoughts as his father, smug and bleary-eyed, went off to bed.

7

Carla made her third visit to Newport in the morning, and realized that the trip was growing shorter each time. Getting too comfortable with the roads, she thought, and she slowed at the toll bridge in Jamestown. As if reading her mind, a state police cruiser appeared beside her, the trooper fixing her with the "thousand-yard stare" so common to soldiers and law officers. Carla flashed a slight smile and kept driving. The trooper lost interest and directed his attention toward other prey.

Michael had been strangely distant with her as they got dressed that morning, even when she asked him what was wrong.

"Just thinking about work," he said. "I'd really like to find an angle on the Worthington murder."

Responding was difficult. "Why don't you check with the police again?" It was the best she could do.

"That's a dead end." Michael's tone was sharper than usual. "What I need is to learn a little more about Hunter and his family. But that's a tough nut to crack."

Michael stopped talking about the case then. They said little during breakfast, and he bussed her cheek before leaving the house for work.

"See you tonight."

She wondered briefly if there was something she was missing, then brushed the thought aside. Paul Carolina was still asleep when she left the house twenty minutes later.

She did not return to Château du Printemps. Instead she visited the public library, looking for microfiche of the local publications. But the machines were occupied by an elderly gentleman researching old stock quotes and a student working on some kind of research paper, with no sign that they'd be free anytime soon. A reference librarian noticed her and offered to help.

"I don't know how you can," Carla said, "unless there's another machine."

"I'm afraid not," the lady said. "But I have a suggestion."

Ten minutes later Carla walked through the doors of the Redwood Library and Athenaeum. The library was private, and loaded with dozens of oil paintings and prints, including several Gilbert Stuarts. Glass cases held historic documents, and the shelves were lined with what appeared to be a significant collection of contemporary and historical works.

But the microfiche, that ancient, dizzying system for conducting research, was what concerned her. She found the files for the Newport paper, then counted back ten years, into the late eighties, and flipped to November. The Sunday editions contained wedding announcements, together with formal portraits of brides, and occasionally grooms. Nearly a dozen faces, all of them radiant, peered out from the viewfinder of the machine. In the month of November, however, none of them belonged to Pippa Worthington.

Perhaps this was not a surprise. It was a second marriage, after all, and couples often chose to keep such matters private. Or maybe there was no photograph.

She moved forward to December, and in the first week she found what she was looking for. A black-and-white portrait of the couple, he in a dark suit, she in a dress of some lighter color. Pippa was a striking woman, her features fine and delicate, responsive to the lens. Still more remarkable was her betrothed. Hunter Worthington, Jr., showed no signs of excessive alcohol or early aging. He was, if anything, younger than his years, looking more like a twin of his dead son or, perhaps, an older brother.

> Château du Printemps was the site of Saturday-evening nuptials for Vanessa "Pippa" Scott and Hunter James Worthington, Jr. The bride is the daughter of M. Walter Bingham and Jane Felder Bingham. The groom is the son of Hunter James Worthington, Sr., and Martha Lane Worthington. The parents of both bride and groom are deceased.
>
> The bride is a graduate of Miss Porter's and attended Mount Holyoke. The groom is a *summa cum laude* graduate of Pomona College and has a Master of Business Administration degree from the University of California at Los Angeles. He is Chief Executive Officer of Johnson Enterprises. The couple will make their home at Château du Printemps.

Johnson Enterprises? The name rang no bells. Carla took careful notes. There was no mention of children, nor of the fact that it was obviously a second marriage for Pippa. Carla thought for a moment and wanted to kick herself for not asking more questions the previous day. But then the Worthingtons were clearly not interested in offering extensive details about their lives.

She left the library and drove to the courthouse on Eisenhower Square. The building was jammed with people attending hearings in the district and superior courts. Carla walked through the metal detector and turned right, heading into the family court clerk's office. She spent almost an hour reviewing a file captioned *Scott v. Scott.* In another half hour, she went to a pay phone and dialed. Then, thinking better of it, she hung up.

Two young women wearing jeans, tank tops, and platform

heels were talking nearby. Defendants or girlfriends of defendants, Carla thought.

"I'm telling you, you can't be using no PD," the shorter one said to her friend.

Defendants.

"But I don't have no money for a paid lawyer," the older girl responded, her voice anguished. "Besides, it's only a suspended sentence."

"Who wants to make twenty dollars?" Carla asked.

The two young women stared at her.

"You a cop?" the short one sniffed.

"No, I just need a favor." She explained what she needed.

"Is this illegal?" the taller one said. " 'Cause I'm in enough trouble on this shoplifting charge."

"It's not illegal. I just need a little help."

"Make it fifty and we do it," the short one said.

"Thirty," Carla said, "and if I were you, I'd stick with the public defender. They're busy, but they know what they're doing."

She dialed the number again, then handed the phone to the shorter girl.

"Yes, this is Miss . . ."

"Parkhurst," Carla whispered.

"Parker, calling from Saks in Boston?"

Close enough, Carla thought.

"We have a question regarding a dress ordered by Ms. Pippa Worthington? Is she available? Thank you." The girl handed the phone back to Carla, who peeled three tens out of a billfold and handed them to the girls.

"Beats boosting," the taller one said. The two young women giggled, then went back to their own conversation.

"Hello." Pippa Worthington sounded more alert this morning.

"It's Carla Tattaglia."

"But you said—"

"I thought it might make sense for us to meet outside your home. Alone."

There was a slight pause before Pippa answered. "No, that's the wrong size. I specifically said size eight."

"How about lunch?"

Pippa sounded frightened. But she was convincing. "No, I'm sorry. I don't expect to be in this afternoon. I have lunch plans."

Carla named an expensive restaurant with a view of the ocean, assuming it would be comfortable, and that Pippa Worthington would know it.

"That's fine, call me later," Pippa said. "My lunch is at twelve-thirty, and I won't be home for several hours."

Carla hung up, and checked her watch. Eleven-thirty. She was wondering what she would do in the next hour when a Newport police officer walked by. He looked familiar to her, but it took a moment to place him.

"Excuse me."

The officer turned.

"Didn't you make an arrest for trespassing yesterday? Out at the Worthingtons'?"

Recognition came across the officer's eyes.

"Yeah, weren't you in the driveway?" The cop's eyes ran up and down Carla in an instant, and he evidently liked what he saw, because he smiled broadly. The look was familiar, in her years as a police officer Carla had run across too many horndog police officers to count. She smiled back.

"I can't believe you remember me," she said. "You were so focused on your job."

The cop smiled again, reveling in the praise. "Are you a member of the family?"

Carla giggled. "Oh no, I work for Mr. Worthington. He wanted me to come down and find out what happened to that woman. Says she keeps bothering him. But—" Carla gave a sigh.

118

"I don't know where I should start. I don't even know her name."

"Well, I might be able to help you with that," the officer said.

He was maybe thirty, Carla decided, with dark hair and eyes, and the sort of bushy mustache favored by so many cops. Why is that? Carla wondered. Maybe it's a macho thing.

The officer flipped through his notebook. "I just dropped the paperwork for our prosecuting officer. Too bad you weren't here sooner. They released her again. Ah, here it is. Brandy. Brandy Shaker."

You've gotta be kidding, Carla thought. Instead, she cooed, "Oh, you're so sweet. Honest, we don't know why she keeps showing up at the house."

The cop nearly blushed. "Yes, she's like that lady who kept breaking into Letterman's place. Although I don't think she's broken in." He flipped a page of notes again. "No, just trespassing. Twice in the past two months. Oh, and one malicious damage to property charge. Someone saw her throw a brick through the window of a Mercedes one night. From like twenty feet away. Pretty strong lady, you ask me."

"Oh my, yes," Carla said. "What happened?"

"Two weeks ago, she got probation. This time, it's probably a suspended sentence. After that, I think she's gonna do time."

Carla put on her best look of shock and indignation. "Serves her right," she said. "I mean, we shouldn't have to be living in fear out at the Château."

The cop peered at her for a moment, and Carla worried that she might have overdone it. But then the officer relaxed again and slipped on the macho smile.

"Well, if you'd like to give me your, ah, number, I can check up on this and let you know how it turns out."

"Oh, you're so sweet," Carla said. She gave him the number for the pizza delivery place a block from her house in Edgewood. "Just ask for Carla," she said. The owner of the pizza joint had a black Labrador named Carla.

"Hey, Carla." She turned just in time to see an officer from the Department of Environmental Management walking past. He worked Aquidneck Island, while she had always been assigned in the western part of the state. She could not remember his name. "How's the wound?"

"Fine, just fine," she said, too quickly. Please don't stop to talk, she thought. Please. The officer nodded and kept going.

The Newport officer was staring again. "Are you okay?"

"Oh sure," she said. "Just someone I met at a party once. I hope you'll call."

The officer's face relaxed again. "Sure," he said. "I'll let you know."

She walked out of the courthouse, climbed into the VW, and waited to see the officer leave the building, which he did. Carla looked up at the clock on the courthouse tower. It would be another forty-five minutes before she needed to meet Pippa Worthington. Carla walked back inside and headed straight for the district court file.

"I'd like to see every file you've got for Brandy Shaker," she told the clerk, who fetched them after she stopped laughing.

The restaurant was perched on a ledge overlooking the eastern approaches to Narragansett Bay. Carla had changed in the car from jeans and a shirt to a sleeveless yellow summer dress with matching espadrilles. It was always good to have extra clothes, she had decided, for unexpected meetings with clients. Especially when the clients lived in Newport.

A waiter dressed in black pants and flaming red jacket escorted her to a table overlooking the water. In the distance Carla could see a small freighter making its way north to Providence, and a string of pleasure yachts, both sail and power, plying the waters between Newport and Jamestown.

The restaurant was of the formal, old-world variety, its clientele carrying the trappings of comfort and wealth. Carla noticed two matrons, both wearing white gloves and tea hats, dining a few feet away. One of the women looked to be in her forties. The other was older. Both glanced quickly at Carla as she was seated, then, satisfied they were dressed better or at least more expensively, went back to their own conversation.

Pippa arrived a few minutes later, in dress and hat similar to those of the women at the next table. Her hair was swept back under her hat, and her eyes were clearer than they had been the day before. All she needs is the gloves, Carla thought.

"I did not appreciate your call," Pippa said. "And I shop in New York more than Boston. Bosworth gave me a strange look."

"Sorry," Carla said. "I'll know better next time."

"I don't think there will be a next time. I'll answer your questions and we'll be done with it." Pippa looked over at the other table. The two women there were staring at her.

"Hello, Mags," Pippa said.

The younger of the two women nodded uncomfortably, but did not respond. Her companion looked away.

"Friends of yours?" Carla asked.

"Once," Pippa said. "It's been a long time."

A waiter came over and offered to take drink orders.

"I'll have iced tea," Carla said.

"Bring me Absolut and tonic," Pippa said. "Double."

Carla looked at the woman across the table. "Do you think we could hold off on the alcohol today?"

"No," Pippa said. The waiter knew when to keep his mouth shut, and turned away. The two women at the next table beckoned him. Carla turned back to see Pippa helping herself to water. Her hand shook as she reached for the glass. I'd better be quick about this, Carla thought.

"Tell me about your first marriage," Carla said.

"How much do you know?" Pippa's eyes darted from Carla to the other table and back again.

"The court file says you were divorced from Claiborne Scott thirty months before you married Hunter Worthington. That the grounds were irreconcilable differences."

"That's what they called it," Pippa said.

"There's also a portion of the file that's sealed. And there are references to other women."

Pippa gave a brave smile. She had placed her hands back in her lap, but her eyes kept moving. "And what inference do you draw from that, Ms . . ."

"Tattaglia. Usually divorce records are sealed because someone doesn't want the public knowing their dirty laundry. Sometimes it's an accusation of child molestation."

Pippa shook her head.

"Or spousal abuse."

Pippa stopped.

"Or infidelity."

Pippa Worthington looked again at her water glass and evidently decided she would wait for something stronger.

"What is it that they say, Ms. Tattaglia? Two out of three isn't bad?"

Carla did not laugh. It was clear that her client was miserable with the subject.

"My ex-husband," Pippa said, "is now living in Provence with a cocktail waitress from our polo club in Palm Beach. She is welcome to him. I'm sure she is better equipped when he tries to drown her in a toilet bowl or break her nose."

The waiter brought the drinks then. He was followed by the maître d', who went directly to the next table and spoke quietly. Even from a distance, Carla could not miss his apologetic tone.

"Excuse me," she said to Pippa, "but am I not dressed appropriately for lunch in this place?"

Pippa kept her eyes on her drink, taking it in both hands and savoring a long sip. "No, dear, they're not complaining about you."

The two women stood up, and the maître d' led them to another part of the restaurant. The woman identified as Mags did not look back at Pippa.

"They were complaining about me. I wear a scarlet letter." Pippa Worthington looked out at the water and drank again. When she set it down, the glass was half empty.

"I grew up here," Pippa said. "Here and in New York. We would summer here, and I went to school in the city. My father was a Bingham, you know. The New York Binghams. And my father's grandfather made our fortune on Wall Street after the Civil War. That's when he built Château du Printemps."

Carla smiled politely. Whoever had designed Château du Printemps should be shot, she thought.

"In the summers we would go to the beaches here. In the evenings we went to parties."

"Sounds very pleasant," Carla said.

"It was. But it was empty. Do you understand?" Pippa stared at her lunch companion then, before consuming the rest of her drink. She looked around for the waiter, who saw them and nodded, heading toward the bar. Carla thought about stopping her. Then changed her mind. Pippa, it seemed, was on a roll.

"Did you go to college, Ms. Tattaglia?"

"Yes," Carla said. Pippa waited, expectant.

"I have a B.A. from Brown in history."

"I went to Mount Holyoke. I studied French literature. Do you like Molière? Racine?"

"They're okay." The waiter brought Pippa's second drink.

"My first husband went to Amherst. I wanted to finish my degree, but you know, things get in the way. Oh." Pippa paused. "Isn't that a terrible way to talk about your daughter?"

Carla did not answer. God, a psychologist could have a field day with this woman. Pippa began to work on the current drink.

"You're not close to your daughter?"

"Why should I be? Perhaps I should have been a spider. People understand when they eat their young."

The waiter appeared.

"You should try the duck here," Pippa said. "Hunter orders it for takeout and has Bosworth pick it up to bring home."

Carla ordered the duck. Her companion asked for soup.

"Don't you want something more filling?"

"No," Pippa said. "It will slow down my drunk." She lifted her glass again. When she put it down she wore a strange smile. "Isn't it funny? I studied French literature. In the original language. My ex-husband can't speak a word of French, and he thinks Racine is French for motor oil. But he lives in Provence and I'm here."

"Why don't you go? Move? Money can't be the problem."

"Because," Pippa said. "Because he won't. Hunter won't." Her speech was starting to slur now. But Pippa's hands no longer shook. "The sailing was too important. The races are too important. Belonging here, it's too important. But we don't belong. I have not since I married him. And he never will."

The waiters had reset the table abandoned by the two matrons, and Carla could see people waiting at the restaurant's door. But the maître d' had chosen not to seat anyone.

A waiter brought lunch a few minutes later. Pippa was right. The duck was excellent. Pippa barely touched the soup placed before her, instead downing another Absolut double.

When Carla was close to finishing she looked at Pippa again. "You mentioned that you wear a scarlet letter. What did you mean by that?"

Pippa drank again. "Are you saying they don't teach Hawthorne at Brown any longer?"

Carla wanted to smile then, but realized it would only encourage her. She was beginning to realize that Pippa Worthington was a rather mean drunk.

Carla said, "I guess what I'm asking you is why you feel you're an outcast."

Pippa Worthington leaned back in her seat, which made her hat slip. She reached up with one hand to right it and managed to knock it off her head. Pippa let out a laugh loud enough to draw the attention of other diners, who just as quickly went back to their lunches.

Carla reached down and picked up the hat.

"That woman you saw me waving to, do you know she was one of my bridesmaids in my first wedding? Now she won't speak to me, and she moves when I come near her."

"Yes, but that doesn't explain—"

"She's heard the rumors."

"What rumors?"

"You'll hear them."

"Tell me."

Instead Pippa Worthington drank again, a long slow pull at the glass before she closed her eyes. Carla reached over and caught the glass as it slipped from her hand, but could not stop Pippa from pouring herself out of her seat and onto the restaurant floor.

8

To call Geoff's on Benefit a sandwich shop would be roughly akin to referring to the *Mona Lisa* as a painting, or Mozart as a pianist, or the Rocky Mountains as a set of large hills. While all of these statements are technically accurate, they fail to account for the individual greatness of the thing described. True, Geoff's is located on Benefit Street, and it is a reasonable assumption that, at one point, someone named Geoff owned it. But there was more, Michael Carolina quickly realized. Much more. Geoff's was an experience. An event. Geoff's was a food emporium with attitude. An extremely bad attitude.

It was housed in a brick building, next to a pizza restaurant and beneath a set of apartments, some occupied by students at the Rhode Island School of Design. A group of kids were parked on the chairs and tables out front, most sporting tattoos and nose rings and the occasional dreadlock. One in particular intrigued Carolina. His frizzed blond dreadlocks sank halfway down his back and joined together in a large, round, convex mat: the do reminded Michael of a beaver's tail.

"Food good here?"

The kids stared at him as if he had climbed up from the gutter. Michael smiled and ducked inside. The aroma was classic deli. There were wooden counters on both sides of him, bolted to the brick walls, and stools for patrons who chose to eat in. A vast pickle barrel lay before him, and he stepped around it to get to the deli counter. But the most fascinating aspect of the place was the signs. There were dozens of them, some printed, others handwritten, advertising sandwiches, and drinks, and insults. "Our hands are in your food," one announced. Another proclaimed the Geoff's Guarantee: "If you are not satisfied with all of your Geoff's product, return the uneaten portion to us and we will throw it away."

A man of perhaps twenty-five, his shoulder-length black hair poking out the back of a Red Sox hat, sliced onions at the counter. The pieces fell in large purple ovals onto a white counter that bore the scars of a thousand different knives chopping briskets and corned beef and tuna.

Without looking up the young man said, "Know what you want?"

"Actually," Michael said, "I was looking for Morgan. Morgan Worthington."

"Mo!!!" the onion cutter shrieked, his eyes never leaving his work. In a few seconds Morgan Worthington appeared from a back room, wiping her hands on an apron.

"What?" She looked first to the onion cutter, then to Michael.

"Are you Morgan Worthington?"

"What do you want?" The tone was just short of hostile.

"I'm from Channel Three. I'm trying to find out about your brother."

The expression on the young woman's face transformed from suspicion to curiosity.

"You're on the news?"

"On occasion," Michael said.

"I've never seen you."

"You're not alone. Our ratings could use a boost."

The answer amused her. She drummed her robin's-egg-blue nails along the countertop. Carolina could not help noticing the tattoo.

"I thought your name was Morgan."

"It is." She waved her hand. "This is my band name." She pointed to a poster on the wall. SARAH HAS A SOCIAL DISEASE.

The poster was made of cheap red construction paper, with the band name printed in black and white and a crude sketch beneath of a woman screaming.

"That's our gig for Friday," Morgan said. "You could cover it for your station, but hey, it isn't exactly family entertainment."

"Gee, that's too bad," Michael said. Morgan smiled sweetly.

"Where did you get the idea for the name? The band, I mean."

Morgan stopped to think for a minute. "I could tell you it was a comment on society. Some statement about the decline of civilization. But that would be bullshit. It was shock value, you know? Like Marilyn Manson with his guts coming out of his mouth? It's all marketing. Gotta get the niche, you know what I'm saying? Who do you like to listen to?"

"I have a thing for Steely Dan," Michael said. "Some of the early Led Zepp's pretty good. And I always liked the Eagles. Did I say something funny?"

Morgan smirked. "You're an old fart," she said. "I guess it's kind of cute."

Carolina wondered whether he was blushing. "Maybe we should talk about your brother."

"Stepbrother," Morgan said. She looked down and began to arrange and rearrange condiments. "He's dead. And I'm tired of talking about him."

Just that fast she was shutting down. Can't lose her, Carolina thought. She's my only shot at the family right now.

He decided to take a risk then, not stopping to wonder if it would come back to haunt him later.

"What, Carla already asked all the questions?"

Morgan looked up and stared. "How did—"

"I know about Carla? Well, I may have lousy taste in music, but I'm a pretty good reporter, Morgan."

She went back to rearranging ketchup and mustard bottles, this time moving more quickly. Her sweater flapped open then, and Michael saw the metal piercing her breasts. Strange, he thought. That must hurt like hell. Morgan was not looking at him.

"If you know about her," Morgan said, "then you must know what we talked about. So I guess we don't need to talk, right?"

"Wrong," Michael said. "I'm as curious as Carla is."

"Yeah, but my steps isn't paying you. How do you know her?"

Michael thought for a moment. "I guess you could say we're friends."

Morgan stopped arranging the bottles and folded her arms. "I'll bet you are."

Carolina paused. Morgan had good instincts, he decided. She also wasn't interested in providing many details about her family. He was going to have to press harder.

"There are a lot of people saying that your stepfather didn't get along with your stepbrother."

"Are there?" Morgan said. "Lots of people don't get along with my father. I don't get along with my stepfather. Being an asshole isn't a crime."

"No, but if an asshole kills someone it is."

The sharpness of the remark surprised her. And it surprised him.

"You really think my steps killed Hunter?" she asked. She sounded different then, like a lost child, almost failing to comprehend what was happening around her.

"The truth is, I don't know," he said. "Your stepbrother doesn't seem to have too many enemies. And your stepfather was seen fighting with Hunter the night he died. But you know, there is this one other guy. Ever hear of Jimmy Mercer?"

Morgan's eyes narrowed slightly. "Another sailor boy, right? Yeah, he hangs in Newport."

"That's the one. Do you know anything about Hunter fighting with him? Over a girl named Ali?"

"How . . . how do you know about Ali?"

There was something in her expression. Was it shock? Fear? He could not tell. But something told him to play his cards close.

"It's just the word on the waterfront," he said. "You know how things get around."

"You're lying." She practically spit the words. "Ali's not in Newport."

Carolina felt as though he were playing poker blindfolded. "Maybe not," he said, "but when she was, I heard she was at your family's house all the time."

Morgan was shaking now. "You don't—Steps would never let that happen. Said he'd die first."

"Why is that? What made him so upset?"

But Morgan Worthington would not answer. She instead turned and disappeared into the back of the shop. Carolina turned and noticed the counterman, still holding the knife he'd used to slice the onions.

"Maybe you should book, man."

And Michael did.

That night he made the dinner: a pair of small steaks with baked potatoes and fresh asparagus.

"This is wonderful," Carla said. "What did you use for marinade?"

"Garlic, salt and pepper, a little red wine, and some olive oil."

"It's great." She picked up her plate and carried it to the sink, then came back and brushed her lips against his forehead. "Where's your father?"

Paul was gone when he'd returned home that night, and there was no note of explanation. Michael shrugged. He did not want to admit to worrying about his father. "I'm sure he'll turn up," he said. "Listen, I'm going to tell him he needs to find his own place anyway."

Carla looked at him. "You don't have to. He's not any trouble."

"You don't sound all that convincing. Besides, he seems to have trouble minding his own business."

"What do you mean?" The expression on her face was innocent, curious. He did not know how he should respond. Finally, he said, "You know, that stuff about my career. About the two of us. I guess I feel he's crowding things."

Her expression softened. "Maybe it's more your feeling than anything else," she said.

"Maybe," he answered. "So how was work today?"

"Fine," she said too quickly. "It's slow, but it's going."

"Ready to talk about your clients yet?"

"What do you mean by that?" Her voice was soft. Too soft, he thought. In that moment he realized he'd said too much, and for some reason it made him laugh. All he could think of was Ralph Kramden, ranting at Norton about how I know you know I know. It was ludicrous, the two of them both pretending that they were not thinking about the same thing. But neither was prepared to admit anything. Carla watched him for a moment, her expression turning stony.

"Nothing," he answered.

"Nothing seems to be very amusing," Carla fumed. She walked out of the room. He heard her climbing the stairs.

I can't blame her, he said to himself. She's trying to do her job. And I'm trying to do mine. And it *would* be funny, dammit, if the goddamed jobs weren't so important to both of us.

He heard the phone ring, and decided to let Carla answer. He was still trying to decide whether to watch television or find something to read or listen to some of the old fart music that Morgan Scott had teased him about when Carla came downstairs again.

"It's the state police," she said. "Lincoln Barracks."

He turned his head sharply.

"They have your father," she said.

* * *

Like most of the other state police buildings in the state, the Lincoln Barracks was old and built of brick. It was set among a grove of trees along what was once a busy highway. But the highway had been superseded by a new and improved Route 146, which sliced a concrete-and-asphalt path north from Providence, past Woonsocket, and up to Worcester, Massachusetts. The waiting area for the public was spartan, but no more so than the quarters for the troopers, who, Carolina could see, were making do with aging desks and chairs crammed into a room enclosed by the old brick and newer bullet-proof glass. A young corporal, dressed in the standard summer uniform of charcoal gray with red epaulets and piping, explained that a detective would be out to see Michael and Carla in a moment.

"Can you tell me what the charge is?" Michael asked.

"He'll be out in a minute," the trooper said politely, but with a tone that suggested further questions would be useless.

It actually was another ten minutes before the detective appeared. The officer was younger than the desk corporal, and did not wear a uniform.

"Mr. Carolina?"

"Yes. What's he charged with?"

"It's one count of disorderly and one of public intoxication."

He felt Carla grip his hand, and did his best not to show his relief. The ride up from Cranston had given him plenty of time to worry about the kind of trouble his father might have found. At least it did not appear that Paul would be charged with a felony.

"Can you tell me what happened?"

"I don't see why not," the detective said. "He was working the poker machines and the dogs over at Lincoln Park. I guess he ran out of cash, but not until after he'd had a few too many. He started trying to panhandle a few dollars off some of the other customers, and a security guard got called in. Then a couple of our troopers. We keep them on site at the track. Your dad got into a little scuffle."

"Is he all right?" Carla asked.

"He has a few bruises, but, ah, nothing serious. Mainly a shiner on his right eye." The detective looked down momentarily, then back at Carla. She knew the look, and knew that Paul Carolina had caught a beating.

"Do we get to see him?" Michael asked.

"Ordinarily, no. But the track isn't interested in pressing charges. And your father just signed a statement saying the whole thing was his fault. So we issued him a summons. He'll be out in a couple of minutes. There is one thing, though."

"What's that?"

"Your old man—your father, he'd better stay away from that track. They don't want him around over there. And when they don't want you, they have a way of showing it. If he does go back . . ." The detective let his words hang for a moment. "I think the charges could be stiffer next time."

Paul Carolina carried an ugly red knot over his left eyebrow. His clothes were the same as the ones he had worn the day before, only wrinkled, soiled, and smelling faintly of alcohol and stale tobacco smoke. When he spoke, his words rolled together in a slur, but his tone was soft, as if he feared that someone other than Michael and Carla might overhear him.

"Those bastards. I ought to sue them."

"To get a jury to pay any attention to you, you'll have to beat the criminal charges first," Michael said. His tone indicated he had little faith that his father would do so.

"Then you can do a story. That track is fixed. Those cops, they're corrupt. You could blow the whole thing open."

"I'm not going to do a story, Dad." Funny, Michael thought. I almost called him Paul. But I called him Dad.

"Why not?" Even with its soft tone, Paul Carolina's voice was angry. He was clearly humiliated, and he was looking for someone to blame. Michael made a convenient target.

"Because even if that track fixed races, there's no proof. A disgruntled gambler who just got arrested isn't exactly convincing evidence."

"What about the cops?"

"The cops were out of line," Carla said. Both Michael and Paul looked at her, but she kept her eyes on the highway. She slipped out of the right lane and quickly passed two cars before turning off Route 146 and onto the interstate toward Cranston.

"So you think we got a case, Carla?" Paul's voice now held a trace of hope, maybe even excitement.

"I didn't say that," she said. "They shouldn't have hit you, but I'll bet anything you did something to provoke it. That's how it usually works. You mess with a policeman, especially a trooper, he's going to come upside you. And just as your son said, Mr. Carolina—"

"Call me Paul, please."

"As I said, Mr. Carolina"—Carla's tone sounded harder now, a bit impatient—"you're not going to make a very credible witness."

They drove in silence until Carla guided her VW off the highway and down Park Avenue. She rolled the windows down and they felt the wind rushing into the car, smelled the salt in the air as they neared her house.

When Carla parked her car, Paul was slow climbing out.

"I guess I'm a little sore." Michael put out a hand to help him, but Paul shook it off.

"I can still take you to one of those walk-in emergency rooms," Carla said.

"I'll just take some aspirin," he said. "That's all a bad witness deserves, right?"

Michael sighed.

"The self-pity is getting a little old, Dad."

"Why don't you go upstairs and get some sleep," Carla said.

Paul turned to go inside.

"Thank you for coming for me," he said. He made sure to close the door carefully behind him. Michael and Carla stood in the driveway and watched him go.

"I should thank you, too," Michael said.

Carla nodded, but made no other response.

"There's something wrong, isn't there?"

Carla nodded again. She looked at him. "I want to know what you meant. About my clients. What were you getting at?"

He could not decide what to do. It was bad enough that she had helped him bail his father out that night. It would be worse if he told her that the old man was eavesdropping on her in her own home. And worse, that Michael knew what his father had heard.

"I don't know," he said. "You just seem so—secretive." Maybe I won't have to tell her, he said to himself. Maybe she will do it on her own.

But Carla did not. "I'm trying to build a business, Michael. My clients need to know that I'm discreet. Especially when my boyfriend is a reporter."

Her features were softened in the dappled half-light, and she pressed her palm against his hand. She cocked her head, and it reminded him for a moment of a bird staring at something it wanted.

"I'm sorry about your father, Michael."

"So am I." He had not allowed himself to be angry until then. Or at least not to feel it. But the sensation was there, as sure as the redness of a sunset, or the darkness that was rapidly covering the both of them.

His father had worked his way into his life once again, played him like a carnival barker, or one of the pseudo-pimps working outside a topless joint downcity in Providence. He'd manipulated his own son, and his son's girlfriend, into giving him a place to stay while he scouted the area and planned his next move. Inevitably, the next move led to a beer and a craps game or, if nothing else would do, a trifecta that hinged on underfed dogs chasing an overstuffed rabbit. Paul Carolina's greatest skill was his ability to use lies and deceit to gain trust. Michael and Carla had trusted, and this made his father's betrayal all the more infuriating. And embarrassing.

But at the same time, he could not escape a profound regret that shot through him and returned and shot through again until he felt as though his insides were a sieve. Was there something I could have done? If I had been a better son, if I had stopped the cracks and the wiseass remarks long enough to try and help him, would it be different? Would it have made a difference?

And when he tried to help me, when he told me what he'd heard on the phone, should I have offered gratitude instead of scorn?

Carla was watching him. Slowly, her hand slipped away.

"What's happening, Michael? You're like a cauldron. I can feel it."

Looking back, he would not know why he said the words then. It was as if her presence alone was enough to draw it out of him, as a poultice pulls poison from a wound. But if that was the reason, he would still not comprehend it.

"I know you're working for the Worthingtons."

The half-light had faded again, working its way to near darkness. He could no longer see any expression on her face. All that was left was the sense of her presence, and the accusation that filled her words.

"What I guess I'd like to hear is how you know."

It would have been easy to make an excuse, to pretend that he had seen her driving in Newport, or noticed her car parked somewhere, or even to say that he'd heard it as a rumor and followed up. But he could not do that. He had to tell her.

"My father picked up an extension. He heard you talking to Balboni. He told me about it last night, as if it were some sort of scoop."

She was silent for a moment.

"I am really embarrassed," Michael said, when she had not spoken for a sufficient length of time to provoke discomfort. "I know what he did was wrong. It wouldn't have happened if he weren't staying here."

"Is that why you've been asking me about my clients?"

She said it softly, calmly, but he could feel the pain in her voice. "I mean, were you going to use it for a story?"

"I don't know," he whispered.

Without touching her, he could feel her flinch. His answer was expected, perhaps, but also unwanted.

"If you had told me I couldn't use it, I would have respected that," Michael said. "And if you tell me not to touch it now, I will. But it's going to be hard."

When she spoke again her words were raw, biting into him.

"The only reason you even know he's a client is—" She stopped, too angry to finish.

"I know. Because my old man is a shitheel who digs into other people's trash."

Which is the same thing I do, he thought to himself. The same thing you do, Carla. Only we get paid to do it.

"Have you used the information?"

"No." In a flash, however, he recalled his unsatisfactory conversation with Morgan earlier that day. "Well, I did mention it to Hunter's stepsister. I told her that I knew you."

"You shit."

"I'm sorry."

"They'll probably fire me now."

"Carla, I really am sorry. It just came out. I have a job to do, the same as you. I try to get information. That's what I do. And when someone gives it to you, it's pretty damned hard to just ignore it."

It was dark now. He could only see her silhouette, her dark hair forming a soft, inverted vase down to her shoulders. She smelled of soap and some perfume he could not quite place.

Her arms were folded, closed. She was breathing in short, rapid spurts.

"This isn't a game. I need to trust you."

"And I need to trust you. You didn't exactly go out of your way to let me know what you're doing."

Even as he spoke the words he knew how ridiculous they sounded. Why should she have to tell him?

But then, he'd always told her about his career, his stories. What he was working on. He reminded himself that they had not been seeing each other that long. That living together had been an experiment. An experiment that was her idea, not his.

How easy it is to rationalize, it occurred to him. But there is no escaping one fact: using a personal relationship was wrong. And the wrong had wounded her.

"I think maybe I should move out for a while," he heard himself saying. "The apartment I was leasing is still open. I can take my father and—" He did not finish the sentence. This was the best solution, at least in the short term.

Or was it?

Part of Michael wanted Carla to object, to tell him not to be ridiculous. That things could be worked out.

Instead she said, "That's fine. I guess that's what we'll do."

They went inside then. Carla climbed the stairs to the bedroom. Michael waited until he heard her close the door. Then he went up and looked in on his father in the spare bedroom. Paul was asleep in his clothes, his body convulsing every few seconds in a series of deep, half-congested snores.

Michael went back downstairs to the couch and thought about his father and Carla, and the different meanings one could ascribe to the word "trust," until the debate faded into a mess of other thoughts and sleep overcame him.

9

Carla made a point of leaving early the next morning, slipping out the front door without checking to see if Michael was awake. She drove into Pawtuxet Village, a collection of small shops, restaurants, and a few galleries near Edgewood. There was a bakery there that she loved but usually tried to avoid, because the bagels and cream cheese had an uncanny ability to add inches to her waist. In the face of personal angst, however, she decided to make an exception.

She promised herself there would be no more tears, too many having been shed privately the night before. The fact that Michael's father had spied on her in her own home was bad enough. But to have Michael use the information! She was still so angry she could see her hand slapping him.

And yet he'd told her. He didn't have to, she knew. Michael wasn't perfect. But damned if he didn't have a conscience.

He even offered to move out, she thought. And I'm letting him. What is going to happen to us?

She finished the bagel, then sipped the remainder of her coffee, enjoying the warmth and mild sweetness of the liquid. It was comforting, though not quite enough. She resolved not to think about Michael again, at least not for the rest of the morning. But the only way to do that, of course, would be to find something else to think about.

Which made the page that came in just then a blessing. If only a temporary blessing.

She found a pay phone outside the bakery and dialed the number.

"Mr. Balboni's office."

"I might have known," Carla said.

"Excuse me?" The secretary's voice sounded confused.

"Sorry. I'm returning a call from Mr. Balboni."

"One moment." Carla listened to the piped-in music of an FM station, one that proclaimed itself as "Southern New England's Salsa King." She caught herself tapping her feet to the rhythm when Rico Balboni came on the line.

"I'm waiting for your report."

So much for pleasantries, she thought. "It's still early. I'm trying to make sure the family members can be ruled out as suspects."

"They *are* ruled out. I know you're new at this," he said, "but I thought that much was clear."

She pondered the insult for a moment, wondering whether it would be better to ignore it. No, she didn't think so.

"If you aren't satisfied with my services, you can replace me."

She could hear Rico's sneer. "How do I know whether I'm satisfied? You haven't produced anything yet. And you won't if all you do is take Pippa out to get her drunk."

Well. It was good to know that Mrs. Worthington kept her attorney, and presumably her husband, up to date.

"I'll be doing some more work today."

"Let me give you a hint. There's a rumor floating around the Newport bars that another sailor is going to do very well at the Olympic trials now that Hunter's son is dead. Name's Mercer. I hear he hangs out at a place called the Porcelain God."

Carla smiled to herself. The hints were getting more brazen now.

"I'll have to check into that."

"Call me tomorrow and let me know what you've learned."

"Nice chatting with you, Rico." She hung up before he could say anything else.

She climbed into her car and started driving south. There was checking to be done, all right. But she wasn't going to start at the Porcelain God. Besides, it was too early for the bars to be open.

Pippa Worthington.

Carla thought of her as she slipped into the high-speed lane on Route 4, whipping past East Greenwich and into North Kingstown. She was a pathetic woman: bright, well educated, but bitter. Wealthy, but miserable, slowly pickling herself in an endless string of martinis. And for all the prestige of her address and social pedigree, Pippa Worthington was incredibly lonely. The behavior of the other women at the restaurant suggested that she was practically an outcast.

But Pippa Worthington had attended the right schools. Her daughter and stepson attended the right schools. To those who fancied themselves to be moving in "proper" family circles, Pippa had an excellent personal family history. So why did she seem so screwed up?

These were among the questions running through Carla's mind as she pulled into a metered space near the Newport Town Hall.

The wedding announcement had said that Hunter Worthington was employed in private industry, a statement sufficiently vague to provoke curiosity. Carla started with the tax records of the assessor's office. Château du Printemps had a hefty valuation, which averaged out to an annual tariff in the mid five figures. But there was no other property associated with the Worthington name.

The clerk's office had listings of all companies with addresses in the city. Carla scanned the W's. Nothing. She remembered Johnson Enterprises. There was a listing for "Johnson, Inc.," together with a PO box. But there was no phone number, and no list of officers or directors.

She called the secretary of state's office and persuaded another clerk to cross-check the name of the corporation.

"We have Johnson Enterprises, a Minnesota corporation doing business as Ton's Worth of Fun."

"Do you have any corporate officers? President?"

"The only officer listed is an H. Worthington."

"What about an address?"

"The address listed is that of the corporation's registered agent, Americo Balboni."

"Thanks," Carla said. It was like driving straight into a wall.

She looked again at the photocopy of the wedding announcement, then went to a pay phone. Pomona College was located in Claremont, California. A woman in the alumni office was just arriving for work. After leaving Carla on hold for five minutes, she patiently explained that the college had no record of a Hunter James Worthington, Jr., ever graduating from the school, much less *summa cum laude.*

Nor did the alumni office at the Anderson School of Management at UCLA.

She made one more call, this time to the secretary of state's office in St. Paul, Minnesota. Yet another clerk explained that requests for information about corporations needed to be made in writing.

"Can you at least tell me whether you have a corporate address? I'm calling from Rhode Island."

After a moment's hesitation the clerk sighed. "The computer lists 1025 Industrial Park Way, in Fridley."

"Thanks," Carla said. The clerk had an interesting accent. "Excuse me, are you from St. Paul?"

The clerk laughed. "No, I'm from north of Duluth, out on the Iron Range."

Carla thanked him again.

She pondered once more the man who was employing her.

He had a presence that she could never quite adequately describe, a way of looking at people that suggested he would always know something more than the next person. He seemed born to a life of wealth and privilege. A patrician in looks, dress, and, generally, demeanor. But he had no visible source of income. He lied about his education. And he had a temper that blew harder and hotter than a cheap radiator.

And Hunter Worthington's speech carried traces of an accent. At first Carla had thought it was Canadian, but now she understood her mistake. For this accent came from just south of the Canadian border, from the vast, ore-rich section of northern Minnesota known as the Iron Range.

She walked down toward Thames Street, checking her watch. It was almost noon, and she wondered when the bar known as the Porcelain God would be open. As she rounded an intersection she recognized the woman she'd first seen outside Château du Printemps two days earlier. Then she smelled her, from fifty feet away. It was enough to make Carla's eyes water.

The woman had the same clothes, filthy khaki pants and ratty sneakers, torn blouse and a well-worn hat. She was screaming at a parked car.

"Avast, Moby! Cap'n'll be askin' for the harpoon in a minute!"

The woman circled the car, a gray BMW with New York plates.

"Best be movin', Cookie, or Wolf Larsen will have ye towed over the side. What?" The woman turned and looked over her shoulder. "Aye aye, Cap'n!" She turned back to the car. "Too late, Cookie, it's the ocean bath for you."

"I loved *The Sea-Wolf,* Brandy," Carla said.

The woman stopped, whipped around, looked at her with suspicion. Carla did not move.

"Wot's that, mate?"

The woman was delusional, Carla realized. The poor hygiene and filthy clothes were only symptoms.

"So who do you prefer, London or Melville?"

The woman stared, quizzical.

"It's Brandy, right? Brandy Shaker?" My God, Carla thought, who in the world named you?

"Who told you my name?"

A horny cop, Carla wanted to say. But she wasn't sure how the woman would react.

"Wolf Larsen. Don't you remember? Before we went after the seals?"

The suspicion on the homeless woman's face eased slightly.

"I always liked London," Carla said. "But London and Melville, they can both be depressing. Still, neither one tops Conrad, if you're looking for depressing sea stories."

The woman had lost interest in the car. Which was good, because Carla feared that she might damage it and get arrested again.

"Call me Ishmael," the woman said. She took a step closer. Her smell was overpowering. Carla forced herself to smile. "I will go in search of the great white," Brandy said.

She's headed out to sea, Carla thought. Got to bring her back. She let a hand sweep around her. "But it's good to be back on dry land, eh, Brandy? Good to make port."

The woman looked around, following Carla's hand. Slowly she seemed to comprehend, and she started to smile. Carla noticed the beautiful, even teeth, and a set of sparkling eyes. Once upon a time, she realized, this lady was beautiful.

But just as quickly, the smiling face transformed into something dark, and wet. A pair of tears made their way down the woman's left cheek. Brandy's face was a storm, but it was nothing compared to the raging pain that must be hidden beneath.

"He said you're a fine girl. He said what a good life it would be."

Carla stared. The woman was in agony.

"Who did? Who, Brandy?"

"Have you ever loved and lost?" She rasped.

The question stopped Carla.

"You have," Brandy said. "I see it. I feel sorry for you. The sea is a cruel mistress."

Before Carla could answer the woman was off again, talking to cars as if they were sailors or fish, lost within her own torment.

Michael heard Carla closing the door, followed by the sound of the Volkswagen starting, then slipping from the driveway.

He overcame the bleary temptation to drift off again. The couch was too soft to afford ready slumber anyway, and he'd had only a couple of hours of decent rest. He dragged himself into the kitchen, measured three cups of water for the brewer, then climbed the stairs to the bathroom like a man mounting a scaffold. He left the water cold, held his breath, and stood under the shower head for nearly a minute. "Penance," he thought aloud.

By the time he'd dressed, the coffee was ready, and his father was sitting on the couch, his fingers clutching at the sides of his scalp.

"I feel like dog shit," he mumbled.

"It matches your appearance."

"You have no respect for me."

"Then we have something in common."

Realizing he'd lost the round, Paul asked for coffee. Michael poured them both a cup. After a few grateful sips, Paul looked up at his son.

"What are you doing today?"

"Going to work. But first I have to pack some things."

"Why?"

Michael looked out the window. Quietly he explained his decision to move out, and the reasons behind it. Paul made no sound for several seconds after he finished.

"Son, I'm sorry for the trouble I've caused you."

He probably is, Michael thought. But that won't change his behavior. My father has dedicated his life to pursuing his own pleasure. Changing that habit isn't going to happen overnight, if it happens at all.

"So where do you think you'll go?" his father asked.

"Back to the place I leased before I moved in here. If it's still open."

Paul drained his coffee cup. "Can I ask you, son, where that leaves me?"

Michael looked at him. "You're broke, aren't you?"

Paul barely nodded. "That damned track cleaned me out."

Michael wondered then whether his father truly felt shame for his actions. Or whether it was merely an act designed to elicit sympathy. The truth, he realized, was probably somewhere between the extremes.

"I guess you're coming with me. But this is not going to be permanent. Not unless you start going to the meetings again. AA and Gamblers Anonymous, or whatever it is."

"I will," Paul said. "I really want to clean up, son."

"And you have to find a job. Now. Today."

"I will. I really will, Michael. I know I can do it."

Michael picked up his own car keys. "I'm going up to pack a few things. Then I'm going to work. I'll call the landlord when I get there." He grabbed a piece of scrap paper and scribbled out an address.

"Michael?"

"What?"

"I need a little money. For the bus. And for walking around."

Without looking at his father, Michael peeled two twenties out of a clip in his wallet. Paul quickly stuffed the bills into his pocket.

"I'll call you, son. I'm going to find something. Have some faith. I'm going to make you proud."

His father was grinning then, carrying that charming expression that must have pulled him through dozens of scrapes and crashes over the years. Faith.

Michael went upstairs, struggling to suppress his doubts.

The blue smoke was already billowing from Shirley's office. Michael looked at Earl, who was idly paging through the *Providence Herald* sports section in a chair outside the photographers' bullpen.

"Looks like there's a fire in there."

Earl barely glanced toward the news director's office.

"Nah," he said. "Just the one she's gonna light under your ass." Michael gave a wry smile and walked through the office door.

"I need a piece from you." Shirley kept the cigarette between her lips as she spoke.

"You know, I used to think that was cool," Michael said, batting away a thick scarf of smoke. "Then I did a story where a surgeon showed me a smoker's lung. In formaldehyde."

Shirley didn't miss a beat. "Too bad," she said. "We could have done a package about that tonight."

Neither one of them smiled.

"Michael, I need a story. This ain't the frigging network."

"I know. I gave it all up for you."

"I'm not amused. You getting anywhere on Hunter Worthington?"

"Some. But I'm not ready to make air."

Shirley's expression twisted into something close to a grimace.

"Are you in pain?" Michael asked.

"No, but I'm dealing with one."

"Sorry."

"Not you. The GM is breaking my balls."

"That's anatomically improbable."

"Well, if I had any he would be. Look, just get me a story. If it's today, fine. If not, then soon, Michael. Or we'll both be out of a job."

He was halfway out the door when she shouted. "Hey, what do you mean, improbable?"

Do You Have What It Takes?
What It Takes to Succeed in the Fast-Paced Food Industry?
If You Do, We May Have a Career for You.

Marketing. *Big$$$ for Aggressive Telephone Sales Representatives.*

Dishwasher. *$6.50 an hour. Nights, weekends.*

Paul Carolina put the paper down and rubbed the ink smudges into his fingertips. The pounding in his head was only beginning to wear off, and with the ease in pain came the dim memory of the night before. He was so sure he could hit the trifecta, that it would pay off into the high five, maybe the low six figures. So sure that he'd bet three hundred on a tan whippet, a brindle bitch running her maiden, and a speckled gray so jumpy that he suspected her kibble had been laced with amphetamines. The brindle took her maiden, all right, but the other two dogs finished out of the money. So he was broke, and no one had the decency to offer him cab or bus fare. The track security called him drunk, and the cops wrote him up for disorderly after he head-butted a trooper. And all his son could say was find a job.

Jobs. Get a job. Any job. A shit job.

He'd held dozens of them over the years. A short-order cook in south Florida. A telephone "boiler room" outside Nashville, until the place was raided and shut down. Barking outside topless joints in Baltimore and New Orleans. Hustling for a few bucks to spend on booze and a few bets, and maybe some female company, though he had never had much trouble where that was concerned.

In between there were a few stints in the can. In Tennessee, after the raid at the boiler room, they brought him in front of a lady judge, a little on the plump side, but not too bad. She peered down at him from the bench.

"You're a handsome man, Mr. Carolina."

"Thank you, your honor. You're a fine woman, too."

Her Honor smiled. Maybe I can catch a break, he thought. A night with her would beat hell out of a night in jail.

"What in the world were you doing in that room, selling those phony magazine subscriptions and pushing those free gifts over the phone?"

He shook his head sadly. "I'm a sick man, Judge. I'm a slave to the bottle and to horses. I can't tell you how sorry I am." Then he looked up and smiled that dazzling smile. "I wish there were a way I could make amends."

Her Honor considered him for another moment with a trace of amusement on her face, the way a spider must contemplate a fly struggling in the nether reaches of the web. "I wish there were a way too, pardner, but I can't think of one. Tell you what, why don't you go back to the county farm? I'll give you three hundred and sixty-five days to think about it."

He spent the year cleaning roads and tilling a vast patch of potatoes and corn. When they let him out he ached every time he looked at a vegetable. The sheriff in charge of the farm shook his hand and told him to find a job. A job. Any goddam job.

That was when he left the South. He'd been to other places in between, even tried AA and Gamblers Anonymous, though not to the extent he had claimed to his son.

Michael. The teenager he'd left behind in Iowa had grown up into a decent man. He had the potential to do something with his life. Paul could see it in him. Hell, he realized, he already *has,* more than his old man.

But there was also the restlessness, the need in his son to roam, to question the authority around him. Michael had never talked about it, but Paul figured it was why he had spent so much time sailing. And why he had come back again. Why he had decided to move out of here, to leave this girl. Michael ought to know better than to run out on a good thing. It usually comes to an end on its own soon enough.

But all in all, Paul thought, he's not so different from me. That's why he gets so angry sometimes. It's not just what he sees in me. It's what reflects back.

He glanced back at the paper again, at the list of low-pay, no-respect bullshit jobs, each one itself a dead end, or part of a maze leading nowhere. They were the reason, he told himself, that he routinely blew money on craps games and bookies and the sullen people working parimutuel windows from Miami to Rockingham. A big score every now and again was the only way to make up for the drudgery.

There was no big score this time. He needed to work up another stake. Needed to convince his son, in fact, that Paul Carolina was still capable of earning a buck. But staring too hard at the paper was bringing back the pounding again. Maybe if he rested for a few minutes.

He was setting the help wanted section down when he saw it. The type was small, the ad short.

High-Quality Landscaping. *Experienced. Cranston, Providence. Wages based on experience.*

There was a number with it. He put the paper aside and closed his eyes. Outdoor work, and it was still summertime. He really didn't like outdoor work all that much, but it was much better in decent weather. And it was close by. People who could afford high-quality landscaping had to have money, and probably did not mind paying decent wages. From what he'd seen on the tube during Michael's reports, there were worse places to be.

Besides, he had the experience. He looked at the number again and walked to the phone. Perhaps that year on the county prison farm was worth something after all.

10

The Porcelain God filled rapidly as the light faded in early evening. Carla watched the peculiar assortment of grunge musicians and their followers, together with preppy boaters. They moved freely but uneasily through the bar, ordering drinks, shouting greetings, and eyeing each other like rival street gangs.

The barman known as Mr. Clean sidled up and tugged at one of his earrings, then gave her a casual leer.

"Another mineral water?"

"Sure."

She'd been there for close to two hours now. The hamburger she'd ordered lay half-eaten on the plate in front of her. The Porcelain God's menu needed work.

Mr. Clean swept up her empty glass and grabbed a clean one. He poured the water from a bottle and set the glass on a piece of toilet paper, torn and folded to form a cocktail napkin.

"Yeah, you're sure living on the edge tonight," he chuckled. "Sure you can handle all this hard stuff?"

"I guess we'll both find out, won't we, Ajax?"

Mr. Clean's expression turned to marble. "That supposed to be funny?"

"Ajax was a Greek hero. It was a compliment."

Mr. Clean hesitated. Carla sipped her new mineral water and smiled.

"Who you looking for?"

Okay, so he didn't study the classics, she thought. But it didn't take a scholar to see she was waiting for someone.

"You know a sailor named Jimmy Mercer?"

Mr. Clean tensed.

"You a cop?"

"Now why would you think that?" She tilted her head to one side and put on her best Orphan Annie voice. "Do I look like a cop?"

"Why do you want to see him?"

"He's a friend of a friend."

Mr. Clean sniffed, as if he doubted her answer. There was a shout then, and Carla looked down to see an impatient patron dressed in black, demanding another beer. Mr. Clean slipped away to attend to him, conveniently neglecting to answer her question.

"You must have a death wish," Earl said.

"No, just healthy curiosity."

They had spent the day on the Newport waterfront, stopping sailors and people who looked like sailors, asking questions about a girl named Ali. No one seemed to know anything. They had visited the Newport Yachting Center, where a young clerk had given them a break.

"I don't know anybody locally by that name. But I remember there was a girl from the Midwest—Wisconsin? One of those states on the Great Lakes. Her name was Alison. She usually finished pretty high in the standings. But that was last year."

"Do you have a last name?" Michael asked. The clerk shrugged.

"I'd check with one of the sailing magazines," she said. "They keep good stats on racers."

A visit to the Redwood Library revealed a slew of sailing periodicals. Michael made a list of every Laser story for the past eighteen months. He worked his way back from the most recent issues, and in a November issue of *Racing Sailor* he found a name.

1.   Charlene McCrea
2.   Laura Stempner
3.   Alison Johnson

An issue of *Cruising Sail* listed Alison as the winner of a regatta near Mackinaw Island, Michigan. An edition of a periodical titled *The Beam* ranked her among the top five Laser sailors in the Great Lakes. But the best was an issue of *Tack and Jibe,* a glossy, colorful record of the yachting world published four times each year. The winter issue had a piece about the annual Laser Regatta held in Key West, Florida, every year. The photographs glistened, capturing the dozens of bronzed men and women driving tiny boats through water the color of jade.

"Nice pictures," Earl said, looking over Michael's shoulder.

There were other photos, of sailors checking rigging before a race. Of still more sailors partying at sunset along the Mallory docks. And finally, of two men Michael recognized: Hunter Worthington III and James Mercer, pushing a screaming young woman off a dock, in the traditional celebration following a race.

Ali Johnson, 19, takes a victory dunking following
her first-place finish in the women's division.

The young woman's body was slender, and she wore what looked like white tennis shorts and a polo shirt the color of a setting Key West sun. Her hair was sandy blond, her eyes brown, her nose small and freckled, and her expression merry. Hunter and Mercer were smiling, too. They knew that she was beautiful.

He rushed back to the yachting center to look up the results of the Laser races from a week ago. But there was no mention of Alison Johnson. She had not placed in the women's division. She had not even registered to compete.

Which brought him back to the Porcelain God.

"We've got to talk to the guy," Michael said.

Earl looked down. "If we live that long. They weren't exactly warm to us last time we were there."

"This is true." But it didn't change the fact that he needed to get to Mercer once again. And this was where the arrogant sailor most commonly was found. But there was another reason to visit tonight, he realized, as he watched the bouncers taking cover charges at the door: the sign announcing that Sarah Has a Social Disease, Morgan Worthington's band, would be providing the evening's entertainment.

Carla finished her third mineral water and realized she would not be able to continue the stakeout without a visit to the ladies' room.

For a bar themed on bathrooms, the real thing in the Porcelain God was remarkably drab, the fixtures chipped or cracked, and lit by a bare bulb. And it was crowded. At least a half-dozen young women waited impatiently for the two stalls to become available. Three more stood before a mirror, two applying makeup, a third adjusting the pieces of metal that pierced her nose and ears. Carla held her breath along with her place in line.

The toilet flushed, and a stall door opened. The woman who walked out went immediately to the mirror for a final primp.

"Hello, Morgan," Carla said.

Morgan Scott turned. She wore a torn purple T-shirt and ripped black denim jeans. Her makeup was of the Morticia Addams variety, and she had dyed her hair a glossy black for the occasion. The nipple rings still poked through the T-shirt.

"Hey, it's the PI lady." Her tone was friendly.

"Thought I'd catch your act," Carla said.

Morgan nodded. "Cool. We're on in about ten. Hey, I met a friend of yours."

"I heard."

"Does Steps know you do it with him?"

The question was so crass, so brazen, Carla assumed it had to be for effect.

"I don't kiss and tell."

The response amused Morgan. She turned back to the mirror for one final adjustment of the rings on her breasts. In the mirror her features seemed softer, more fragile, perhaps, than they were in the cold, harsh light of the rest room.

"Neither do I," Morgan said. "Neither do I."

Michael and Earl found a pair of seats and a ratty table as far from the bar as possible. Earl had agreed to enter the club on the condition that they avoid contact with Mr. Clean.

Michael could see the shaven-skulled bartender. He was pulling on a tap, his free hand shifting glasses underneath without ever stopping the flow of beer. Mr. Clean's eyes were roving the room, his mouth twisted into something resembling an ugly pink scar.

Earl followed Michael's gaze. "I'm telling you, that guy was seriously abused as a child. That or he abused everyone else. Stay clear of him."

This would not be a problem if Mr. Clean did not notice their presence. Still, it might make it difficult to look for Mercer. They turned their heads away from the bar, which irritated the skinny waitress who had appeared at the table.

"What is it, my breath?"

"Uh, no," Earl said.

"Drinks?"

"Two beers, whatever's on tap," Carolina said. "When does the band come on?"

The waitress shrugged. "I'm not the entertainment director."

She sauntered off. As she did, the growing crowd led out a roar, as the members of Sarah Has a Social Disease made their way toward the stage.

There were four of them: a tattooed drummer sporting a Mohawk, a slender bass player with bangs that dropped past his eyes, a guitarist with a greasy goatee, and Morgan Worthington, her face the color of cinders, but her step as light and bouncy as a teenybopper's.

"Great crew," Earl said. "Think they take requests? I've got a yearning for Cole Porter."

The band stepped up to the stage, while Morgan grabbed a microphone.

"Hello, fuckers. I'm Sarah."

The crowd, preppies and grunge alike, roared approval.

"Cool, SARAH. . . ."

"Sing, bitch. Sing."

With no warning, the guitarist dragged a hand across the strings, and sound blasted from the speakers like grapeshot from a cannon. The drummer grabbed his sticks and began beating his snare while the bass player fiddled with two knobs before plucking at the G string. What emerged was an assault on the eyes and ears such as Michael and Earl had never heard before. It was brutal. It was vicious. It was lousy.

"Ever hear of original sin?" Michael shouted. Earl looked back, brows raised.

"As a concept?"

Michael nodded. Then he screamed, "I think this must be what it looks and sound like."

Earl nodded sadly.

The tune, if it could be called that, bore a twisted resemblance to "Runaround Sue," but with a faster rhythm. The guitarist and the drummer wailed backup vocals while Morgan seemed to plead indecipherable lyrics into a microphone. Bodies in front of the stage jigged to the beat like insects in a frying pan.

The first beer was thrown before the band hit the song's second bridge. It caught Morgan full in the chest, splashing her face and making her blink. Still, she kept singing. Her nipple rings flapped against her shirt and sprayed tiny bits of foam back at the crowd. A man in the center of the pack, tall and sun-bleached, made a guttural noise and pumped his fist in the air.

"Hello, Jimmy," Michael said.

Jimmy Mercer was dancing, if it could be called that, with a pretty auburn-haired girl who looked dangerously close to being underage. The lanky sailor towered over her, waving his arms and sloshing a drink from a white plastic cup on the both of them.

"You see him?" he shouted to Earl.

Earl followed his gaze. "Yeah." The photographer pointed to the bar. "Do you see him?"

Mr. Clean stared at Mercer. When the two of them made eye contact, Mr. Clean pointed, then curled a finger in a beckoning motion. Mercer stopped dancing and began to edge his way through the swell of people toward the bar. The auburn-haired girl kept moving, unaware that her partner had abandoned her.

Carla saw Mr. Clean as well. And the young man now coming toward him. He was good-looking, but there was something hard about him, a sort of cruel expression on his face. It did not change as Mr. Clean pulled him close to say something in his ear. And to gesture toward Carla. The man was watching her now. He had the look of a salesman trying to decide on the right approach with a customer.

Carla winked at him. Come on, Jimmy, come talk to me.

This caught the man by surprise. But it worked. He grinned and began moving toward her.

"Shit," Michael said.

Earl saw Mercer. "Isn't that your girl—"

"Yeah." Or ex-girl, he thought.

"What's she doing here?"

Carla's attention was focused on Mercer.

"Probably the same thing we are," Michael said.

The crowd inside the Porcelain God packed the dance floor to overflowing. The interior of the club was a blend of bodies, fluids, and drinking cups, a human Hydra, complete with nose rings and Bud Light. Sarah Has a Social Disease whipped the mass of bones and flesh to a rolling boil.

Beer was tossed freely, at the band, between dancers, and onto patrons seated at the wobbling tables. Here and there a few revelers stopped to vomit, which only heightened the screams and a weird sense of panic among those nearby. A woman fainted in the middle of it all, and was lifted into the air and passed overhead, ultimately landing in a crumpled heap on a table that collapsed from the weight.

It would never be clear where the first punch came from, nor even to whom it was directed. Soon enough, however, there followed a string of them, as the Hydra grew restless and began to beat on itself like monks doing penance in a medieval abbey. The cops, of course, would not be so poetic, instead referring to it as another riot at the God.

"Are you Jimmy?" Carla asked when he got within shouting range. Her back was to the dance floor now.

"Who are you?"

"Carla." She handed him a card. He slipped it into his pocket without reading it.

"Can we talk someplace?"

"About what?"

"Hunter Worthington."

Whatever warmth had existed in Jimmy's expression vanished.

"I thought you were looking to score." He ducked then and

a flying beer narrowly missed his head before crashing against the bar. A group of preppies pushed past, knocking Jimmy against a stool and then down to the floor.

"Some other time maybe," Carla said. She held out a hand to help him up. Still more people were screaming now, and the swirling mass of people in the center of the club seemed to rock back and forth, a human wave trapped inside a water tank. The backwash rolled up against the crowd, upsetting the balance on Carla's stool.

Michael saw Carla sliding to the floor. The band was no longer playing. Instead the drummer and the guitar player were systematically destroying their instruments. Morgan, or Sarah, or whatever she was called, was dry-humping a microphone stand and giving a low moan with each thrust. A string of curses flew up from the crowd, and people began to push for the door.

Earl grabbed Michael's arm. "We've got to get out of here."

Michael climbed out of his chair and fought his way toward Carla, Earl a step behind.

There were feet everywhere, stomping, grinding, seeking anything solid to stand on. Carla had to fight to keep a boot off her throat. Two feet away she could see Jimmy Mercer struggling to do the same.

"Got to stand up!" she shouted to him.

"Can't!" he gasped as a foot landed squarely on his solar plexus. For the first time, Carla wondered whether she would be able to get out of the club.

Michael fought off a heavyset kid wearing Doc Marten boots and three steel rings through his eyebrows. The kid took a swing and missed.

"Lemme through, asshole," the kid rasped.

Earl pushed the kid from behind. "Who's stopping you?" The kid nearly fell, but kept his balance and stumbled off.

"Pretty soon and this place could be dangerous."

Michael gave a wan smile.

A steady line of people were pushing past the bar, most of them on their way out of the club. A few fell, screaming when they did. The people around them did not stop to help them up. Michael and Earl pulled a young woman in a torn summer dress to her feet and pointed toward the door. They did the same with her date, a pale young man with limp dark hair, white shorts, and a tennis shirt. All the while Michael kept looking to the bar, to the spot where Carla had fallen. She had not reappeared.

He pushed through another group of grungers and past the skinny waitress, now shrieking at the top of her lungs.

"Sorry we didn't leave a tip," he said, turning her toward the door.

"Yeah, but you never brought our beer," Earl said.

The waitress screamed louder and pushed toward the door.

Then they were through. A crowd of men and women were milling by the bar.

"Get the hell away!" Earl shouted. The crowd looked at Earl and Michael, panicked. They pushed forward, and a split developed.

Carla was on the floor, pulling on Jimmy Mercer's arm. But the sailor had gone fetal, trying to protect himself from the stomping feet.

"Let me get him up," Michael said to her.

Carla turned and peered at him, a look of surprise growing on her face.

As they lifted Mercer, he groaned and hugged his chest.

"I think he broke a rib," Carla said.

Before Michael could reply, a splash of blue-and-red strobe flashed through the club. A police cruiser, lights burning, had pulled up to the club's door. The arrival only created more panic in the club's patrons, who were now pushing to escape.

Yet another group of preppies banged into them in their rush toward the door, and Carla and Mercer were nearly knocked down again.

"Somebody's gonna get killed," Earl said.

Michael looked around. In the dim light he could see only one other exit sign. But the sign was burned out, and blocked by the two amplifiers. The band had disappeared from the stage, its members most likely mixed with the customers now rushing to get out.

"Get everybody behind the bar," Carla said.

She was right. Together, they lifted Mercer onto and then over the bar. Michael and Carla pulled themselves over, and Earl followed. The Porcelain God was still filled with the noise of people screaming and stampeding. But they were no longer in danger of being crushed or trampled.

"What's this shitheel doin'?"

Michael turned to see Mr. Clean hefting a baseball bat. His face was almost a shade of purple in the mix of blue-and-red strobe. The bartender swung the bat, missing Michael's head by inches, but connecting with the bar and shattering wood and splinters everywhere.

"Be cool!" Mercer pleaded. "I said be cool!"

Mr. Clean held the remnants of the broken bat in his hand. "I ain't going to jail. You the asshole called the cops on us?"

"We didn't call anyone," Earl said.

"We just wanted to talk to Jimmy," Michael added.

The answer seemed to enrage Mr. Clean once again. His eyes bounced from Mercer to Michael and Earl to Carla.

"This bitch work with you?"

"No," Carla said. She took a step back from them all and lifted her shirttail away, revealing a small nine-millimeter. "Now put down the bat, Ajax."

Mr. Clean blinked. Slowly, he put the broken bat handle aside. "Knew you was a fuggin' cop."

"I'm not a cop. I'm a PI. But since the cops are coming in, I think you'd better untwist your knickers and see if we can get some help for your friend."

Mr. Clean glanced down at Mercer, who was still hugging his ribs. The two of them exchanged a look that Michael was sure conveyed some sort of message.

"I said to be cool, Myron."

Two Newport officers finally managed to get into the room then, and Mr. Clean shrugged, as if he no longer had a choice.

Michael looked at Earl. Who arched his brows.

"Myron?"

The first cruiser was joined by two more, along with a uniformed lieutenant who presumably handled second-shift command. Together the cops rounded up the scattered remainders of the crowd from the Porcelain God. The officers tried to obtain statements as to how the riot started.

"I dunno."

" 'S a fight, 's what I heard. Didn' see nuttin'."

"I think someone didn't like the band, man. But hey, Sarah rules, know what I'm sayin'?"

"No, Officer, I don't know what happened. D'you have a smoke? And a light?"

The lieutenant walked up to Carla, shaking his head. "I suppose you didn't see anything?"

"I saw plenty. But I don't know how it started."

"My officers tell me you used to be a cop."

"That's right," Carla said evenly.

"Hell of a place for an ex-cop to be drinking."

"I was working," Carla said. She handed him her PI license. The lieutenant looked it over carefully, then returned it.

"On what?"

She did not answer him.

"Well, that's fine," the officer said. "Let me tell you, I got three people in the hospital now, one with a concussion, one a broken arm, and the last one may have a busted jaw. This friggin' club is a menace. You don't wanna tell me what you were doing here, I guess that's your right. But don't be coming around later looking for any favors from our department."

"I'm crushed," Carla said.

Michael watched the exchange from a distance. He turned to Jimmy Mercer, who was being worked on by an EMT.

"You really ought to go to the hospital," the paramedic said.

"I'm fine." Mercer snapped the words out, and the action made him wince. "I'm telling you, I'm fine." He glanced at Michael through heavily lidded brows.

"You still here?"

"I still wanted to ask you something."

"I got nothing to say to you."

"When are you going to tell Ali about what happened to you?"

Mercer started to say something, then stopped, then paused long enough to convince Michael he'd touched a sore spot.

"Who's Ali?" Mercer finally asked.

"You're not very convincing."

Jimmy Mercer kept looking at him, eyes smoldering.

"Don't yank my chain, Jimmy. I saw the picture from the magazine. The one where you and Hunter threw her in the water? Nice shot. How come she wasn't here last week for the regatta?"

"I don't know what you're talking about, Mr. Reporter."

"Didn't you hear what the man said?"

Mr. Clean had appeared at Mercer's side.

"Actually, I did, Myron," Michael said. "I just don't believe it."

Mr. Clean scowled. "You don't know me well enough to use my name." He turned to Mercer again.

"You gonna be okay? You leave for a race tomorrow, don't you?"

Mercer grimaced and nodded.

"Because you got to keep up with your career. You know what I'm saying?"

Mercer threw another look at Carolina.

"You know what I'm talking about?" Mr. Clean's tone was even more menacing then.

"Yeah," Mercer said. "Yeah. I'm ready to sail."

Mr. Clean leaned over and placed a stumpy pinky finger on Michael's chest. The power behind it was astonishing.

"Time to back off, newsman. You ain't welcome around here."

Michael blinked. But he did not move. Mr. Clean looked around him, as if noticing for the first time that there were cops standing outside the Porcelain God. Without another word or a look back at Mercer, he stalked off.

"Helluva friend you got there," Michael said.

"Mind your own business." Mercer would not look at him.

"Where are you racing?"

Mercer did not answer, but in the silence Michael remembered the article from the sailing magazine. The annual race in Key West. He made a note to check the date again.

"For whatever it's worth," Michael said, "you're in no condition to sail. Especially in a single-handed race."

"I didn't ask for your opinion," Mercer said. "Now fuck off."

Michael walked away. The police were taking photographs of the broken windows of the Porcelain God. Earl walked up with his videocamera and began rolling tape of the exterior.

"Heads up, Michael. I just got off the phone with Shirley. She's sending a van, and she wants a live shot for eleven o'clock."

Wonderful, he thought. At least the station will get something good out of this.

From the corner of his eye he caught Carla looking at him. They walked toward each other.

"Are you okay?" he asked.

"I'm fine," she said, her voice a little cold. "What were you doing here tonight?"

Her tone surprised him. "I should be asking you the same thing."

"I was working," she said.

"So was I. You have a problem with that?"

"I have a problem with you spying on me."

Michael looked down and fought the urge to snap back at her.

"After what my father did, I can understand why you might think that. But I wasn't spying, Carla. I came to talk to Jimmy Mercer."

"My, what a coincidence," Carla said, her tone now sarcastic.

"You think I'm lying?"

She looked at him, unsmiling, arms folded across her chest. "You wouldn't be the first in your family," she said. The moment the words were out, she regretted them.

Michael cocked his head slightly. He seemed to be about to respond, but was interrupted by a strange giggle.

Morgan Worthington was watching the two of them.

"Whoa, true love hits the shoals, eh?"

Her black shirt was torn, but the nipple rings were still intact. Morgan's hair hung limp and uneven on both sides of her face, and she wiped her arm across her forehead, denying a small cut over her right eye the opportunity to clot.

"That's how Moms and Dads started. Moms and Steps, though, they get a lot rougher. At least, he does." She smiled faintly.

Carla spoke softly but firmly. "This is a private conversation, Morgan."

"And this is a public street, Miss Private Eye." Morgan's hard gaze shifted to Michael. "Great show, eh? I love it when the band trashes the guitars. It's wicked original."

"Ever hear of The Who?" Michael asked dryly.

Morgan gave him a quizzical look.

Earl appeared. "Van's here, Mike. Gotta write something and edit tape if we're going to make eleven."

Michael turned to look at Carla. Her face was softer now, but not enough, he guessed, to make further discussion appropriate. Besides, there was no time.

"I've got to go," he said.

"Fine. Do not quote me."

The anger in her voice was still there. He shrugged.

"What makes you think you said something worth reporting?"

Carla watched him walk off in the direction of the Channel Three van. I shouldn't have taken so many shots at him, she thought. But what the hell was he doing here? And that last remark. Bastard.

She did a quick survey of the scene. Jimmy Mercer had managed to evaporate, with the bartender known as Mr. Clean. The police were still mopping up, but it was already clear that no information would be coming from them.

Which left her with Morgan, who was still watching her.

"What happened to the rest of the band?"

"They cruised." She said it as if she did not care. "I'll probably see them tomorrow."

The girl was so strange, so desperate for attention. Carla sensed she did not want to go home, and would use almost any excuse to avoid that possibility. That presented an advantage. The key to any good interrogation was knowing what the subject wanted.

"So you've met Michael before?"

"Yeah. He's cute. You shouldn't be fighting with him."

Carla ignored the remark. "What did he talk to you about?"

Morgan hesitated. It was clear that the subject was delicate.

"You know, you've got to be careful what you say to reporters," Carla said. "You never know what they're going to do with information."

"You mean you don't trust him?"

Carla paused for only a second. "I'm very careful with what I share with him about my work. And you're part of my work." Well, that's the truth, she thought. I didn't answer her question, but I told the truth.

"But if you want to be sure you didn't go too far," Carla said, "you should tell me what he asked you about."

Morgan stared at her, trying to decide what to do.

"He asked about Ali," she said. "But I didn't tell him anything."

Carla said nothing. The next question was too obvious to be asked.

Morgan gave a small sigh. "Do you have any money? I want to get a beer."

"Sure."

"Good. Then I guess I'll tell you about Ali."

11

Y ou're going where?"

Michael tucked the plane ticket back into a duffel bag. "Key West."

Shirley threw a baleful glance at the luggage and slowly shook her head.

"Come on, Shirl, it's not the bag's fault."

But she would not look at him. This was not like her. She was usually more confrontational.

"You've got more nerve than a stripper at a Baptist revival," she said finally. "You've been working this story for a week, and we have zip."

"Hey, I got you that live shot last night, right?"

"I *ordered* you to do that live shot, remember?"

Michael offered the most pleasant smile he could muster. "I did a good job, didn't I?"

Shirley reached for her cigarettes. "Sure. Yes, you're just fine on the air. The problem is, you're never on. And now you want to take off again to look for some kid named Ali." She lit up again, took a drag, and noticed him frowning. "Don't start. Don't you dare start. If I ever get lung cancer, it'll be because you drove me to it."

Michael held his tongue.

"In case you haven't figured this out, you're not working for a network, or even a top ten station. This is Providence, forty-third market, squeezed between Hartford and Boston. And you work for Channel Three, which stands for number three in the ratings. That means we have to do more with less, understand?"

"Yes, boss." He said nothing more. She was weakening, he knew it. So she was entitled to a little free-form rant.

"I know what's going to happen," Shirley went on. "The GM is going to catch the show tonight at six, and he's going to call down here and ask where the hell you are. And I'll either lie, which I hate doing, or I'll tell him, which I hate even more. Know why?" She did not wait for an answer. "Because he's going to tell me to fire your ass. And frankly, I wonder sometimes if he's right."

The words hung there for a moment, and Michael wondered whether she meant it. Shirley took another drag, and blew a perfect O ring. They both watched it hang there and disappear.

"If it makes you feel any better," Michael said, "you might want to think about what happened the last time I went to the tropics."

"I remember." In fact, he'd located a missing banker who'd looted a loan and investment company on Federal Hill. The story had earned the station a string of awards, and more respect than the number one and number two channels had between them.

"The thing is," Shirley said, "that was then. Does the phrase 'What have you done for me lately?' sound familiar? The GM sings it to me every morning."

"I didn't know you were so close."

Shirley made a face. "Even I have standards, Michael. I may be a television whore, but I'm not a real one." She sighed. "You'd better bring something good back."

He picked up his bag and looked out from her office toward the assignment desk. Earl stood waiting. The chief photographer winked and pointed at the window, where a cab had pulled up.

"One more thing."

"What is it?" Shirley was beginning to look irritated again.

"Earl's coming too."

They could still hear her screaming as the cab pulled out toward Green Airport in Warwick.

Carla was in the air before Michael walked out Channel Three's door. Northwest took her to Detroit, where she connected for Minneapolis–St. Paul. It was hard not to think about Michael. She regretted accusing him of spying, but the facts had certainly fit. How could he be working the exact same part of the case? The coincidence, she decided, was astonishing.

Or was it?

The sky page she wore vibrated against her belt, and she checked the readout. The jet was equipped with cell phones in each bank of seats, and the connection was swiftly made.

"Funny, I was just thinking about you," she said when Rico Balboni came on the line. He did not bother to ask why.

"I'm waiting for your progress report."

"I tracked down Mercer last night."

"And?"

"It was a riot."

She briefly explained, omitting any details about her conversation with Morgan.

"This Mercer guy sounds promising," Balboni said as soon as she was finished. "What's your next move?"

"I'm doing some background on friends Mercer has," she said. Technically, I'm not lying, she told herself.

"Keep it up. Something tells me you're on the right track." Balboni hung up. Carla replaced the cell phone in the center seat and gazed out the window at a sea of brilliant white clouds.

The story Morgan had told her the night before was as perplexing as it was bizarre. And it gave Carla a second reason to visit Minnesota.

"Hunter and Ali met at one of the regattas," Morgan had said. "A couple of years ago, down in Virginia or the Carolinas, I don't remember. Or maybe it was the Great Lakes. If that matters. Anyway, Hunter said she was a real cute girl, and when she came to Newport for another race, he introduced me to her. He was right. She was really a doll."

"I thought you weren't close to your stepbrother," Carla said.

Morgan Scott offered a rueful smile. "Living where I live, with Steps the way he is, and Moms the way she is, the less they know the better. I keep things to myself. Anyway, Hunter had a thing for Ali. And he wasn't alone. Jimmy Mercer did, too. They both fought over her. I think Ali loved the attention."

"I can see why," Carla said. "Two handsome young men from old money—What's so funny?"

"You think Jimmy is from old money? That's a load. He tells people that, feeds them a line about coming from Fairfield County. It's all bull. You know where he gets his money? Jimmy's a dealer. He sells coke and marijuana. Works out of the Porcelain God with that bald-headed bartender, Myron."

"You mean Mr. Clean."

"Yeah, Myron's been telling people to call him that ever since he opened up the bar. He and Jimmy deal to the kids on the waterfront, the preppies and the sailors and the grunge types. Anybody with money. Jimmy wants people to believe he's just another rich-kid sailor. But he isn't. He's a dealer who likes boats."

Carla nodded, stashing the information away. "Getting back to Ali . . ."

"Like I said, Jimmy and Hunter were both chasing her. Hunter won. He was crazy for her, and she fell for him. But you know, Newport isn't exactly a fairy tale."

"What does that mean?"

"Steps. Steps went crazy. Said that Ali wasn't welcome in the house, that he'd cut Hunter off. He swore his son would date some farm girl over his dead body."

"Farm girl?"

"Yeah. Ali was from Minnesota."

* * *

She kept thinking of that conversation as the jet passed the northern reaches of the Mississippi on its final approach to Minneapolis–St. Paul. The day before, Rico Balboni had all but ordered her to look at Jimmy Mercer. This morning he was encouraging her to do more. Did her client have a theory? Or did he already have proof?

On the ground by ten-thirty, she threw her carry-on over her shoulder and hailed a cab. The driver was talkative, punctuating his questions with long looks in the rearview.

"Where you from? First time to the Twin Cities? Business or pleasure? What line you in?"

She smiled politely, and remembered a headline from the *Star Tribune* at a newsstand inside the terminal. "I'm from Baltimore. In town for the Orioles' series. Thought I'd stop in on an old friend."

The cabbie launched into a lengthy complaint about the failures of Minnesota pitching, and the fact that the team wasn't the same since Kirby Puckett had left the game. Carla looked out the window, nodding and smiling every block or two.

The corporate offices of Johnson Enterprises were located in Fridley, a northern Twin City suburb. "Friendly Fridley," a sign proclaimed on the way into town. From what she could see, Fridley was a blend of neat middle-class houses, working-class bars, and small industrial buildings, some of which looked as though they had fallen on hard times.

But not the warehouse where her cab stopped. It was the size of half a football field, constructed of white brick and surrounded by a high chain-link fence topped by barbed wire.

She looked at the cabbie. "This the right address? 1025 Industrial Park Way?"

The man grunted yes. "You want me to wait, right?"

"Yeah."

She wore jeans and an oversized red T-shirt tied in a knot at the waist. Travel clothes. Designed for comfort, but she liked the way they looked. Apparently the guard at the entrance gate did, too, opening the door of a small guardhouse and directing his comments at her shirt.

"Hey, baby, you here for a shoot?"

"Excuse me?"

"A shoot. You know—" He stopped, finally raising his eyes to meet hers. "What are you here for?

"I came to visit the corporate offices of Johnson Enterprises."

"And who are you?"

"I'm Amanda Worthington," she said. "I was visiting in Minneapolis, and I wanted to surprise my brother."

The guard looked at her curiously.

"Who's your brother?"

"Hunter. Hunter Worthington. The president of Johnson Enterprises. I'm sure he'll be interested to know how you treat guests here." She started to walk inside.

"Wait." The guard said it firmly, smugly. From his tone she could tell that he was not impressed by the threat. "Ain't no Hunter Worthington works here."

"No? This is Johnson Enterprises, isn't it?"

"Sure is. Ain't no Hunter Worthington, though." The guard began to smirk. "Tell you what—why don't you go on back to the cops and tell them to try harder next time." He folded his arms across his chest and stared at her, menacing, but nevertheless amused.

She walked back to the cab.

"That didn't take long," the cabbie said. "Your friend ain't there?"

"I guess not," she said.

The cabbie drove, still glancing in the mirror, obviously intrigued by this twist in the life of his latest fare.

"Where to, then?

"Take me to the police station."

She introduced herself to the Fridley police chief, told him she was looking for information about Johnson Enterprises, and was quickly passed off to a detective, who in turn told her to have a seat in the station lobby.

"I need to make a call," he said.

In twenty minutes the detective was back, joined by a square-jawed man in his early forties, sporting cotton dockers and a blue blazer. He was prematurely gray, and his hair almost matched the color of his eyes.

"I'm Bob Nelson. Federal Bureau of Investigation, Minneapolis." His voice was smooth, his enunciation perfect. The Fridley detective seemed to defer almost automatically.

"Carla Tattaglia." She held out a hand and hung on long enough to show him she was not intimidated. "I'm just looking for some information about Johnson Enterprises."

Nelson turned to the local detective. "Is there a room we can use?"

"Sure." He escorted them into a cramped squad room in the back of the station house and opened the door to an even more cramped room that looked as though it might once have been a large closet.

"We use this for interviews," the detective said. He raised his eyebrows at Nelson. "I figure you won't need me for this?"

"I don't think so," the agent said. "It was good of you to call us."

The detective shrugged, not at all unhappy with the dismissal. "Let me know if you need something." He closed the door, leaving Carla and Nelson seated in cheap plastic chairs, with a matching cheap plastic table between them.

"Maybe you can start," Nelson said, "by telling me why you're interested in Johnson Enterprises."

"Maybe you can tell me," Carla answered, "why a simple request for information from a local department gets me a sit-down with the FBI."

They stared at each other.

"The bureau," Nelson said, "is not in the habit of sharing information with private investigators."

"And I'm not in the habit of sharing information about my clients," Carla said. "But I'd like to point out that I didn't ask to see you, remember? I just wanted a little information from the locals."

Nelson did not respond immediately. But he did not argue.

"Maybe," Carla said, "we can both put a few cards on the table. I'm investigating a murder in Rhode Island. The dead kid's name is Worthington, and he comes from money. Now, what can you tell me?"

Nelson scribbled some notes on a pad, then looked at her.

"I handle missing persons," he said. "The president of Johnson Enterprises disappeared last year. She vanished without a trace."

"What do you mean, she—" Carla stopped. She. The president? "What's her name?"

"Johnson. Barbetta Johnson. You've never heard of her?"

"No. Should I?"

"Only if you're into hardcore sex. Barbetta Johnson is the head of the largest pornography distributor in the upper Midwest."

Special Agent Robert Nelson, Carla learned, liked to hear himself talk. While this would be tedious on a date or at a cocktail party, it was quite helpful in the context of an investigation. The mild look of shock she offered delighted him, and he went on for the better part of fifteen minutes.

"Johnson's her married name, of course. Yeah, Barbetta grew up in Minnesota, from what we can see. Broken home, no father, mom living on welfare in one of those little towns up in the Lakes Area. We're reasonably sure she was abused when she was young. Funny thing is, she didn't stay that way. Social Services moved her to a foster home, and she got lucky. The foster parents really cared about her, made sure that she went to school, stayed out of trouble. She wound up graduating high school and got a scholarship to the University of Minnesota. That's where it fell apart again."

"What do you mean?" Carla didn't know where the agent was going, but she wasn't about to stop him.

"She dropped out after her freshman year. Lost contact with the foster family. She'd been running with some guy, and they decided to elope. Derek Johnson. They went to L.A. This is like 1970, 1971, when the porno business is about to explode. Within a few years, she starts turning up in skin flicks. Derek produced them." Nelson gave a sad smile. "Barbetta made quite a name for herself. They used to do ripoffs of classical literature. *The Whoremaster of Venice, Much Ado About Coming, A Tail of Two Cities.* My personal favorite is *Of Mice and Menage à Trois.*"

"I've never been much of a fan," Carla said dryly.

Agent Nelson laughed, and the sound was full and rich. "Maybe it's an acquired taste. When you're doing an investigation you come across this stuff. Anyway, about twenty years ago, she and Derek move back here. They set up their own company to shoot films and distribute the product. Johnson Enterprises. And yeah, I think the double meaning is intended."

Carla did not smile. "Please, go on."

"Well, Barbetta gets pregnant, and she has twins. A boy and a girl. She's full partners with her husband, and the business is going like gangbusters. They're making money hand over fist, and they've got enough cash to hire decent legal talent whenever the community starts making a stink about public morals, or obscenity, or whatever. And then it all crashes down."

"How's that?"

Nelson watched her carefully.

"Derek dies. He was with their son, and one of their top male stars, guy who called himself Dee Bonaire."

Carla smiled lamely. "Very original."

"Yeah. They were driving on a highway on the north shore of Lake Superior. They had a house up there for the summertime. The car he was driving went off the road and into the lake. What did you say the name of your client was?"

He asked the question smoothly, quickly. Carla began to speak, and stopped.

"I don't recall telling you the name of my client."

Nelson came close to looking unhappy just then. He folded his arms and leaned back in his chair.

"Aren't you going to finish?"

"Sure." Nelson gazed at the ceiling for a moment, then turned back to Carla. "So Derek Johnson, his son, and Dee Bonaire were all drowned. Or so the story goes. The car and the bodies were never recovered."

"Why not?"

"Ever been on the north shore of Lake Superior? It's absolutely beautiful. Rugged. Windswept. And right in front of it is some of the coldest, deepest water on the continent. Perfect place to lose something forever."

She could see where he was going, but the story he was telling was two decades old. Something more current would be helpful.

"So what happened to Barbetta?"

"Oh, she was devastated by what happened, I'm told. She quit appearing in the skin films. But she kept right on producing them. She changed the business name of the company to Ton's Worth of Fun, but the movies were still the same: hardcore porn. She fought off an indictment for transporting obscene materials about twelve years ago."

Nelson's voice had an edge to it, as if he were truly angry about this development.

"By any chance," Carla said softly, "were you involved with the indictment?"

Nelson did not answer her. Which was answer enough. No wonder he was so interested in Barbetta Johnson's disappearance.

"Right after the dismissal," he said, "she started donating a lot of money to women's shelters, rape crisis centers, things like that. It almost made her respectable, and the local cops decided it was easier to lay off her. And then, last year, she disappeared."

The story was intriguing, Carla had to admit. "How did that happen?"

"She kept the cabin after her husband died. Her car was found on the north shore of Lake Superior."

Carla smiled. "Let me guess. In the exact same spot where his went off the road?"

Nelson smiled back. "You could have been an agent, Ms.−"

"Tattaglia."

"Right. Only hers didn't go off the road. The keys were still in it. And that's as much as I can share with a private investigator from Rhode Island without getting something in return."

He'd given her a lot, that was certain. It would have taken days to acquire all that information by digging on her own.

"I think it would only be fair at this point," said Nelson, "for you to tell me why you're looking at Johnson Enterprises."

He was right. But I agreed not to reveal my client's identity, she thought. Even if I'm already wondering whether cutting his nuts off would be a service to humanity.

She decided that there might be a way to get around the question without lying.

"Before I do, tell me the name of Johnson's daughter."

He stared at her. "We don't think she's involved in her mother's disappearance."

"Fine. Humor me."

"It's Alison. Alison Johnson."

Bingo. "What kind of cars do FBI agents drive in the upper Midwest?"

Nelson looked puzzled. "What the hell kind of question is that?"

"The kind you ask when you want to go somewhere."

* * *

Special Agent Nelson drove a gray Grand Marquis with two doors, a cell phone, and a pile of fishing gear in back. He drove fast, sliding in and out of slower traffic on Route 394, taking them out of Minneapolis and west toward Lake Minnetonka. Carla fiddled with the radio stations for a moment.

"Where's Garrison Keillor?"

Nelson grinned. "Never listen to him. Besides, I don't think he works weekdays—at least, not on the radio."

He was good-looking, she decided, and apart from the cheap crack about porno film titles he seemed decent enough.

"Is that a spinning rod?" she asked.

He glanced at her and nodded.

"What do you like to fish for?"

"Pike. Muskie. Walleye. I've got a little place up north. You fish?"

"Salt water, mostly. We go after striped bass, shad, blackfish. Catch one on a fly, there's nothing like it."

Nelson looked impressed. "I wouldn't have figured that," he said. "Maybe if we wrap this up quickly we could go make a couple of casts. There's a couple of nice places out this way."

"Sure."

"Then, if you're staying over, I know a nice restaurant where we could grab a bite."

"Maybe we should talk to Alison Johnson first."

Nelson smiled again. "No problem."

The Johnson house was about a mile west of Wayzata, a suburb built on the shore of Lake Minnetonka and filled with the trappings of affluence: expensive late-model cars; handsome, well-dressed men, women, and children, sprawling single-family homes surrounded by trimmed green lawns. The house was hidden from the street by a vast spread of maple and oak leaves and a brick wall perhaps six feet in height. But the gate was open, and Nelson eased his Mercury along a black-topped driveway and parked in front of a gorgeous yellow Colonial with white door, windows, and shutters.

"Not exactly what you'd expect of a retired skin queen," Carla said.

Nelson chuckled. "Believe me, every nail was paid for with a peep show or a double feature."

They walked to the door together. Nelson rang the bell with the ease of someone who'd visited the home before. In a moment it was opened by a small, gray-haired woman with dark eyes and brown skin, and wearing a maid's uniform. She stared briefly at Carla, then Nelson, recognizing him instantly.

"No one's home."

"You mean Alison?" Nelson asked.

The woman dropped her eyes, as if confessing to a crime.

Nelson clucked his tongue and looked at his feet. "Can we come in, Juanita?"

"The mistress, she no want strangers in the house."

Nelson's voice was gentle. "The mistress, she's not here. She's been gone for months."

"I know she don't like police."

Nelson paused a moment. "Thanks all the same." He turned to Carla. "Too bad no one wants to hear our news."

"What news?" Juanita's voice climbed half an octave. "You have heard from the mistress?"

"Well, we really can't say," Nelson said. "Miss Tattaglia here, her work is highly confidential, and she can only speak with family."

Juanita stared once again at Carla, withholding approval, but still curious.

"I am like family," she said.

"Why don't we go inside?" Nelson said. This time the maid opened the door.

The house was spotless, and tastefully decorated with oriental rugs, antiques, and fine art. A series of matching seascapes hung from the walls in the foyer. Juanita led them down a hallway to a small study, furnished with a desk and credenza holding a small computer. In front of the desk were three wingback chairs. The maid sat in one of the chairs and folded her hands in her lap, watching Carla and the agent anxiously.

"Where is Alison?" Nelson asked.

"Mees Alison, she is sailing. Always sailing. What is the news?"

"I didn't know Alison wasn't here. I'm not authorized to share information with anyone other than a blood relative."

Juanita looked surprised. She pursed her lips, realizing that she'd been fooled into admitting them into the house.

"I've been wanting to talk to you, Juanita," Nelson told her. He took another chair and leaned forward, resting his elbows on his knees. "I think you know where your boss is."

Carla looked around her. The office walls were loaded with photographs of a blond girl. A girl sitting behind a tiller, fit, intense, looking at some unseen competitor. The same girl, now a young woman really, smiling and shaking someone's hand as she accepted a trophy.

"This is Alison, right?" The maid nodded, with no small measure of pride. "She is beautiful, no? Like her mother." Juanita looked down again. "Once upon a time," she whispered.

Nelson kept his voice low. "How long have you worked here?"

"Fifteen year. I do all cleaning. Cooking."

Carla turned back from the pictures. "Did you raise Alison?"

"No. Mees Barbetta, she is good mother. She love her daughter. She always give her the best."

"How did Alison get involved in sailing?" Carla asked.

"Seex, seven years ago, Mees Barbetta, she send her daughter for lessons. On the lake. At first, Alison no want to go. But then it take with her." Juanita gazed at a photograph of Alison, the one in which she accepted a medal of some sort. The maid's pride in the young girl was unmistakable. "Alison is wonderful sailor. Maybe next year she go to the Oleempics."

Nelson had said nothing during this exchange. It was clear to Carla that his interests were in something other than Alison's athletic career. Still, his next questions showed he was listening, evaluating, and exploring possibilities.

"Ms. Johnson was proud of her daughter too?"

"Oh jess, she very proud, she love her daughter very much." Juanita looked pleased now. The question was easy to answer.

Suddenly Nelson's tone grew harsh and accusing. "Then why did she leave? Where did she go?"

"She no leave. She deesappear," Juanita said softly.

"Mothers who love their children don't just get up and walk away." Nelson stood up and leaned forward, the difference in body language intentional, designed for maximum intimidation. "You've been with this woman for nearly twenty years. For you not to know something would be crazy."

After a brief pause, Juanita murmured, and twin tears rolled down each side of her face.

"Jess. Crazy." But she offered nothing more.

Nelson looked at Carla and, almost imperceptibly, raised his eyebrows. Carla nodded.

"I guess we'll have to consider her a suspect," he said. "She's not cooperating at all."

"No!" Juanita's face was loaded with anguish. "I tell you all I know."

Nelson got up. "Yeah, well, I don't believe you. Maybe you'd better talk to an attorney." He turned and walked out of the room. Juanita sobbed quietly.

Carla waited a moment, then slid a hand across Juanita's shoulder. "I don't know him too well," she said. "But I think he means it."

"I tell you, I know nothing."

But there was something in the way the maid spoke. Carla decided to play a hunch. "What was Miss Barbetta like before she disappeared?"

"What you mean?"

"How did she behave? Was she upset about something?"

Juanita looked away. "The last few months, they were bad. Very bad. Mees Barbetta, she was changing."

"How?"

"She would not eat. She would not sleep. She stay up late, watching movies. Her old movies. All night long."

"What kind of movies?"

Juanita flushed. "You know. Mees Barbetta, she was very beautiful when she was young. She would watch, and she would talk."

"Talk to who?"

"To the movies. She was not well."

"Do you know whether Miss Barbetta knew her daughter had a boyfriend?"

The maid flinched. The question had struck home.

"Nobody is good enough for Mees Alison. That is what Mees Barbetta say."

"And what did Miss Alison say?"

"Mees Alison is young. She is not happy. She is like her mother. No one tell her what to do."

The questions had caused the maid to stop crying. She watched Carla intently, the tears drying slowly on her face.

"Who's paying the bills around here?" Carla asked.

"Alison. She take care of everything."

"When will Alison be back here?"

"I don't know. She is gone away for a few days."

"Where did she go?"

Juanita made a sound then, as if something were caught in her throat. She turned her head toward the desk for a moment, then back at the floor.

"She is in Florida. At the sailing races." The little maid got up and walked to the desk, opened a drawer, and removed a sheet of paper. The document was a copy of an itinerary from a travel agency in Wayzata.

"She come back sometime next week."

Carla pulled a notebook out of her pocket and scribbled down flight and hotel information. From the corner of her eye she could see Nelson lurking in the hallway. He'd been listening to everything the maid had to say. "If you hear from Alison," she said to the maid, "I think you should keep this visit we had confidential."

Juanita agreed. "Please, you will tell the other agent to leave me alone? I swear I know nothing."

On the way out of the house, Nelson reverted from hard-ass special agent to friendly Minnesota boy once again.

"You were good in there. Picked right up on what I was doing."

"Yes, quite a team," Carla said. "Scaring the daylights out of a maid to get to a couple of scraps of infromation."

Nelson sighed, climbed into the Grand Marquis, and started it up. They pulled out of the driveway and cruised back through Wayzata's small business district. "I'm not always proud of it," he said quietly. "But you do what you have to do. I didn't hear you object when I started the Mutt and Jeff routine."

He was right, she knew.

"It didn't produce much," she said. In fact, the interview had given Carla some ideas, but she was not about to share them.

"You don't think so?" Nelson gave a small chuckle. "I interviewed Alison twice, right after Barbetta disappeared. Didn't get a thing out of her. At least you established that Barbetta was having trouble with her little girl."

Carla did not respond. She was sure the agent would develop his own theories from the meeting.

Off to the right she could see Lake Minnetonka. They passed the Wayzata Yacht Club, where a few clusters of people were rigging boats for an afternoon sail.

"I've lived in Rhode Island most of my life," she said. "Never really thought of Minnesota as a place that produced great sailors."

"Well, I guess we should never assume anything," Nelson

said. He smiled, with a confidence that was almost, but not quite, annoying.

When Carla did not reply, the agent spoke again.

"Before we came out here, I'd mentioned dinner."

The offer was tempting. Carla did not look forward to spending a night alone in a strange city. But a meal could easily lead to further temptations. And for all the problems she'd had with Michael, Carla wasn't quite ready to try something new.

"I think I need to get back to my hotel. Maybe some other time." Like I'm planning to come back here, she thought. Still, Nelson took it well. They drove back toward the airport, Nelson chatting about Minnesota fishing, Carla listening politely and wondering how fast she could get a flight for Key West.

"Make sure youse get that shit down good. Dese people, they want fresh flowers. An' youse got to spread a lot of shit if youse wanna smell them roses."

"Yes sir," Paul Carolina said, guiding a trowel across the flower bed. The boss man laughed and bit off the end of a Cuban cigar.

The boss's name was Urbano Scungio. What was left of his thinning black hair was slicked back and glued to the sides of his head. His nose was broken, his eyes were bagged and too far apart. His skin was browner than new saddle leather. His workers, his customers, and even his wife called him Urb.

"Urbano's Luscious Landscapes" was plastered in bright yellow letters on the sides of his trucks, the front of his mowers, and the bright yellow T-shirts of his employees. They sweated and grunted in the sun, hauling peat, spreading fertilizer, and raking the flower beds of customers all over western Cranston.

Urb was coarse, profane, and uneducated. He was, however, Paul was learning, extremely shrewd, and politically sensitive to the needs of customers.

"Gotta move. Gotta move. Gotta new guy today, a referral." Urb made the word sound like "refurral."

185

"No problem, boss." Paul finished with the trowel and stood up. The work was back-breaking, to be sure, but he kept the aches hidden behind a smile. Urb showed a spread of tobacco-stained teeth and blew a cloud of smoke into the summer air. He turned and walked back toward his truck, shouting to two other workers trimming a set of hedges.

"Keep it up. Gonna take a ride with Paulie here." It was clear that Urbano Scungio had taken an instant liking to Paul. They were roughly the same age, and Paul was one of the landscaper's few employees who did not speak with a Spanish accent. They climbed into Urb's shiny new pickup, his pride and joy, the metallic blue paint practically glowing.

"Youse want a smoke, Paulie?" Urb slipped a Cohiba out of his pocket and handed it to his new employee.

Paul Carolina hated to be called Paulie. But a job was a job, money was money, and a Cuban cigar was one step closer to the good life.

"Thanks, Mr. Scungio."

"Urb! Call me Urb." The weathered gardener stepped on the accelerator and the Ford lurched, sending a mower crashing into a bag of fresh fertilizer. Urb seemed not to notice. He drove fast, avoiding smaller cars with last-minute swerves, punctuating each arrival at a stop light with a stomp on the brake, so that each new stop and start was commemorated with small patches of rubber. Paul hung on for dear life.

"So's youse are from Tennessee, right?" Urb puffed another patch of blue cloud into the air.

"No, that's just where I learned the agricultural business," Paul said.

If Urb heard him, it did not seem to sink in. "Great state, Tennessee. They done great gettin' the Oilers."

"Oilers?"

"Ya know, the football team. Now they're called the Titans, I think. I'm a Pats fan, myself. Got season tickets. We was tryin' to move a team down here from Foxboro, but it didn't fly. They was gonna move to Hartford, but now it looks like they'll stay in Foxboro awhile. You follow pro ball?"

"Oh sure," Paul lied. The last time he'd watched a professional football game his team had failed to cover the spread. The name of the team escaped him now. The memory of beating it out of town to avoid paying an angry bookie still lingered.

"Great game. Coaching pro ball, it's a lot like landscaping. If youse wanna have a great season, y'need the right personnel."

Paul considered this a moment, tugging at his Cohiba. Urb slid the truck through an intersection off the state road and turned left. In a few minutes they were passing a slew of large houses, dressed with stone pillars or fronted by red brick. The driveways were marked by brick and stone monuments, some with statues of lions, dogs, or more ambiguous carnivores.

"Right now, I think I got the right personnel," Urb said. "New client. New talent. Gonna be a great fuggin' day."

As if to make his point, Urb jammed on the brake once again, nearly sending Paul through the windshield.

"Sorry," Urb said. "Almost missed my turn." He swerved to the right, and the truck leaped past a stone gate. Paul noted that the mailbox was housed in a thick foundation of concrete. It read BALBONI on the side.

12

Michael had never quite been able to place the color. Perhaps it was because there never was just one. At least, not for very long.

Sometimes it was green, and at others it was closer to the palest shade of blue, the kind of blue seen only in the tropics and subtropics, like a patch of sky filtered through a glass and then poured, in liquid form, on top of the ocean bed. And then there were other days, when it was overcast, when the water seemed to take a darker shade, a wet, salted blend of sandalwood. The strangest thing about it was that he could never catch the color in the act of changing. It just happened, subtly, without warning, until suddenly he realized it had happened again.

Michael wondered sometimes whether it was really the water at all, or just a reflection of the mood and temper of the people who lived along the stretch of islands called the Florida Keys. Especially on the one called Key West.

"What's the matter with you?" Earl was seated on the bed of the hotel room, cleaning a camera lens.

"Not a thing," Michael said. He stood on a small balcony, watching a fishing boat coming in from the Gulf. The boat sat heavy in the water, weighed down by the catch in her hold. "Why do you ask?"

"Because you have this faraway expression, like you climbed inside yourself. This what Key West is supposed to do to you?"

Michael turned his attention outside again. The fishing boat was slowing down, her bow drifting to the right as a crewman grabbed a line on the foredeck, making ready to tie up and unload fresh fish. Down below, a group of tourists were standing on a pier, sporting the latest in T-shirts and conch jewelry fresh from Duval Street.

"Key West is whatever you want it to be, I guess. I was here a few times when I was chartering boats a few years back. It was always a great party town, and a great place to relax and rest between charters." But there was a lot more to it than that, he knew. The island had been the home of salvagers and smugglers, writers and artists, pirates and confidence men. The city had seen outrageous booms in the wealth of its citizens, as well as the misery that accompanied the changing fortunes of an island economy. Through the years, Key West had persevered, offered sanctuary to adventurers and misfits alike, each one taking something different from the swirling blend of palm trees and sand and conch shells found at the southernmost landfall in the continental United States. But that was more, certainly, than Earl was either ready or willing to hear.

The tourists were now photographing each other, each one taking a turn behind the camera while the others posed in front. Michael looked at an older man sliding his arm around a younger man's shoulder. The resemblance between the two was unmistakable. Father and son both smiled, enjoying the moment.

"How are your kids?" Michael asked.

Earl looked up, mildly surprised, to make sure Michael was speaking to him. "Fine. I called them this morning." He turned his attention back to the camera again. "Erin's all excited about trying out for the swimming team this year. Does a wicked backstroke, and she's gonna nail the two-hundred-meter this year. I bet she gets her time under two minutes."

"What about your son?" Earl's oldest child was sixteen, tall, handsome, and mildly retarded. For years the photographer had been fighting with teachers, psychologists, and school administrators to get the best programs for his son, often taking time off from work to attend meetings and counseling sessions. Some of the other station photographers grumbled about favoritism. But then, Earl was private about his son's problem, telling only his boss and a few others at the station. Shirley brushed the other photographers' complaints aside, and as a result had won her chief photographer's undying loyalty. Michael, flattered that the older photographer trusted him with the secret, mentioned it rarely.

"He's okay. Wants a car, because he sees other kids getting their licenses. I told him he needs to wait a few more years. He told me I don't know what the hell I'm talking about." Earl snorted and shook his head. "Typical teenager." But Michael could hear the pride in his voice. Earl was delighted that his son showed signs of independence.

Earl carefully replaced a lens cap and snapped a battery onto the back of his camera.

"Ordinarily, I'd be curious about why you're asking about my son," he said quietly. "But I think I know the reason."

Michael folded his arms. "Do you now?"

"I think this story is eating at you. You see this rich, domineering bastard who slaps his boy, who seems to be trying to control him, and then looks indifferent when the kid turns up dead. And, for reasons I'm not entirely sure of, it pisses you off more than usual."

Michael stared at the photographer for a moment. "His old man is probably the top suspect in his own son's murder. I'm surprised it doesn't piss you off more than usual."

"At one point, it probably would have," Earl said. "But I've learned something over the years. There are all different kinds of ways to take care of your family. You can love them, you can help them, you can try like hell to protect them. But in the end, you can't change who they are. See, when you looked at that guy on the dock, you saw somebody smacking his kid. And I saw that, too. But I also saw a guy who hasn't learned what I've learned yet. And that doesn't make me feel anger. It makes me feel pity."

Michael did not respond. Instead he looked over the balcony again. The tourist group he'd seen before was gone, replaced now by another group, taking more pictures and chattering about who knew what.

Earl slung a bag of tapes and spare batteries over his shoulder. "Don't we have to go find that girl you've been talking about? Alison?"

"Yeah." Michael grabbed a notebook. Then he walked over and placed a hand on the strap of the bag. "Let me take that."

And Earl did.

Rico Balboni's house was a monument to ostentation. It was perched on a small bluff that offered a broad view of Cranston, with the larger office buildings of downtown Providence poking through the distant haze. The exterior was white brick and rose to three stories, with a series of arches and windows dotting the front. The front steps alternated between pieces of white and dark brown marble, each looking so clean Paul was afraid to step on them. The front door was painted a glossy black. A large pineapple-shaped door knocker made of polished brass was bolted to its center.

Urbano noticed Paul's expression.

"Like this?" Urbano chewed on his cigar. "This is class. This is where we wanna be. Working with class."

Urbano paid no attention to the marks he left on the marble as he walked to the door and slammed the knocker. It was opened by a dark-eyed woman dressed in a white thong and high heels. The polish on her talon-length nails matched what little there was of her swimsuit, and her hair was teased high enough to brush the doorframe.

"Oh," she said. "You must be the lawn guy."

"Yes, ma'am," Urbano said, slipping into his best fawning tone.

The woman appeared to be in her early twenties. Paul saw no sign of tan lines on her. She did not smile.

"You scuffed the steps," she said. Urbano looked down and saw the marks on the marble.

"Sorry, ma'am," Urbano said. He knelt and began to wipe the dirt away with his hand. Paul was glad he was still standing on the white brick walkway.

"Next time go to the garage," she said. "You can walk around back to see Rico." She closed the door before Urbano could respond.

"Fuggin' housegirl," Urbano said, marching to the back of the property. "She think we're some sort of field hands or somethin'? She'll be outta here in a month, when the owner starts breaking in a new catcher's mitt."

Paul nodded grimly, wishing Scungio had left him at the previous job.

They made their way between a pair of overgrown hedges that led around the side of the house and through to the backyard. The hedges opened to reveal a lawn that was in better shape than the gardens, but still showed signs of crabgrass. Fifty paces farther on lay a terrace that held the swimming pool. A man in his mid-fifties lay on a chaise longe, his eyes wrapped in designer sunglasses, his sun-damaged skin glistening with tanning lotion. The man held a cell phone up to his left ear, arguing with someone on the other line.

"She's where?"

The thong-clad woman emerged from the house carrying two drinks. Her stiletto heels made her walk as though stepping on eggshells.

"Well, I'm sure she has her reasons, Agent. What did you say your name was again?" Rico's voice continued to rise. "No, I really don't think I can discuss this with you right now. Why don't I speak to my client, and I'll get back to you."

Rico punched the cell phone and shut off the call. "That

bitch," he said, his voice rising now. "That bitch was supposed to do nothing."

Urbano cleared his throat. The sound was roughly akin to a Harley starting. Rico jumped. The thonged woman nearly spilled the drinks, and glared at the landscaper. Then, slowly, she licked the condensation gathering on each glass, watching Paul and Urbano the whole time. Rico Balboni accepted his drink from her, but did not appear to notice.

"You the landscaper?"

"Uh, yes sir, I'm Urbano."

Balboni looked mildly annoyed. He slid off the seat, leaving an oily patch behind him.

"Yes. I don't have time for work outside the home, and we need help."

Scungio nearly bowed. "Yessir. Of course, sir."

"You were recommended."

"Very kind, sir. I do my best."

Balboni looked the two landscapers over, his eyes betraying no hint of satisfaction or dissatisfaction. Then, sighing, he slipped into a pair of beach shoes and started toward the hedges again, Scungio following like a lap dog.

It took at least five steps before Paul realized where he'd seen the man before. It was the way he walked. No, it wasn't a walk as much as a preening strut. The man had done the same thing for a television camera a few days before, when he entered the Newport police station.

Urbano glanced back at Paul, tossing his head impatiently, conveying a message to hurry up. And Paul Carolina did, ignoring the woman watching him from the lounge chair, still licking her glass and sucking on her drink.

Paul watched but did not listen as Rico gave directions on how the hedges should be trimmed. Urbano nodded vigorously, agreeing to whatever the customer wanted. Finally Balboni turned to Paul.

"You get all this?"

"Uh, sure." He managed not to laugh at the glistening gut jutting out above Rico's swimming trunks.

"You better," Balboni said. "I ain't gonna be telling you twice." He strutted off toward the chaise and picked up a cell phone.

"Just keep trimmin'," Urbano said to him as they unloaded clippers and an electric trimmer from Urbano's truck. "Keep lookin' busy. You can drag the job out all afternoon."

"Where are you going?" Paul asked.

Urbano smiled and dug a lighter out of his pocket. "I'll be back by five. I got a business to run."

Carla's pager went off in an airport lounge in Orlando. She paid for her beer, left too much tip, and hauled her bag to a pay phone cubicle facing the boarding gate for the connecting flight to Key West. The plane, a vintage double-prop, did not inspire confidence. Nor did the gangly, pimply faced man in the pilot's uniform shamelessly and unsuccessfully flirting with the pert little ticket agent.

"Balboni."

"You wanted to speak to me?" The ticket agent, stone-faced, stamped a boarding pass as the pilot hovered behind her.

"Where are you?"

"I'm out in the field," Carla said. "Still gathering information."

"I asked where you were." Balboni's voice held all the warmth of an ice cube. In the background she could hear a whirring noise, like the sound of a power tool.

"I'm in the field," she said. "Where is not your concern."

"It is when I'm paying you, and when my client is paying you. And when I get a visit from FBI agents asking why I have you working in Minnesota."

Nelson. That bastard.

"Naturally, I was surprised, because I didn't know you were

working in Minnesota," Balboni said. "They said you were pretty quiet about who your client was, but that you were looking into a homicide. I'm sure it took him all of two or three hours to find your bank records and find out who has wired money to you lately."

"I have other clients," Carla said. It was a weak lie, she knew.

"I doubt it," Balboni said. "You're just getting your feet wet. And I'd bet your retainer that you don't have any other homicide cases." Balboni's tone grew sharp. "That's one of the reasons we hired you."

The ticket agent had finished with passengers now and appeared to be reviewing a manifest. The pilot, giggling now, was bumping up against her. Carla could sense the woman's annoyance.

Balboni went on, "The agents wanted to know who my client is, Ms. Tattaglia. I don't like it when federal agents start asking questions about my clients. I think it's time you tell me what you're doing."

"Running down a lead," Carla said.

"I'll expect you in my office in the morning. I'll have Mr. Worthington here, so we can get a full report on what you're doing."

"I won't be there."

"You should make it your business to be there. I have a lot of clout among the local defense bar. I'd hate to see your new career fall apart before it's even begun."

The ticket agent was now calling the flight for Key West over the loudspeaker.

"We'd like to begin our preboarding process with all passengers—Quit it!—with all passengers who are over age sixty-five or accompanied by small children." The agent, tears in her eyes, turned toward the geeky pilot, who still hovered over her. The words "I'm warning you" filtered into the microphone.

"Is that your flight?" Balboni said.

Carla did not respond.

"If you are not in my office in the morning, you're fired. Do you understand?"

"I understand," Carla said. "I just don't know why you don't want me to do what you hired me to do."

The pilot was directly behind the agent again, rubbing up behind her, oblivious to the disapproving stares of the waiting passengers.

The tormented agent looked ready to explode. "We'd like to begin boarding all passengers now on flight 1063 for Key West—That's it!" The agent dropped the microphone and spun once more on the pilot, who seemed both surprised and delighted to have provoked such a stern reaction. The adolescent grin on his face evaporated when the agent drove her heel into his instep. The pilot howled, grabbing for his foot, as the young agent swung a roundhouse right that landed just below the man's rib cage, doubling him over. The little agent, not yet satisfied, finished the man off with a kick to the groin, sending him sprawling to the floor. A few of the female passengers applauded.

Rico Balboni was calling out from the receiver, "Hello? Hello? Are you listening to what I just said?"

The ticket agent picked up the microphone again. "Ladies and gentlemen, there will be a short delay while the airline locates a new pilot and I look for a new job." With that she replaced the microphone and stormed down the concourse.

Carla hung up the phone. As the young ticket agent passed her, the two of them exchanged glances.

"He had it coming," Carla said.

"Frigging job isn't worth it," the agent said, blinking away a tear.

Carla watched her continue down the concourse. "I know what you mean," she said. "I know what you mean."

The temperature was approaching ninety and it was humid, which made the hedge leaves feel thick, even pasty, as Paul

Carolina cut them. The metal blades on the trimmer made a harsh, unpleasant sound. Bits of branch flew, occasionally hitting Paul on the arms and face. Perspiration poured off his forehead and down his shirt, staining the back and the underarms.

"I could use a beer," he said out loud, though no one could hear him.

But you can't. You told him you'd get a job. Told him you'd stay on the wagon. That was the deal.

He felt another bead roll down his nose, then drip onto the hedge in front of him. It made him wonder what proof his sweat was . . . forty? Sixty? Eighty?

Urbano Scungio was gone, off to bow and scrape before another customer somewhere else in Cranston. Paul was left alone, ordered to finish trimming the hedges before day's end. Rico Balboni had spoken animatedly on the phone, then jumped into the pool. After five minutes of sloshing about he was back on the chaise, broiling next to his thonged companion.

But Rico Balboni was restless, tossing and turning as though he suffered from insomnia.

Man, these people are strange, Paul thought. The thonged woman got up just then and walked to the pool, slipping off her heels before sliding her legs into the water. She was careful to keep her hair from getting wet. The woman turned and caught Paul staring. She gave a half-smile, acknowledging his look, then lightly splashed water across her chest.

"Come back in with me," she pouted in Rico's direction.

But Rico was on the phone again.

"Yeah, this is Balboni. Get me Worthington's number." After listening for a moment the lawyer clicked the phone again and dialed once more. Paul moved along the hedge, trying to get closer to where Balboni was standing.

"Yeah, Hunter? You got a minute? There's something we should talk about."

* * *

Hunter Worthington sat by his own pool, with his own drink and his own phone.

He did not, however, have a thonged bimbo by his side. Instead there was Bosworth, strutting out of Château du Printemps, clad in a red-and-black-striped two-piece swimsuit straight from the Gilded Age. Hunter watched the butler as he kicked off the beach sandals and mounted the pool's diving board. Bosworth executed a near-perfect swan dive, surfaced, then blissfully began a breast stroke across the pool.

"You hired this bitch," Worthington said when Rico finished speaking. "I want her taken care of."

Bosworth flipped onto his back and squirted water out of his mouth. Worthington listened to his lawyer's feigned dismay. Attorneys. They were good for next to nothing.

He looked up at the mansion that had come to be his home. Thought of the places he had been, the money he had made, and the sins he had committed. Was it worth it? Hell, yes. Would it be better if he gave it all away?

Rico Balboni had finished speaking. There was only the dull half-empty, half-full silence that accompanies dead air in a telephone call. Calmly, without another word, Hunter Worthington, Jr., terminated the call. Bosworth, in the shallow end, stood up. He flicked water off the straps of the top of his striped suit and eyed his boss curiously.

Hunter Worthington eyed him back.

"I'm not giving shit away," Hunter said.

A thousand miles south the sun burned hotter but the humidity was eased by a light Gulf breeze. The palm fronds swayed, and a string of signal flags fluttered outside a yacht club perched near the end of a new marina. In Key West, it would be a good day for racing.

Michael could tell that the regatta would be similar to that held in Newport. As a warmup for the Olympic trials, it drew hundreds of sailors from across the United States, along with a few scattered entries from Canada and Mexico. The entrants were all gathered at the marina, located in the waterfront section of town known as the Truman Annex. Once the Navy had owned this section of Key West. Now it was being privately developed, and the sailors wore docksiders and shorts in lieu of dungarees and white swabbie caps. The racers busied themselves stretching sails, adjusting rigs and lines, and watching for signs that might betray a change in the direction of the wind.

Earl and Michael nosed their way along the piers, searching for Alison Johnson. The camera Earl carried did not attract attention; there were at least two other crews working their way through the assembled fleet, interviewing sailors and taping preparations for the first race. Still, after more than half an hour of searching, Alison had not been found, though several people claimed to have seen her.

Gradually, the boats began to raise their sails and pull away from the dock. A small crowd, approximately the same size as the one from Newport, watched them go. Soon there were fewer than a dozen boats remaining.

"It would help if we asked one of the race officials," Earl said.

"I tried," Michael said. Indeed he had, but the race organizer, a surly-looking gentleman who declined to remove his Vuarnets even in the shade afforded by a canopy at the dock's edge, had demanded to know why Michael wanted to speak with one of the sailors.

"You're from Providence, right?"

"That's right."

"We've been warned that a reporter from your town is prying into personal matters about Hunter Worthington. Why don't you let the authorities do their job?"

Maybe because they haven't done anything, Michael thought to himself. Instead, he said, "We just want to cover the race."

The official sniffed. "I doubt it. Perhaps you should leave."

"You can't keep us off these docks," Michael said.

"Maybe not. But I certainly don't have to help you."

Michael didn't bother to explain the full exchange to Earl. "Let's just say the officials are less than enthusiastic about our presence."

They walked toward the remaining cluster of Lasers making ready to set out. As they moved farther down the dock a familiar face came into view.

"And I think I see the reason why," Michael said.

Jimmy Mercer had just raised his sail. It flapped lazily in the breeze as he tossed a life jacket into the boat's tiny cockpit.

"If the wind picks up, it could get interesting," Michael said.

Mercer's head whipped around. "What would you know about it?"

Michael did not look at him. Instead he devoted his attention to the sail. "You probably ought to straighten out that telltale now, Jim. There probably won't be time once you're out at the start line."

Mercer practically sneered. "I don't need racing advice from some reporter who doesn't know enough to mind his own business. Fuck off."

"Who's that, Jimmy?"

The voice was young and female, and came from behind another sail.

"No one," Mercer said, too quickly.

A moment later she appeared, her bleached hair poking out from a baseball cap, wearing sunglasses and white sunscreen smeared across the bridge of her nose. Still, there was no mistaking her.

"You must be Ali," Michael said.

The young woman stared at him. Despite her appearance, Michael could tell she was beautiful, her face oval, her lips full, her limbs brown and slender. She cocked a hip, her posture conveying a confidence that suggested she was both used to and comfortable with being admired.

"Do I know you?"

"You don't want to know him," Jimmy said, his tone brittle. "He's just some jerk reporter trying to dig up dirt on Hunter."

At the mention of Hunter's name, Ali Johnson's expression changed. Her lips closed together, and she turned her gaze toward Jimmy.

"I don't have any comment," she said. "I want to be left alone."

"You heard it," Mercer said. "Now get the hell out of here."

Alison Johnson was the reason Michael had come to Key West. It was just bad luck, he knew, to meet her for the first time in the presence of Jimmy Mercer. If he failed to get an interview with her, Shirley would pull him off the story for good, or at least until an arrest was made.

Still, crisis tends to create opportunities.

"I'm sure you'd like that, Jimmy, since you've never been straight about where you were when Hunter died."

"Screw you," Mercer snarled. He reached down to release the line that held the Laser close to the finger pier. "It's none of your business where I was."

"I met Jimmy the morning they found Hunter, Ali. He acted surprised, said it was the first that he'd heard of it. Then he asked what boat Hunter was found on. The funny thing is, I'd never mentioned that Hunter was found on a boat."

"Shut up," Mercer said. He intended the words to be harsh, but they sounded weak and hoarse.

Alison Johnson did not react immediately. Michael glanced back at Earl. The photographer had had the good sense to put his camera down, to avoid alarming the young woman in front of them.

"You said you were at the hotel, in bed," Alison said. "That you didn't know how it happened."

"I was!" Mercer sounded desperate. "Come on, Ali, there's only a half hour till the start."

"Maybe he was at the hotel," Michael said. "But your friend knows more about what happened to Hunter than he's let on."

"Fuck you, Carolina." Mercer pushed his Laser away from the dock, then laid a hand on the boom, forcing the boat's mainsail to catch the wind from the bow. The maneuver was called "backing the sail," and it had the intended effect of pushing the little boat away from the pier.

"Come on, Ali," Mercer pleaded. But Ali did not move. Instead she stared at the reporter, unsure what to do.

"I really would like to talk to you," Michael said. "But I don't want you to miss your race."

His words seemed to pull her out of a trance. She turned to look at her own Laser, still waiting. The other boats were gone. Alison Johnson was the only woman left on the dock.

"I guess I should go," she said.

"Could we meet later?" His question hung in the air what seemed like a long time. Please say yes. Please.

Alison Johnson walked back to her boat. She undid the dock lines and dangled a foot inside the cockpit to keep the boat in place.

"I don't want any camera," she said. Then she gave them a place and a time.

They watched her guide the boat down the channel as the breeze freshened and the sun's reflection on the water grew as white as her sail.

The bus from Cranston had blown its air-conditioning, which meant a twenty-minute sweat before Paul Carolina was deposited at Kennedy Plaza in Providence. He started toward College Hill, ignoring the calls of a panhandler.

"Yo, man, li'l change for something to drink?"

God, cold beer would taste great right now, he thought. He crossed over the river, passing Three Steeple Street. The week before, he'd stopped for a quick one after a job interview. He'd wound up staying for two hours, drinking manhattans and trying to hit on one of the waitresses.

He walked past. Maybe tomorrow, he thought. Just not right now.

By the time he got to Michael's East Side apartment it was nearly five-thirty. He opened the refrigerator, hoping to at least find soda. No luck. In their haste to move in, no one had gone to the store. Paul drew a glass of water from the tap and threw open a window.

The words came back to him again. The words spoken by the side of a pool in western Cranston.

"I'm sorry it worked out like this," Rico had said. "She's become a liability." Then the words in reply, loud, incomprehensible, but the tone rich in accusation.

"I can't hear things like that, Hunter," Rico saying back into the phone. "I've already fired her, but if you think you need to do something more . . ." And Rico letting the words hang in the warm, humid air, full of menace, all the more so because Balboni uttered them in such a matter-of-fact way.

Paul looked to the kitchen table, to the note his son had left that morning.

Dad,

Have to go out of town for a few days.
Good luck with the job search.

Love,
Michael

It felt strange, reading it again. When was the last time my son told me he loved me? he wondered, and could not remember. It must have been back in Iowa, when I was still working, he told himself. Before the gambling and the alcohol took hold. It pleased him and made him sad. He would have to wait to tell him about the job, and the strange luck that had led him to the house of Rico Balboni.

"You take care of it," Balboni had said. "I don't need to know about it."

The words made him uneasy. There was an attitude there, an expression that went beyond anger, or indignation. Paul could remember the look on men who would fight at the prison farm over a lower bunk, or a choice job assignment. There was an indifference, a ruthlessness, that covered Balboni's face like a glaze.

He grabbed a telephone book, flipped to the end of the white pages, and found the listing for Michael's station.

"Channel Three."

"Yeah, uh, I'm trying to reach Michael Carolin—"

"He's not here today. On some kind of assignment." The voice on the other end sounded rushed, anxious to end the call.

"Well, this is his father. How do I reach him?"

"Is this an emergency?"

Paul thought for a moment, but his mind became clouded. The apartment seemed bare, almost like a cell. And the voice on the end of the line was dull, uninterested in helping him.

"Hello? Hello?" There was a curse, and the line disconnected.

Paul replaced the phone softly on its cradle. What did it matter, anyway? Balboni was probably thinking of getting a new investigator. That was it. And wouldn't Michael be angry at him for listening to other people's conversations again?

"It's so damned hot in here." He thought again about a cold beer. There was a Mexican place down on Hope and Olney that served Corona and Tecate, with wedges of lime crammed into the bottle, or hooked on the side of a frosted glass.

He reached for the keys, slamming home the deadbolt when he closed the door to the apartment. Maybe just one, he thought. He felt better already.

Two hours, twenty-three dollars, and six Coronas later, Paul went for a walk again. This time it was toward Thayer Street,

204

down past the pharmacy and the Greek and Asian restaurants, the theater that showed the independent films, and the clusters of kids with their lips and noses pierced, their bodies tattooed, and their hair dyed unnatural colors.

He stopped to watch a man wailing harmonica in front of a bookstore, watched a man playing three-card monte outside a convenience store. He thought about playing. Then he thought better. It was dark now, and he could not go home. Not yet. The apartment would be dark, too. But there would be no one there. And besides, the warm buzz was beginning a slow, bumpy fade.

He went back up the street to the Greek restaurant. He chose Budweiser this time, and drank two more. No one at the bar seemed interested in conversation. The bartender was engrossed in a Red Sox game on the television.

He thought about Balboni again, yelling into the phone. About his son, breaking up with that girl.

"Hey, you all right?" The bartender was young, dark-haired. "You look like you just lost your best friend."

He did not answer the man, instead laying another ten-spot on the counter, money he could not afford to spend on beer. The buzz would be enough now to get him home and into bed, enough to knock him out until there was light again in the morning.

Then he saw the pay phone on the way out the door. He stared at it for a moment, until an impatient couple asked him to step out of the way so they could enter the restaurant.

He called information, and dialed the new number Carla had set up for her investigation business.

"You've reached the office of Carla Tattaglia. Leave your name, number, and a message."

"Yeah, it's Paul Carolina. I bet you're, uh . . ." He stopped for a moment. "I just want to say I'm sorry for what I said, to Mike, I mean, for listening to you. You know."

He was speaking slowly, trying hard to think of the words,

but they seemed to slide away from him before he could get them under control.

"Anyway, I've got this job now. And I met one of your clients. Sort of. I mean, I know who he is. From television. Anyway, I think you should call me. He seemed kind of angry. With you. Something about Minnesota."

Two more men had entered the restaurant, and grunted at Paul in annoyance.

"Move it, pal."

He thought there was something more he should say. But the physical presence of the two men was distracting. It was not until after he had hung up and was walking down the street that he remembered the peculiar way Balboni had sounded when he talked about doing something more. By then he was out of quarters, and walking down an East Side street toward the apartment.

Maybe when I get home, he said to himself.

13

Carla's flight was delayed nearly three hours as the tiny airline located a new pilot to replace the one neutered by the ticket agent. By the time the plane made its approach to Key West it was early evening. The party and charter boats were heading into open water to catch the sunset. Anyone who'd been racing, she guessed, had no doubt returned to shore. She found a pay phone and called the guesthouse reported on the itinerary provided by Alison's maid. Yes, Ms. Johnson was a guest, a cheerful male voice told her. No, she was not presently at the residence. "I'm sure she's off with her little sailing friends," the man said. "May I take a message for her?"

"No thanks." Carla hung up. It would probably not be helpful to announce her presence in advance.

She took a small bus from the airport into the center of Key West, taking a seat that faced the interior. The driver was a Latino who listened to salsa on an AM channel, the music brassy, pounding, and loud. An older couple wearing matching straw sunhats seemed delighted by the ambiance. Two young sailors, Navy duffel bags stowed beneath their seats, appeared bored. A man in his mid-forties, his hair windblown, his face weathered and creased, gave her a once-over. He wore jeans, docksiders, and a gray shirt with maroon piping at the edges of the short sleeves. The man smiled at her. Carla pretended not to notice. The man shrugged and turned his attention out the window.

The bus dropped her on the eastern end of Duval, at the corner of South Street.

"I can take you to a hotel," the driver offered.

"Rather walk," she answered. It was easier than explaining the strange feeling that someone had just sharpened a lens upon her. She crossed through a walk to a hotel on the beach, where a clerk seemed only too glad to offer a room; despite the regatta, it was still off-season. A lone bellman, delighted at the chance for a tip, practically wrestled her bag from her.

"In town for business or pleasure?" He jumped to press the elevator button before her.

"Business, I'm afraid," she said.

"Too bad," the bellman said. "You should try to get out a little while you're here."

Just as the doors closed she saw the middle-aged man from the bus walking into the lobby.

Michael and Earl watched the sun set from Mallory Dock.

"Is this what they call a tourist thing?" Earl asked, as they stepped around a crowd gathered around a performer with a small herd of trained housecats. He wore shorts and a tan fishing shirt with the sleeves rolled to the elbows.

"I guess you could say that," Michael said. He tugged at the tails of his own shirt until they flapped outside the blue cotton pants he'd bought that morning. Tropical garb, Earl had teased. Warm-weather fashion.

They had spent the day waiting for Alison Johnson to complete the day's racing. The thought of getting tape of her on the water had occurred to both of them and been rejected. No sense spooking someone who'd agreed to talk to them. Instead, Earl visited the military museum at Fort Taylor and bought souvenir conch shells for his family. Michael tried to call Carla, decided against leaving a message, and went for a walk through town.

"We need more assignments like this," Earl said.

"We need a story," Michael responded, "or I'm going to be unemployed."

They left the small summer crowd that had gathered at the dock and made their way up Duval Street, bypassing T-shirt shops, ignoring the barkers for struggling restaurants, catching a few sounds emerging from bars and nightclubs already revved for the evening. Ali Johnson had named a place off Simonton and United, a block away from Duval. Michael checked his watch. Eight-twenty. Another ten minutes.

Earl watched the people coming toward them, a blend of drifting young people, older gay men, and the inevitable tourists. "You want me to stick around, right? When you talk to her?"

"You mean *if,* don't you?" The lengthy delay before actually talking to Johnson had conjured up all sorts of fears about how the interview would go. What if she knew nothing about Hunter Worthington, or simply claimed that she knew nothing? Even if she was cooperative, would her information advance the story? Worse, Ali Johnson had just spent a full day on the water, in close proximity to Jimmy Mercer. He had had more than ample opportunity to get her to change her mind about giving an interview to a TV reporter.

"Stop worrying," Earl said. "She's gonna talk to you." They had turned left off Duval and were nearing the corner of Simonton. The foot traffic had slowed considerably, though there were still a few people moving on the dimly lit sidewalks, each one briefly illuminated by the headlights of slow-moving cars.

The guesthouse where Ali Johnson had said she was staying was a Queen Anne, built of Dade County pine and garnished with a porch that wrapped around three-quarters of the house. Rooms on the upper floors were brightly lit, and music could be heard coming from somewhere inside. The porch itself, however, remained dark.

Earl and Michael turned from the sidewalk and stopped in front.

"Nice," Earl mumbled. "Looks like one of those places in the rich part of Fall River."

"Actually, that's one of the influences. New England, I mean." The voice was female, and came from the far end of the porch. Michael climbed the steps and looked to his right. There at the far end of the porch were three rocking chairs, facing the street. In the middle chair was the silhouetted figure of a woman.

Michael took a step. "Alison?"

The figure did not move. But when he moved closer she spoke again, and this time the voice was easier to recognize. "Did you bring a camera?"

"You said not to," Michael said. "Though I'm hoping that later you'll change your mind."

He was close enough to see her now. She wore a summer dress, probably orange or yellow, and cut just above the knee, along with a pair of beach sandals. Her eyes and lips and the edges of her face seemed like black points in the darkness, lightened by the dress, her skin, and the blond hair that hung loose and long down to her shoulders. Michael thought she smelled like a new bar of soap.

"Where's Mercer?"

"He doesn't stay here," Alison Johnson said. "He's probably off getting drunk. Or maybe buying a pound of reefer."

The uncertainty that he had seen during their brief meeting this morning was gone. Alison Johnson spoke with a calm assurance that suggested she would be in control of her emotions, or at least she would try to be. That was what she had gained from waiting all day before meeting them.

As for the crack about Mercer, Michael could not tell whether she was joking. He looked at Earl, who shrugged.

"Why don't you and your friend sit down?"

Michael took a chair. Earl followed, and half-nodded to Michael as if to say, "It's your show."

But it wasn't. Control clearly belonged to the young woman, who peered at them and said, "I want to talk about Hunter."

And for the next hour, she did.

Carla tipped the bellman ten dollars.

"Thank *you,* ma'am," he said. "Please let me know if there's anything else I can do for you."

"There are two things," she said. "First, if you call me 'ma'am' again I may have to kill you."

"Sure. Sorry, ma—I'm sorry. It won't happen again."

"Good. The second thing is that I have an old boyfriend who won't take the message that it's over. I think he just followed me into the hotel when we got on the elevator."

"You want me to call the police?" The bellman seemed eager to please.

"No, I don't want to do anything that drastic just yet. What I need you to do is take a look down in the lobby and see if there's anyone waiting down there. Look for a man in his forties, wearing a gray shirt with red trim on the sleeves. If you see him, I want you to let me know."

"Yes ma—sorry. Sure." The bellman closed the door softly.

The room, like so many others in the Keys, was painted and decorated in soft pastels, peach, white, and aqua being the predominant colors. Carla opened the sliding door to the balcony and gulped in the air. It was thick and wet, and smelled different from up north. Saltier, perhaps. The heaviness of it felt good after the blast from the air conditioner. She looked at a stand of palm trees in front of her, and watched as the whisper of a breeze seemed to shuffle the fronds. How nice it would be, she thought, to be doing something besides working.

The phone rang once.

"There's no one down here," the bellman said. He held his breath, and Carla smiled to herself.

"Go ahead, say it."

"Thanks, ma'am. It's force of habit. I checked the lobby, and the clerk at registration. Whoever you saw is gone."

"Do you know that I used to be afraid of the water?" Alison Johnson gave a light laugh. "My mother would take me to swimming lessons when I was a little girl. Private lessons. I'd cry and cry. But she kept sending me. Made me go. She made me learn how to sail, too. Eventually I fell in love with it. I wanted my own boat before I wanted a car."

Michael nodded, impressed. "Why did your mother do that? Make you sail, I mean."

"I don't know. She said I'd need it someday. But she never explained. Eventually I wasn't afraid of the water anymore. And the sailing, it just took. It was like learning to fly, I guess. Not with an engine, but like with birds. Using the air to be free."

Alison Johnson was poised, calm, and clear-headed. She looked carefully from Michael to Earl and back again, watching them as she spoke. And her voice had a lilt to it, as if she were reciting poetry.

"This is the first time I've talked about him, you know. The first time since he died."

She stopped for a moment. Earl shifted in his seat. Michael made no sound, instead giving the young woman time to compose herself.

"I met Hunter at a race near Mackinac Island. Do you know northern Michigan?"

"I was there once," Michael said. "Cold water and fresh breeze."

"You do know," Alison Johnson laughed. "I love the Great Lakes," she said. "My parents had a place on the north shore of Lake Superior. That's colder still."

"What made you notice him?"

"Well, he was good-looking." Even in the shadows he could tell that she was smiling. "And he was the best sailor. Jimmy's always telling people that Hunter was overrated, but the fact is that Hunter won most of the time. He had a sense for where the wind was going to be, when it was going to shift. And he always made the adjustment a little bit before everyone else. Jimmy's a good sailor, but Hunter . . ." She smiled. "Hunter was great."

"I hear the same is true about you," Michael said. "At least, that's what the magazine article said."

"Anyway," Alison continued, ignoring the compliment, "there was this fish boil when the race was over. They do that up there, kind of like a clambake in Rhode Island. And I had this plate of boiled whitefish, with cole slaw, and a big plastic cup of Diet Coke. And I was walking with it, trying to get to a place to sit down. And I spilled the Coke. All over Hunter's dinner."

There was a lilt in her voice, a lightness, that suggested she relished the memory. "Why do I get the feeling that wasn't an accident?" Michael asked.

Alison Johnson chuckled. "You catch on fast, Mr. Carolina. I wanted to meet him. It seemed like a way to do it that would keep him humble."

"Did it work?"

"It did. I offered him my plate. I never liked fish that much anyway." She laughed again, but as she did, her tone changed. "We got to talking then, and that was that." Her voice trailed off then, as if the story ended there. But it did not.

"You must have been torn up when he died," Michael said.

"I wanted to be with him," she said. "If I had been with him, it might have been different."

"What would have been different?"

"Hunter took a lot of risks. It's what helped make him such a great sailor." Alison reached up to her face and brushed away a strand of hair that Michael could not see. "He took risks to see me. But when we got together, we were both so . . . comfortable. Even after a few weeks, we could finish each other's thoughts. It was like we had known each other forever, that's how good we were."

"Can we back up for a second?" Michael looked at Earl. The photographer was listening closely, and Michael had noticed him shift in his chair. "Why was it a risk for him to see you?"

"Because of who I am," Alison said. For the first time, her voice betrayed traces of acid. "I wasn't going to fit into the Worthington household."

"Why not?"

"Because Hunter's father would never let his son marry the daughter of a porno queen. Even when—no." She gave a bitter laugh. "*Especially* when she was pregnant."

Carla changed to a pair of tennis shorts and white sandals, along with a blue silk blouse she'd picked up in the airport waiting for the connection to Key West. Florida gear. She pulled her hair into a loose pile, then let it fall again around her shoulders. Did it really matter how she looked to talk to Alison Johnson?

"She'll talk to me no matter how I look," she said to the mirror.

The hall outside her room was deserted, save for an elderly couple arguing about whether they should turn on the air conditioner. Carla smiled at the couple. Embarrassed at being overheard, they stared until she was past them, then resumed arguing.

She looked at the elevator, but the man who had entered the lobby was still on her mind. Instead, she turned around and walked to the other end of the hall, where a red neon exit sign had turned pale, as though its light would soon fail from fatigue. She went down the stairs quickly, stopping briefly at each landing, but hearing nothing.

The stairs spilled into the lobby directly across from the elevator. She cracked the fire door and peered out. The bellman

had earned his tip. There was no one in the lobby.

Still, she continued down another half flight, to another door that opened onto a footpath surrounded by palms. The path led to the hotel pool in the back and to the main entrance in front. Carla emerged at the entrance, wishing there were more traffic around for camouflage, but glad that no one seemed to be around. She set off toward Duval Street, trying to think of where she needed to turn to find the guesthouse where Alison was supposed to be staying.

After twenty steps she thought she heard a sound behind her, but decided it would be better not to stop. There were people up ahead, their bodies briefly illuminated as they passed before the lights from bars and restaurants. After another fifty steps she began to blend into them. After twenty-five more she was in the midst of a small crowd.

There was a café on her right, and she stopped to look at the menu posted on a board in front. The position gave her a chance to look quickly behind her, but the glare from the café lights made it impossible to see anyone more than a few yards away. She took her time, glancing at the menu, then her watch, and occasionally up the street, as if waiting to meet someone. But no one familiar appeared.

She turned and began walking again, until she saw the cross street and turned right. It was only a few blocks away, if the directions were correct. She moved fast, listening for the sounds again. There were only the shouts from people on Duval Street, and a few notes of music from the nightclubs and bars.

The street ahead grew progressively dimmer as she edged away from the commercial district. A middle-aged gay couple, blissful and holding hands, passed her without speaking. Across the street a small crew of young people yelped and laughed as they walked back toward Duval.

Carla saw the lights from the upper floors of the large Queen Anne and glanced at the number on the house next to her. This had to be it. Alison, daughter of Barbetta Johnson and her long-

lost husband, Derek. Sailor. Minnesotan. Lover of Hunter Worthington before his untimely demise. Surely a secret would unfold from this meeting.

She turned onto the walkway and started up toward the house. The music and noise from Duval had ebbed to a dull buzzing sound, pierced occasionally by a scream or a blast of music. And the sound of precision metal, pieces machined and polished and oiled to make one clean action as a round was chambered.

Michael leaned forward. Ali Johnson was crying now, her tears making two long thin streaks down her face.

"It was Hunter's baby?"

The girl was silent for a moment, first uncrossing, then recrossing her legs. "When I told him, he didn't know what to say. We weren't exactly expecting it, you know."

Michael was silent. From the corner of his eye he saw Earl turn his head.

"Someone's coming up the walk."

Alison seemed not to hear them. But she had stopped crying now. "I think he was going to ask me to marry him. But I couldn't—it wouldn't have worked. Not yet. We were both too young."

She uttered the words with determination, as if she had already made a decision.

"Did you tell your mother? About the baby?"

Alison nodded. "She screamed at me. Told me I'd ruined my life, the same way she had. That was two months ago. The next day, I went to school. When I came home, she was gone. I haven't seen her since. Two weeks later I called a clinic in Minneapolis and made an appointment. I thought maybe if I didn't have the baby, my mother would come back."

Michael was careful not to show any reaction. "Is that why you missed the Newport regatta?"

Alison looked as though she might cry again. Instead, she

took a deep breath. "The procedure only took a few hours. But I wanted to rest after that. And I didn't want to see Hunter."

"Did Hunter know you'd decided not to keep the baby?"

"I never got the chance to tell him," she said. "He died before I could—"

The popping noises that interrupted were like oversized firecrackers, used in some strange celebration. Only the sounds were accompanied by shards of glass and holes ripped into the wooden frame of the porch. Michael fell to the floor, looked to his right, and saw the dim illuminations that signaled the firing of each new round.

The first two, no, was it three? They were a blur, but he definitely counted four more before there was a pause. The silence lengthened to the point of being unbearable, and then it was clear that at some point he would have to move.

"Michael?" Earl's voice sounded hoarse, which seemed appropriate. He had slipped off the porch and into the yard.

"You all right?" Michael asked.

"I think so. You?"

"Michael?" The voice froze him. He heard a bush move, and a branch crack. There was another burst of music from Duval, which faded as quickly as it had come.

"Well," Michael said, "that's one hell of a way to say hello."

Carla might have laughed then, if he had not sounded so shaken. That and the fact that Earl had still not moved.

Neither had Alison.

He turned to his left. She was still in the chair, rocking slightly, her legs still crossed, and her dress fluttering in the whisper of a breeze.

A Key West officer was on the scene in less than a minute. He was quickly joined by no fewer than three cruisers from the Monroe County sheriff's department, their headlights and red-and-blue strobe bars garishly illuminating the front yard of the guesthouse. A rescue vehicle arrived next, and two paramedics rushed down the path to check on Alison Johnson. In a moment one returned to the pool of headlights in front of the cruisers, shaking his head.

"One shot," the first one said. "Went in under her arm. Probably a ricochet."

Carla told a sweating deputy sheriff about the man who had looked at her in the van, then appeared in the hotel lobby. The deputy keyed a radio microphone on his belt and broadcast the description to a dispatcher.

The deputy adjusted his belt and looked at her carefully, trying to decide how much he should believe. "Did you see him behind you on the street?"

"No. But I didn't tell anyone I was coming here."

"How did he miss you?" Carla shrugged. "I hit the bushes. Guess I was lucky."

"How do I even know he was looking for you?" The cop was smart, Carolina decided. He was changing subjects, keeping the witnesses off balance, yet not jumping to any conclusions.

"You don't," Carla said. "But it's the only thing I can think of."

The deputy removed a handkerchief from his back pocket and gently patted his own forehead. He carefully tucked the cloth away and peered at Carla.

"You gonna recognize this guy if we catch him?"

Carla pursed her lips, trying to conceal her amusement at the deputy's delicate gesture. "I'll do my best."

The deputy swung his gaze to Michael. "What about you? Any thoughts you wanna give me?"

"I'd be looking for a guy named James Mercer. He's one of the sailors here for the regatta Alison was in. I think you want to find out where he is."

"And why would that be?"

"Because he wasn't tremendously pleased that I was talking to the lady who just got shot."

"Uh-huh." The deputy sniffed approvingly. "I'm gonna need you to tell me where you're staying around here."

Michael looked at Carla as she told the deputy the name of her hotel. She had a scrape on one arm where she had attempted to break her fall. He reached out and touched her softly.

"Are you all right?"

She nodded. "Are you?"

At the same moment both had realized how close the bullets had come. The deputy watched them, scratched himself, and cleared his throat.

"Sorry to interrupt, but is there anyone else we should talk to?"

"Yeah," Michael said. "His name is Earl." In fact, Earl had bolted for the hotel within seconds of the paramedics arriving. A fresh crime scene needed fresh video, and fresh video required a camera. "He'll be right back," Michael said.

At that moment another deputy gave a shout, walking into the flood of red, white, and blue light. In his hand he held a pencil, and dangling from the pencil was a small automatic handgun of indeterminate caliber.

"Found this down about half a block," he said to the deputy questioning Carla and Michael. "It's still warm."

The larger deputy looked the gun over. "Got a serial number?"

"Think so."

"Run it."

Earl returned, and began rolling tape. He was joined moments later by a still photographer. The two of them worked every bit of the area in front of the guesthouse. As they did, the radios of the deputies squawked.

"All available units, we have a report of a theft of a car on Simonton at South Street. Suspect seen fleeing in a 1996 Camry, red in color, Florida tags Roger Zebra Kevin six six five. He's described as white male, mid-forties, wearing blue jeans, gray shirt, and boat shoes. Unknown direction."

"That's the guy who was on the bus with me," Carla said. The deputy with the congested sinuses looked at her again and then at his notes. The dispatcher squawked again.

"All units, we have a report of a hit-and-run on Route 1, northbound. Driver is a white male in a 1996 red Camry. Struck a parked car and didn't bother to stop. Last seen heading north. Partial plate reads Kevin six six. Think that's our thief."

The sweaty deputy keyed his own microphone. "Dispatch, this is ten twenty-one. Notify all units this guy could be involved in the shooting. Repeat, the hit-and-run driver could be involved in the shooting."

One of the other deputies trotted to his cruiser, fired up, and sped off. The congested one stared at Carla. "That was a good ID you made. You're a private investigator?"

"That's right."

"How long were you a cop?"

"Long enough."

The deputy smiled slyly.

"And you're sure you didn't see the guy behind you on the street here?"

Carla smiled in return. "Are you suggesting something, Officer?"

"Not at all," the deputy said, too quickly. "If he's the right guy, though, we don't have anything to tie him to this shooting."

"I'd try for a paraffin test," Carla said. "Or maybe you can persuade him to confess. I bet you've done that before, haven't you?"

The cop grinned. "Yeah, us good old boys just love beating suspects. It's one of the more rewarding aspects of the job. Now if you'll excuse me, I need to speak to that news cameraman over there."

"The strangest truths are said in jest," Carla said, watching him go.

"In that case," Michael said, "I need to think of a joke with 'I missed you' as the punchline."

They looked at each other, and in a moment, folded together. As Michael put his arms around her he could feel Carla shudder.

"I couldn't see him," she said softly. "But I knew there was something wrong. It was like walking blind, and knowing that you're almost at the cliff's edge."

He kissed her forehead. "You have good instincts," he told her. "That must be why you followed me here."

Carla looked up at him and saw that he was smiling. "I'm sorry I said that, Michael."

"It's okay."

She kissed him, hard. The deputies and paramedics watched while trying not to. In a few minutes a forensic van pulled up, and two technicians climbed out. Earl finished his statement to the deputy and came toward them.

"Seems like they're going to be here for a while," he said. "You want to call the station?"

Michael looked at his watch. It was past ten o'clock. There would be no way to feed tape, and besides, how did the story relate to Rhode Island?

"The ex-lover of a dead Newport sailor dies from a stray bullet in Key West . . ." he said out loud.

Earl set his camera down. "You sure it was a stray?"

"No." He looked at Carla. "There's not much of a connection here," he said. "Too bad there isn't some way to see if things tie together."

He did not look at Carla. But then, he did not need to.

"I can take a hint when you hit me on the side of the head with it," she said.

Earl suppressed a chuckle.

"Perhaps an arrangement can be made," she said. "Earl, would you like to have a hotel room to yourself tonight?"

"Sure. He snores, you know."

"I know."

Earl looked at Michael. "What do I say if the boss calls us?"

Carla slipped her hand onto Michael's arm and slowly began to guide him away. "Tell her," she said, "that your reporter is meeting with a source."

Twenty minutes later a Monroe County deputy sheriff spotted a red 1996 Toyota Camry at a stoplight on Route 1 in Matecumbe Key. The officer activated his lights, only to see the car accelerate through the intersection, barely missing a pickup truck. After a fifteen-mile chase the Camry left the road, slamming into a tree, then rolling three times before coming to rest in a clump of mangroves.

The deputy drew his weapon and approached the car slowly. As he neared it the car caught fire, and the officer backed away. Only then did he hear a moaning sound to his right, and shining his light he quickly spotted a man of perhaps forty-five, wearing blue jeans and a torn gray shirt with maroon piping on the sleeves. At first, the man appeared to be lying down, but closer inspection revealed that he was impaled on a broken section of mangrove. Fearful of moving the suspect until help arrived, the officer stood by and watched him bleed.

Only after the man had been declared dead on arrival in a hospital in Key West was it determined that he had a wallet containing a faculty ID card for a school called St. Ives Academy and a driver's license for one Charles Nathan of Portsmouth, Rhode Island.

14

The sheriff's office disclosed Nathan's identity at nine in the morning. By noon, Earl and Michael had made arrangements for a live shot with a local satellite company and had fed video from a small studio in the middle of Key West.

"Too bad I don't have a picture of this guy Nathan," Michael told Shirley on the phone.

"We're working on getting one from St. Ives," Shirley said.

"They won't be much help. That school wants publicity like a hen wants a fox. Try one of the newspapers, see if they photographed him at a regatta."

"Will do," she said. "Do the cops have anything hard to tie this guy in with Carla? Or Alison Johnson?"

"Best I can get is that they're looking at both. But no one will say it's one investigation. It's my guess they'll trace the gun. And they'll check to see whether Nathan fired a weapon recently."

"I'm impressed," Shirley said. "You should have been a cop."

Carolina smiled. He did not tell his boss that Carla had supplied the information following a session of rapturous lovemaking.

"Any idea why Nathan would be following Carla?" Shirley asked.

"We're not even sure that he was," Michael answered. It was at least possible that the shooter was aiming for Alison Johnson. Or—

Shirley finished the thought. "Any chance someone was following you?"

Michael thought of Jimmy Mercer again. He'd made trouble in Newport, and had tried to keep Alison from talking. There was something strange about him that Michael had never been able to place.

Still, the money was on Carla. And the odds got better when she met him at the hotel following the noon live shot.

"I just left our friend the deputy from last evening. The cops picked up Mercer at a bar just before midnight."

"And?"

"And they've been leaning on him ever since. Says he doesn't know a thing about Alison's death. Actually looked pretty surprised by it."

"He looked surprised when I told him about Hunter, too. Do they believe him?"

Carla gave a small shrug. "He cried his eyes out when he heard she was dead, or so I'm told. That gave the cops an opening. They asked for permission to search his hotel room, and he gave it. I guess he forgot that he'd left two pounds of fairly high grade reefer in one of the dressers. When the deputies found it, Jimmy confessed that he's been running dope for Mr. Clean. Uses regattas like this one to meet up with suppliers."

"Is that right?"

Carla showed traces of a smirk. "It's amazing what people will tell you when they think they're suspected of murder."

Carla finished packing her bag. The glass door to the hotel balcony was open, and he felt the breeze coming through. Outside, through the trees, was the slash of sand that the hotel called a beach, and beyond, the mixture of gray and green and pale blue that marked the beginning of the water.

"All right," he said quietly. "So Jimmy Mercer is a dope peddler. That doesn't move me any closer to figuring out who killed Hunter Worthington."

Carla finished packing his bag. "Or his girlfriend," she said. "I'm about ready to leave. Is Shirley expecting you back today?"

"Same flight as you," Michael said. He picked up her bag. "Can I carry this for you?"

Carla picked up the phone. "I haven't checked messages at home. Can you wait a minute?"

When she heard Paul Carolina's slurred voice she played the message back to Michael. And then once more.

Michael called his apartment in Providence. He had not yet installed an answering machine. The line rang twenty times before he hung up.

Carla called the sheriff's office from the Key West airport.

"Got a line back on that gun we found," the deputy told her. "It was purchased a year ago by one Charles Nathan at a gun shop in Fall River. Oh yeah, the paraffin test shows gunpowder traces on his right palm. We're checking his travel itinerary right now, but I'd say the chances are real good he was looking to curtail the work of one Eyetalian-American private eye."

The deputy chuckled when he said this.

"You really are hysterical, Deputy. Perhaps you should consider a second career in comedy."

"That's what my wife always says. Think I got talent?"

"Nah," Carla said. "I just wanted to get even for you calling me Eyetalian." She hung up.

The commuter plane to Miami had three seats to a row: a double on the right and a single on the left. Earl had the single.

"This is cozy," Carla said.

Michael nodded. "Too bad we're not alone. The sheriff get more on Nathan?"

"He got enough." She filled him in, which did not take long. When the plane lifted off, they both looked out the window as the islands turned into brown-and-green pieces of a map once again.

225

"Perhaps we should consider our next move," Michael said.

"Perhaps we should." Carla pressed the button on her seat, only to find that the seat back would not adjust. "Of course," she said, sliding downward, "I think my next move is somewhat limited, since I'm almost certain to be fired when I get back to Providence."

Michael looked at her in mock horror. "Whatever gave you that idea?"

"The attempted assassination was a clue," Earl mumbled. Michael and Carla stared at him patiently until he turned to look out his own window.

"The fact is," Carla sighed, "I have completely screwed this case up. Balboni will put the word out about me in Providence. I doubt I'll ever get another client."

"There may be a way to deal with this," Michael said. "Of course, we'll have to trust each other."

There was something unsettling in his expression, as though he were betting on a long-shot horse, or dodging cars in heavy traffic.

Carla cocked an eyebrow. "I'll share my bed with you, sir. I'll even tell you what I've been up to, at least when it looks like my own client is trying to do me in. But you're supposed to be a journalist, remember?"

"I remember. And we both still need to know who killed Hunter Worthington, right?"

The answer was so obvious she did not bother to reply.

"So tell me what you think of this," Michael said. "You too, Earl."

They listened. They told him what they thought. They argued. Made counterarguments. And compromises. By the time their connecting flight began descending on Providence, they had a consensus.

"All in all," Michael said, "it's a good plan."

"Not a plan," Carla said. "An accord."

She ran a hand lightly along Michael's arm, which caused Earl to shake his head.

"You two'd better move back in together."

"Why do you say that?" Michael asked.

"Because if you don't, you'll probably wind up killing each other."

Later that evening, Jimmy Mercer returned to Providence. Instead of traveling by commercial flight, however, he flew courtesy of the United States government. Once he was on the ground, a DEA agent equipped him with a body microphone and fifty-five pounds of high-grade marijuana, neatly packed in twin steel suitcases.

Jimmy took a cab to Newport and went immediately to the Porcelain God. Fifteen minutes after his arrival, the Newport police, supervised by Captain Cicero, executed a search warrant with the assistance of the DEA. From the club's office they seized a drug ledger, a digital scale, assorted steroids and other pharmaceuticals, and four thousand dollars in cash. Both Mercer and the club's owner, one Myron Barbour, also known as Mr. Clean, were taken into custody. Cicero made a show of cuffing Mercer in front of the cue-ball-headed bartender.

"Mercer, you fuckin' rat."

"The fuck are you talking about, Myron?"

"I ain't fooled. You set me up. And don't you ever fuckin' call me Myron."

Jimmy Mercer was terrified. He shook his wrist bracelets. "These look like something I want to be wearing? I'm goin' down, same as you."

After Barbour had been escorted to a police cruiser, Mercer looked to Captain Cicero and his DEA handler.

"Think he bought it?"

"Probably not," Cicero said. His elation at making the bust was outweighed only by his contempt for the snitch who'd made it possible. "Tell me something. The reporter from Channel Three ran a piece about you pretending not to know that Hunter Worthington was dead. Seeing as you're cooperating, you want to tell us how Hunter was hanging from that yardarm?"

Mercer hesitated. "This covered by my cooperation agreement?"

Cicero glanced sideways at the DEA agent, who gave an almost imperceptible nod. "As long as you didn't kill the kid, Jimmy, or have someone do it for you, I'd say you're covered."

Jimmy sniffed once, loud enough to make Cicero wonder if his brains were falling loose.

"We were coming back from a run, Mr. Clean and me. Brought a small load in from a boat maybe twenty miles out, and north of Block Island. Just reefer, about 10 pounds and a little bit of coke. Just under a key."

"Fair to say you like to sample your product?" Cicero asked.

Jimmy nodded. "It's a fringe benefit of the job."

The DEA agent chuckled.

"Go on," Cicero said.

"Okay. See, Myron—Mr. Clean—was pissed about the size of the load. He wanted more. Bigger loads, more money. That's why I went to Florida—to score from another source."

The DEA agent appeared interested, but Cicero was impatient. "What about the body?"

Mercer licked his upper lip. "My partner was using his own boat. He's got a slip not too far from where *Stream* is moored. It was like, five a.m. So we're moving, got the engines down low, looking around to make sure no one's watching out for us. And that's when we saw the body, right up there under the spreaders. I almost shit my pants."

"So it was already strung up when you saw it?" Cicero asked.

Mercer nodded.

"How'd you know it was Jimmy?"

"I didn't. Not then. But later, when that reporter starts questioning me, tells me he's dead, I figured it out. Said I'd go on camera just to throw him off. If I hadn't mentioned the hanging, he never would have known. God, I can be so stupid sometimes."

Neither Cicero nor the DEA agent argued the point.

"You see anyone else?" Cicero asked.

"Nah. The boat was like, I mean *totally* quiet. Saw some cabin lights, but no one else. It was weird, him twisting up there, like one of those movie scenes, you know? I was gonna call the cops. Anonymous. But Myron—my partner—he said he'd break both my arms."

Mercer wore his best "I'm sorry" expression, one he'd been practicing ever since he'd turned snitch. It was the face informants wear when they're still hoping for a slap on the wrist, and some stern words like "don't do that again."

"Well, I wouldn't worry," Cicero said after a moment. "Myron's gonna be off the street at least five years."

"Maybe a lot more if we can hang a continuing criminal enterprise rap on him," the DEA agent said. "That should give you plenty of time to move out of Rhode Island. That is, after you finish your own sentence."

"I thought I got a walk," Mercer said, shocked.

"No one ever promised that," the agent said. "We just said we'd talk to the judge about you. Hell, not even Sammy the Bull got a walk. You won't do no five years, but you'll do time."

Cicero was smiling now. He was feeling much better. "I were you, Jimmy, I'd look on the bright side."

Jimmy turned to the captain. "What's that?"

"You just helped Newport get rid of two scumbags instead of one."

Carla and Michael took a cab to her Edgewood home, where a check of the answering machine revealed a new message from Rico Balboni. His tone was on the far edge of polite and the near side of brusque.

"I'm calling to advise you that your services are no longer required on behalf of my client, Mr. Worthington. However, we are expecting a final report of your activities. You can forward that to my office. I also expect that you will destroy all notes related to your investigation, or turn them over to my office."

"Fat chance," Carla said, when the message ended.

"Does this change our plans?" Michael asked.

"Hell, no. We need to follow through." She popped the tape out of the answering machine, shaking her head in disgust. "Do you believe the nerve of this guy? Worthington had to have something to do with the shooting. That message from your father proves it—"

Carla's face turned ashen. "Michael, have you spoken to your father?"

They took her car, beating a few yellow lights, ignoring a few red ones, and were at his apartment in fifteen minutes. There were dirty dishes in the sink, but otherwise the house was clean. The beds were made, the towels in the bathroom were dry, and a stack of boxes from Michael's move earlier in the week stood unopened in the living room.

And Paul Carolina, his clothes, his bag, and even his toothbrush were gone.

15

n the morning Carla drove to a video superstore on Route 2 in Warwick. A cheerful young clerk, upon spotting her, stopped fingering his pimples and approached.

"Can I help you find something?"

"Yes," Carla said, deadpan. "Do you have a copy of a *A Tail of Two Cities?*"

The young man looked puzzled. "You mean they made a movie of that?"

"Several," Carla said. "The one I'm talking about is a porno film."

The clerk pursed his lips. "I don't think so," he said.

Carla looked at a list she'd jotted down.

"How about *The Whoremaster of Venice? Much Ado About Coming? Of Mice and Ménage à Trois?*"

"I better check the catalog," the clerk said. He scurried behind a desk, then disappeared into the adult section while Carla glanced at newly released titles. In a few minutes the clerk was back with two films.

"We need a credit card to guarantee the rental," he said.

"I'll just buy them," she said, sliding a hundred-dollar bill across the counter. "That won't be a problem, will it?"

The clerk tucked the bill in a cash drawer and watched her leave. "Maybe I should have taken more English lit," he said, to no one in particular.

Morgan Worthington opened the door to Château du Printemps. Her hair bore no traces of dye, her body no signs of piercing. Without makeup, and dressed in cotton slacks, a cotton sweater, and canvas tennis shoes, she looked more like a model from a Talbots catalog than a grunge rocker aching for the cover of *Rolling Stone*.

"Hey, Madame Private Eye," she said, in a not unfriendly way.

"What happened to Bosworth?"

"Gone. Gone with Steps. Want to come in?"

Carla did. She waited for Morgan to shove the door closed, then followed her through the great house.

"Moms is in the study. We're discussing her rehabilitation."

"Excuse me?"

Morgan offered a sad smile. "Drying out."

Pippa Worthington looked like she needed it. She was parked in the same seat where Carla had first seen her, the ever-present pitcher of what appeared to be martinis beside her, half full, ice melting.

"Hello, Mrs. Worthington."

"Don't call me that," Pippa said, without looking up. "My daughter thinks I need to detoxify. Do you think I need to detoxify?"

Carla paused a moment before saying, "I think your liver might appreciate a rest."

Pippa slurped at her drink again. Then she placed her drink down, either not noticing or ignoring it when it sloshed over her fingers.

"Weren't you fired?"

"Your husband said I was."

"Then why did you come here?"

"Because you didn't," Carla said. "Say that I was fired, that is. And even if Hunter the Third wasn't your son, I have the feeling you cared about him."

Pippa Worthington did not respond. But she also did not drink.

"I brought something for you to look at," Carla said, pulling the videocassette out of a plastic bag. Morgan looked at it curiously.

"Is that a–?" She stopped.

"Why don't you show me your VCR?" Carla asked.

The set was flimsy, cheaply built, like something even Sam Fuller would have rejected when shooting a low-budget war epic. The plants in the background showed their brown cardboard edges where the green paint from the designer's brush had not reached. In the foreground was a bench, crudely constructed, and with a set of garish red pillows on top. The words A MIDSUMMER NIGHT'S CREAM were suddenly superimposed across the screen, then vanished. STARRING BARBETTA JOHNSON AND DEE BONAIRE.

In a moment a young woman skipped onto the screen. She was dressed in a negligee and sported a wreath around her shoulder-length hair. She gave a tittering laugh, and began a speech peppered with "thees" and "thous" and the line "Lord, what fools these mortals be."

"Do you know her?" Carla asked.

Pippa Worthington stared at the television screen, but did not respond.

"She looks familiar," Morgan said. "But I can't place her. How old is this?"

Carla looked at the box. "The film was released in 1975." Morgan was right. The actress did look familiar.

So did the man who appeared next, also wearing a wreath, as well as a white sheet in the style of a Roman senator. In response to the negligeed actress he launched into his own spiel of "thous," "thees," and the occasional "forsooth."

"Oh my God," Morgan giggled. "That's Bosworth."

The giggling escalated into outright laughter when actor and actress disrobed.

"Wow, he's hung like a buffalo," Morgan said.

As the couple began copulating, Carla shut the VCR off.

"Hey." Morgan looked petulant.

"You can watch it later," Carla said. "I need to speak with your mother."

Pippa Worthington had not moved. She continued to stare at the television screen, now blank. "I'd like another drink," she said.

"No. Pippa, look at me."

She turned, her face anguished.

"Your husband is a pornographer," Carla said slowly. "The woman in that film is his first wife. I don't think they were ever divorced, so I guess that makes him a bigamist, too. In any event, he used to make movies like this one and distribute them all over the country. More recently he's had an interest in straight porn, videos and hard-core stuff. They shoot them in a warehouse in the upper Midwest. Stuff that would turn your stomach."

"Wouldn't turn mine," Morgan sniffed.

"Shut up, Morgan," Carla snapped. "You're so damned busy trying to shock people you don't even realize that your mother's in pain."

Surprise crossed Morgan's face like a ringing slap. She said nothing. Instead, after a small pause, she sat down next to her mother, sliding a hand onto her shoulder.

"My mother didn't know about this," Morgan said.

"That's what I've always figured," Carla said. "The man you know as Hunter Worthington wasn't *summa cum laude* at Pomona College. He didn't even go to Pomona College, and he didn't go to UCLA. I'm not even sure he's from California. He used to be a porn producer, and I think he's still involved in distributing films out of a giant warehouse outside Minneapolis. Which happens to be the home of his first wife. And their daughter, Alison."

Morgan Worthington managed to turn an even lighter shade of pale.

"You mean my stepbrother and Alison . . . ?"

"Incest happens in the best of families," Carla said. "And the worst."

There was a silence then, as heavy and hard as the marble on the floors and the fireplace. Carla glanced at the martini pitcher, its ice now fully melted into the gin. Pippa Worthington seemed not to notice.

"I suppose you expect me to go to pieces," she said, her voice thin and brittle. "Maybe you'd even like to see that."

"No, ma'am," Carla said. "I'd just like to know what happened to your stepson. And to find out, I want you to tell me about your husband."

Pippa looked up then, her eyes heavy-lidded from the gin.

"He said that I charmed him. Captivated him. Can you imagine? But I wasn't drinking so much then. I was just a divorced woman with a little girl, and a fortune wasted by Morgan's first father."

"The one who's in France?"

"The very one. Hunter came into my life. He had that peculiar butler, but I could overlook that. He said he could restore the Binghams to their rightful place in Newport society."

"What Moms means is he had money," Morgan said.

"It was more than that." Pippa's voice was breaking now, and her anguish was enough to quiet her daughter once again. "He could be charming, you know. He had style, and he knew the right things, even if he tried too hard." Mother peered at her daughter then, hoping for some sign of confirmation. "That was always his problem. He wanted acceptance too much, you know. Wanted to belong. But in Newport, wanting to belong is a dangerous thing. It's precisely what makes people cast you out. That was what disgraced us. That and—" A look of revelation came over Pippa's face. "Do you think they knew? Do you think people knew how Hunter made his fortune?" Her face colored then, and she looked down. The thought of others knowing such embarrassing information seemed to be more than she could bear.

There was silence again. Morgan moved her hand and lightly stroked her mother's head.

"Do you want anything, Moms?"

For an answer, Pippa asked, "Do you know what he said to me? When he asked me to marry him? 'I'm your Jay, and you're my Daisy. Only we will have a happy ending.' That's what he said."

"Pippa." It was an awkward moment, Carla knew. But there was no chance that the scene would get better, and a good bet that it would get worse. "I need to know where your husband was the night that Hunter died. If he had something to do with your stepson's death, you've got to tell me."

Morgan started to speak, and stopped again when her mother raised a hand.

"I know you would like me to tell you that he left that night," Pippa said. "That he went somewhere and returned with a length of rope, or burns on his hands from hauling line. But I can't. Because it isn't true. In a strange way, I wish that he had gone. But he was here, drinking, with me."

"It's like she told you the first time," Morgan said. "My stepfather is a bastard. He's pickled nearly as much as Moms, and he can be as nasty as they come. You've seen it. But he was here that night. At least he was when I got home."

Carla decided that if they were lying, they were both very good at it. But more likely, they were simply too drained not to tell the truth.

"Where is he now?"

"My husband has decided he'll be sailing the Newport–Bermuda Race." Pippa picked up her glass again. "He's moved onto *Stream* to make preparations. I think they're starting in another day or so."

"End of the week, Moms," Morgan said. "Bosworth's going with him. I hope they both drown."

Carla thanked them. Morgan nodded absently, still stroking

her mother's head. She made no sign that she would see Carla out.

"Do you think my husband was right?" Pippa asked suddenly. "About Jay and Daisy?"

Carla thought for only a second.

"You're better than Daisy Buchanan ever was. But your husband isn't fit to shine Jay Gatsby's shoes."

Pippa Worthington smiled slightly, and reached for the martini pitcher.

Carla walked out of Château du Printemps. Maybe I'm wrong about her, she thought. But I know I'm right about him.

Michael was just finishing a memo on the Key West death of Alison Johnson when the phone rang.

"Well, I made the visit," Carla said.

"How was Mrs. Worthington?"

"Like a lost little girl."

"What did she think of the film?"

"I think the alcohol helped to dull the pain. Her daughter was amused that the family butler used to have another career."

"I'm sure. Anything else?"

"Yeah. Morgan seemed to think that Barbetta Johnson looked familiar. But she couldn't say from where. Neither can I."

"Maybe I should take another look," Michael said. "For professional reasons, of course."

Carla chuckled. "Looking for pointers or something?"

"Do I need them?"

"Hardly. Anyway, the illustrious husband isn't there. He's off with Bosworth, getting their boat ready for the Newport–Bermuda Race."

"Is that right?" The information was mildly surprising to Michael. Hunter Worthington III might have been an outstanding sailor, but his father?

"Well," Carla said, "I've done my share. Now it's your turn to deliver."

"Just so," Michael said.

"Where are you going to start?"

Michael thought for a moment.

"With a surprise inspection."

It was close to twilight when they found *Stream*. The gorgeous Little Harbor had been moved from her mooring into a slip at a marina just off Goat Island. The man Carla had identified as Bosworth the butler appeared in a sport utility, unloaded several crates of food and liquor into a hand truck, and wheeled it down to the yacht. Hunter Worthington stepped briefly above the deck and assisted in the unloading. Then Bosworth returned to the sport utility and driven off.

Earl sniffed. "So this guy thinks he's Ted Turner?"

"Larry Flynt with a boat, more likely," Michael said. "Seems like the right time for a visit."

"Why don't we go in with the camera rolling?"

"Because he'd throw us off his boat in a heartbeat," Michael said. "I want to get something meaningful out of this guy."

The wireless microphone Michael wore was taped to his chest. Ordinarily, he did not like to record interview subjects secretly. But this occasion presented a unique set of problems, not the least of which was Worthington's status as a murder suspect. His father's strange message to Carla and the bizarre appearance of Charles Nathan in Key West both pointed to Hunter Worthington. That and the man's demonstrated capacity to lose his temper.

Earl wore a dubious expression. "I'm just not so crazy about you going in alone."

"So listen in, and if it gets hairy, call the cops," Michael said, in a tone that suggested more confidence than he truly felt. "I'll be fine."

"Are you reassuring me, or yourself?"

"Both."

He stepped out of the van they had parked at the edge of the set of piers, where Earl's camera pointed out the side door. There were few other cars parked in the lot, and the blacktop seemed to absorb the orange rays from the halogen lamps that came on at the first sign of twilight. He walked down the steps of the floating dock that rose and fell with the tides.

"If you can hear me, Earl, let me know."

After a pause, he heard the brief, familiar sound of the van's horn. The wireless was working. A minute later he was standing alongside *Stream*. The yacht was simply magnificent, her teak decks bleached nearly white, the gelcoat on her hull glistening, even in the near-darkness. It was a boat built for beauty and luxury, not for racing. Still, the Newport–Bermuda Race was not the America's Cup. And if Hunter Worthington wanted to get away from it all, he would do so in comfort. Michael's opinion on this was confirmed when he spotted a dozen cardboard boxes of supplies set across the cockpit. There were canned goods, piles of fresh fruit and vegetables, and loaves of bread. Another box held what looked like enough steaks and chops to feed a navy. Finally, there were two cases of wine, and another case with a mixed supply of liquor poking out.

"Who's there?" Hunter Worthington, Jr., had emerged from the yacht's cabin. He asked the question harshly, and, Michael thought, with a trace of apprehension.

"I'm from Channel Three. I hope you have enough room in your icebox for all that meat. Be a shame if it spoiled."

"This is a private marina. You're trespassing."

"I don't think so. There weren't any signs posted."

Worthington did not respond. The light from the cabin displayed him in silhouette, wearing a baggy pair of cotton trousers and a sweater. His hair was tousled, and his feet were bare.

"I'd like to talk to you."

"I have nothing to say."

"You might after you hear about the story I'm preparing, Mr. Johnson."

If Michael had choreographed the next moment, the man standing on the top step of the cabin hatchway would have done a double take, perhaps frozen, maybe feigned curiosity at the use of the new name.

Instead, he seemed to relax, even offered a slight smile through closed lips.

"Well," he said. "As you've already seen, I need to attend to these supplies."

It was the perfect noncommittal answer. The man climbed all the way into the cockpit and laid his hands on a box.

"Would you like a hand?"

"No." Hunter lifted and turned, then nearly fell as he tried to climb down the hatchway steps, treating them like a set of stairs.

"Do you really think you're ready for the Bermuda race?"

Now the man turned and stared.

"What makes you think I'm not?"

"For one thing, the way you're going into the cabin. Try backing down them, like with a ladder."

Hunter Worthington, Jr., put the box down. He turned and backed part of the way into the cabin before picking it up again.

"I'm surprised your son didn't show you that," Michael said.

Worthington kept backing down.

"Or your daughter."

Worthington disappeared for a moment, and Michael could hear the dull sound of the box being set down again, only this time a bit too hard. Worthington emerged again, his face a mask.

"It's obvious you won't go away," he said. "You might as well come in."

"Mind if my cameraman comes along? He's waiting in the car." Michael did not expect the man to agree. But Worthington needed to know that the reporter had not come alone.

"This invitation is exclusive, Mr.–"

"Carolina."

"Yes. It's just for you. Would you mind handing me one of those boxes before you come in?"

Earl was not pleased. It was one thing to stand on the dock and talk to a pornographer and suspected killer. It was quite another to go inside the man's boat. Still, the audio reception was clear. And a cell phone next to him made it easy to summon the police.

The knock at the door of the van made him jump. He was generally used to distraction when driving one of the news trucks with the Channel Three logo splashed on the sides. But the van was unmarked. He left the camera rolling and opened the door.

"Hello?"

There was no one. At the same moment he heard a banging sound, metal striking metal, from the other side of the van. But there were no windows. Earl jumped out and circled the front. Probably some punk thinking about stripping the hubcaps, he thought.

"Hey, cut it out," he said, just before the blow hit him in the back of the head.

"I still have nothing to say," Hunter Worthington said. "But you seem to have a great deal to tell me. So go ahead."

He was seated now, on a plush banquette in the middle of the Little Harbor's main cabin. The boxes were strewn across the galley, with a few more piled at an ample navigation station equipped with the latest electronics. *Stream* was capable of almost any voyage, Michael realized.

"Our story will say that you are the founder of and continue to be involved in a Minnesota company that produces and distributes pornography. We are also prepared to report that you are living under a false name, that your true name is Derek Johnson, and that you faked your own death in the late 1970s, along with that of your son and a male film star named Dee Bonaire, who now calls himself Bosworth."

The stony expression on Worthington's face did not change.

"Shall I go on?" Michael asked. Worthington shrugged.

"I've also interviewed a young woman named Alison Johnson. You may have heard of her. She was murdered recently in Florida."

"I've seen the news," Worthington said.

"I understand she was romantically involved with your son, and that you disapproved. Which would make sense, since they appear to have borne a striking resemblance to each other."

"Are you finished?"

"I have lots of questions, but basically, that's my story. That and the fact that investigators are looking for a link between you and your daughter's alleged killer, Charley Nathan."

"That was an accident!" The words were the first real sign of emotion that Hunter Worthington had displayed.

"How would you know whether it was or not?"

But Worthington would not answer him. He quickly seemed to regain composure. During the pause that followed, Michael felt the boat rock, ever so slightly. Had Bosworth returned? Earl was supposed to use the horn if someone approached the boat. But no horn had sounded.

Carolina decided to turn up the pressure. "You sent Charley Nathan to Key West, didn't you? Sent him to get rid of the investigator you hired. Funny, he seemed like a decent guy. It must have taken a lot to persuade him to go to Florida. Maybe the promise of a perpetual endowment of the St. Ives sailing program. That'd guarantee his job for life, wouldn't it?"

Worthington's silence spoke volumes. Michael's theory, it seemed, was not far from the truth.

"What I still don't get," Michael said, "is why you were so angry at your son the night he died. I mean, if you didn't kill

242

him, then you must be going through hell, thinking that the last time you saw him alive you slapped him."

The remark stung. Worthington licked his lips, then spoke in a low, steady voice.

"You may think I'm a man without morals, Mr. Carolina. You're wrong. I loved my son. I didn't want him to ruin his life. I didn't raise some hillbilly. He could have had any girl. Girls with money. Status. Privilege. Maybe I can't, but he could. The one thing he couldn't do is marry his own sister. Especially if she was pregnant." Worthington stopped again, realizing he'd gone too far.

"It never would have happened," Michael said.

"Of course it would," Worthington snarled. "She got pregnant to trap him. That's what women do."

"She aborted the baby," Michael said. The expression on Worthington's face was difficult to describe: it was a blend of surprise, sadness, and no small amount of relief. Then, realizing that Michael was still watching him, Worthington turned hard again.

"If you air that story, I will own your television station, as well as anything of value that belongs to you or that woman my jackass lawyer told me to hire as an investigator. I will hound you wherever you go, whatever you may do. I will attach your wages, seize any asset. You will live the rest of your life as a pauper."

"The last time I checked," Michael said, "truth is a defense to libel or slander. And somehow I don't believe that you really want to go to court over this."

Worthington stared at an expensive-looking rug on the floor of the cabin.

"I want you to assume," he said, "that a man has a past. That he needs to start a new life. A moral life. That he wants his child to have a moral life."

"You didn't have just one child."

Worthington continued to look at the rug with the intricate

weave. "It's not easy to have a moral life. Not when you want to assure the best for your child. Not when you want to start over. You have to make a break. Get away from the temptation. Tell your son that his mother is dead. Pretend your daughter no longer exists. You have to sacrifice to achieve respectability."

Michael did not move. And Hunter Worthington was absolutely still.

"You didn't exactly start fresh, though, did you?" Michael asked. "You're still taking money out of that company. Your first wife always knew you were still alive. She must have known where you were. From what I hear, she may never have gotten over your 'disappearance.' How many years has it been?"

For the first time, Worthington's voice cracked. "As I said, you must sacrifice to achieve respectability. You must compromise." Worthington continued to look at the rug. But now his left hand rubbed the leg of his cotton trousers. Rubbed, then pinched the fabric. Michael watched the fingers constrict, and relax, as the cloth twisted and wrinkled.

"How long has it been since you talked to your wife, Mr. Worthington?"

"I left her this morning."

"I mean your first wife. Barbetta Johnson."

Worthington's fingers continued to pull at the fabric of his clothing. The yacht made a slight rocking motion, and there was the faint, high-pitched screeching sound of a rubber fender pressing against the dock.

"I'm begging you not to air that story," Worthington said.

"I'm afraid I have to," Michael said, knowing it would sound cruel. Worthington showed no reaction. As much as he loathed the man in front of him, Michael felt a trace of sympathy.

"Would you like a drink, Mr. Carolina?"

"No thank you."

"Then perhaps you wouldn't mind getting me one. There's a bottle in that box, and some cups."

244

Michael rose and went to the box. Inside was a bottle of twelve-year-old scotch and a set of plastic cocktail glasses. He pulled the bottle out and turned toward Worthington. His hand no longer tore at the cloth of his trousers. Instead it was wrapped around the handle of a gun.

"Does this mean you don't want any ice?"

"Your story cannot air, Mr. Carolina."

"Well, under the present circumstances, I'm willing to discuss that." Worthington did not smile. He did not frown. And he did not drop the gun.

"Did I mention my friend with the camera?" Michael asked, still holding the bottle. "His name is Earl, and he's waiting for me in the parking lot."

Worthington remained frozen, the barrel of his weapon still aimed at Michael's chest.

"Don't do this, Mr. Worthington. Don't make a bad situation worse."

"I'm not going to make it worse. I'm going to make it better." Worthington's voice cracked again. "I loved my son. I did not kill him. But you and everyone else believe that I did."

"I'm willing to listen," Michael said. "But first you have to put the gun down." God, Earl, I hope you can hear this, he thought. I hope you've already called.

"I'm not putting it down, Mr. Carolina. We're going to go see your friend. We'll just walk down the dock together, and you can tell him I've agreed to an on-camera interview. You will invite him to join us here. Now set that bottle down slowly, and keep your hands where I can see them."

Michael did.

"Put your hands in your pockets. Do what I say or I will shoot you like a dog."

Worthington stood up. "You're going to climb the ladder. One step at a time. And I know it's not good seamanship, but I want you to do it backward."

Worthington was on the edge of violence, Michael realized,

but he wasn't stupid. The awkwardness of climbing out of the cockpit backward would make it impossible to run. Slowly, he backed toward the hatchway ladder and began to climb. Worthington kept the pistol trained on him. When he reached the top step, Worthington said, "Back up, and sit down."

Michael followed the instruction. Worthington climbed out of the hatch, face forward, his eyes never leaving Michael. When he was almost in the cockpit, Worthington stopped.

"Stand up again. Keep your hands in your pockets and turn your back to me. Remember what I said in the cabin, because I'm going to be right behind you."

As Michael turned he saw a shadow. There was a gunshot, and a cry erupted from Worthington. Michael froze. Then there was an oath, and he felt a sharp pain on the side of his head.

He was falling then, and it seemed to last a long time, like something out of a Peckinpah film. Then there was coolness, and wetness, and salt, enveloping him, and shocking his senses. But the pain on the side of his head made it all quite surreal. It took another few seconds before he realized he would like to breathe. He rolled to his side, and he rose, and sucked air, knowing that somehow he was still alive as he heard the screeching noise of boat fenders rubbing against a pier once again.

The man known as Bosworth Dempsey, who formerly had worked as an adult film star who called himself Dee Bonaire, had been loyal to Derek Johnson all his life. They had met in Los Angeles more than twenty-five years ago when Bosworth stepped off a bus from Yuma with dreams of becoming an actor.

"I'm getting good vibes," he said upon meeting Derek Johnson in the bus station. "Definitely good vibes."

The acting career took off immediately, though not the way Bosworth expected. Still, work in adult films offered a good living. Flat-footed since birth, Bosworth was able to wear flip-flops, something his parents, devout Christians, had always prohibited. Besides, Bosworth's new boss even wanted him to fuck his new wife. On camera, even.

But adult film work, he discovered, could grow tiresome. There were too many hours spent in bathrobes on cold, dreary sets in cold, dreary warehouses. And like an athlete, after years of performing on cue, Bosworth's timing began to slip. There were even a few embarrassing incidents when he shot blanks. So when, after years in Los Angeles, and still more in Minnesota, his boss decided to disappear, Bosworth stayed true. Derek Johnson paid him well. The butler's job in Newport required no heavy lifting, and he got to wear a tux. He also considered the position the acting role of a lifetime. He enjoyed developing his "character" with the flip-flop shoes and the vintage bathing garb that he occasionally wore in the pool of Château du Printemps.

"I got good vibes, boss. Really good vibes."

Lately, however, the role had taken some strange turns. First there was the strange business about "eliminating" the private investigator hired by the boss's lawyer. Then there was this weirdness involving a sailing race. Bosworth knew next to nothing about sailing, and his boss knew even less.

Which did little to explain why, upon pulling his sport utility back into the marina parking lot with still more groceries, he saw *Stream* backing from the marina slip.

And a man lying slumped on the ground next to a plain white van.

And another man, soaking wet, nearly stumbling as he made his way along the pier.

As he heard the wail of a siren in the distance, Bosworth realized that perhaps the show was finally coming to a close. "Bad vibes," he mumbled aloud, as he climbed back into the sport utility and started the engine. "Definitely bad vibes."

* * *

There was no fog at dawn.

This made it easy for the Newport police, still investigating the injuries to a TV news crew and a report of a gunshot at a Goat Island marina, to spot the Little Harbor yacht known as *Stream* adrift near the rocks by Fort Adams. The yacht was a major hazard, having collided with several other craft moored in the harbor and caused extensive damage.

Of course, it was also a crime scene, when the officers noticed that the body of Hunter Worthington, Jr., was hanging from the spreaders.

16

The ER doctor at Newport Hospital was thirty, his hair receding, the circles under his eyes evolving slowly into shopping bags. He wore a dubious expression as he looked at Michael, sitting on the edge of an examination table.

"You should be lying down, Mr. Carolina."

"I'm fine, dammit. Where's Earl Taylor?"

"The cameraman? He's got a mild concussion. We'll be keeping him until tomorrow. But he should be all right. You should worry about yourself."

"Are you releasing me?"

"Only if you have someone to take you home." The doctor was patient, but firm.

He looked toward the door of the ER unit and saw Carla hurrying toward him. "I do."

Their embrace was fierce. "Shirley called me from the station. She's parking the car. Are you okay?"

"He's got a bad bump on the back of his head." the doctor said politely. "He said he was knocked off a boat. Do you think you can persuade him to get some rest?"

"No," Michael said.

"Yes," Carla said at the same time. They looked at each other. "I'll try to take care of him, Doctor."

The physician nodded. "I'm writing a scrip for some pain-killers. I'll be back in a few minutes."

249

"He's dragging this out," Michael said, when the doctor was gone.

Carla saw Shirley walking through the entrance then, and waved her over.

"It's okay, Shirley, I'm fine."

"I don't know whether to hug you or slap you," the news director answered. She looked like a worried mother for a moment. "Why didn't you call us?"

"Earl was supposed to be backing me up. But I think he ran into some complications." He told them about the interview gone awry. "I don't know how much of the tape was saved."

"I have another crew down on the waterfront right now," Shirley said. "They can look for the van. And the GM sprang for a helicopter to get aerials of Worthington's boat."

"I need to get down there," Michael said.

"You need to go home," Shirley answered. She turned to Carla. "Will you take him home?"

Carla gave a smile. "If he'll let me."

Shirley gave Michael's shoulder a squeeze. "I'll call you tonight. I need to go check on Earl."

"Tell him I asked for him," Michael said. When she was gone, he turned to Carla. "You don't want to go home."

"I don't?"

"No. You want to find out what happened down at the waterfront, just like me."

"Is that right?"

"Damn right that's right." He gripped her arm and slid off the table.

"How do you feel?" She asked.

"Like I've been in a train wreck," he answered.

"A shipwreck seems more appropriate." Her voice turned gentle. "The story isn't going to go away, Michael. You can follow it tomorrow or the next day."

But the words did not ring true. And when they looked at each other, they both knew it.

"Another hour or two isn't going to kill me," he said. "I want to see this through."

The all-too-familiar TV news crews were parked at Fort Adams, cameras set up and trained on *Stream*. The reporters from the competing stations looked at Michael curiously. The crew from Channel Three, a rookie reporter and photographer both assigned to the morning and noon shows, seemed genuinely surprised.

"Are you all right?" the reporter asked. "Shirley said you were in the hospital." Her name was Eileen, and she was less than a year out of Columbia Journalism School. Michael had heard that she was smart and ambitious, though perhaps a bit naive.

"You should know better than to believe a news director," he said. "But if you tell her I was here . . ." He let the rest of the sentence hang, and then shuffled off to get a closer look at the grounded yacht.

Eileen looked puzzled for a moment. "He seems pissed," she said to Carla, who half-grimaced in agreement. "Just give him some room. I don't think we'll be here long."

With the tide ebbing no one had noticed in time to keep the yacht from going aground. *Stream*'s hull was now tilted at an extreme angle. Hunter Worthington's body continued to twist in the early-morning breeze, the policemen unsure how to bring him down without tipping the ship farther and risking injury to the officers. Several boats were circling at a distance, watching the commotion, and there were a few dozen observers on shore. Among them Michael recognized a few from the Newport Harbor waterfront. And farther down, next to the rocks, was the peculiar woman who'd destroyed his live shot the night that the Laser regatta had ended. She held her arms wrapped around her, her gaze frozen on the yacht and the police boats.

"Remember her?" he said to Carla.

Carla looked at the woman, who appeared to be shivering.

251

"Yeah. Her name is Brandy, I think. Kind of pathetic, isn't she?"

Michael stared at the boats, but they were too far away for him to make out the people aboard. He turned his attention back to those on land.

The same thought hit them then. Carla took his hand, gripping it so tightly it made the tips of his fingers white. For a moment, Michael did not speak. When the words did come, they were slow, as if each one was a labor to produce. "There wasn't any tender."

"Tender?"

"There wasn't any tender. *Stream* didn't have a small boat to launch to come ashore. And a water taxi would have reported any problem."

Carla glanced at the body of Hunter Worthington. "So whoever hauled him up probably had to swim."

They turned back toward the homeless woman. She was still shivering, still staring at the yacht, and this did not change as Carla and Michael approached. When they were less than fifty feet away, they both stopped.

"Look at what's next to her," Michael said.

The weapon was familiar. After a few seconds Michael realized it was the same one Worthington had trained on him the night before. How had she disarmed him? Then he remembered her grip. The woman, he realized, was unusually strong. Strong enough, perhaps, to knock a man down. Definitely strong enough to do it with a heavy metal winch handle. And strong enough to slip a rope around a limp man's neck and haul him into the air.

"Brandy?" Carla said. The woman did not answer.

They stepped closer. Still the woman did not move. But now they could see that her clothes, the same khaki pants and weathered blouse, were dripping. Her hair hung around her lined face in tangled strings. When they were within twenty feet, they could see her lips moving, though no words could be heard.

"Don't go closer," Michael said.

"Brandy?" Carla said again. The woman kept staring at the yacht. She was shaking now. Carla took another step, and heard the words, raspy and thin.

"Oh, Billy Budd. Oh, dear Billy. Oh, Billy Budd, we've done what we have to do. Oh, Billy Budd, oh, dear Billy."

Her words were singsong, a chant, repeated in almost a whisper. But the voice was familiar now. Carla had heard it the day before. And with the sound, the face was more easily recognized.

"Barbetta?"

The woman paused for a second. Then she resumed the chanting.

"Oh, Billy Budd. Oh, dear Billy."

Carla took two more steps, with Michael coming behind her. Carla stopped and held up her hand to warn him: don't. She took another step, and was now less than ten feet from the woman, and the gun that lay next to her on the rocky shore. From the water there was a shout. Someone in one of the police boats was watching them now.

"I won't hurt you, Barbetta."

". . . done what we had to do, dear Billy. Oh, dear Billy . . ."

Carla took another step. The woman continued to chant, but her voice was fainter now. Suddenly she looked at Carla, her face taut and alert. "He needed killing."

"Who did?"

"That bastard swinging in the breeze," she said, her tone not quite matter-of-fact. There was a trace of satisfaction blended in. The woman was content. "I killed him before, you know. When he was young. And if I have to, I'll do it again."

Carla barely breathed. "You killed him before? When, Barbetta?"

"It seems like just a few days ago. I saw him on the docks, saw him on that boat. I waited for him. During the races, I waited for him. And then one night, when the races were running, I watched him go out to the boat. He was so young, so handsome. Like the days when I first met him. When he said we'd have a life together.

"I waited till he was on that boat. Till the lights were on. That's when I swam out and climbed aboard. He must have heard, because he was out and looking, calling out. Wondering. I think he was afraid. I wanted him to be. That's when I hit him. Watched him go down. Then I hauled him up, just like Billy Budd. It should have been enough. It should have been enough."

The woman had made no move to the gun, but it was still within easy reach. She shivered again, and then relaxed. "Oh, Billy boy, dear Billy . . . oh, my poor son." The woman was sobbing now, slipping away into grief. Carla weighed the risk of reaching for the gun. It was still too far away.

The woman gasped, and twisted toward her.

"He was my son, you know. I killed him."

"Yes," Carla said. "But you thought you'd killed his father."

Barbetta Johnson opened her mouth, her face creased and dirty, a thick film of flesh and soil stretched over demons screaming inside. But there was no sound. The sobs were all the more painful for their silence.

Carla took another step and plucked the gun from the rocks. She threw the weapon, and it landed without any detectable sound on a small patch of sand.

The woman blinked, offered a weak smile, and relaxed her arms. It was then that Carla noticed the patch of blood, still wet, on the left side of her chest.

"Michael, she's been shot."

Suddenly Barbetta began to laugh, the noise like a dull saw cutting through knotty pine.

"The sins of the fathers are visited on the sons," she said. "And the mothers on the daughters."

17

They crossed the Pell Bridge without a word, drawing down the visors to ward off the rays of the fading sun. Michael handed Carla the tollbooth fare and leaned back in his seat as she accelerated down the two-mile stretch that would take them over the Jamestown Bridge and on to the western side of the bay.

"I suspect she'll wind up in the forensic unit at Pinel," Carla said, referring to the state mental hospital. "I don't think the women's prison is equipped to handle her."

"You really think she was delusional?" Michael asked. "Even if she thought she was killing her ex-husband, she still intended to kill. The law can't permit that."

"You're right. It's called transferred intent. If she kills someone by mistake, thinking it's someone else, it's still murder. That's the law. But you're forgetting something."

Michael turned toward her. "What's that?"

"Hunter Jr. was a dirtball who corrupted his first wife and then abandoned her, not to mention trying to have me killed. Juries have a funny way of forgiving defendants whose victims deserved to die. Besides, by the time she gets to trial her lawyer will make her sound crazier than John Hinckley."

"You feel sorry for her, don't you?"

Carla hesitated only a moment before asking, "Don't you?"

"Some. A little. Not as much as for her children."

Carla did not argue.

A Cranston police cruiser was parked on the street when they pulled into the driveway. The two young officers at the front door turned and walked toward them, one holding a piece of paper in his hand.

"Does a Paul Carolina live here?" the first officer asked, gently slapping the piece of paper against his leg.

"He did," Michael said.

"Do you know where I can find him?" The second officer's tone suggested he did not expect an affirmative response.

"In all honesty, no," Michael said.

"What's he done?" Carla asked.

"We have a warrant from the district court," the first officer explained patiently. "He failed to appear for a pretrial yesterday."

The state police case, Michael remembered.

"If he turns himself in, the judge might cancel the warrant fee," the first officer said. "Plus he won't have to spend a night in jail."

"If I see him, I'll tell him," Michael said. The officer, evidently satisfied he was telling the truth, said goodbye and climbed into his cruiser. Carla unlocked the front door, while Michael watched the patrol car drive off.

"Do you want something to eat?" she asked when he had come inside. But Michael did not answer her. He found a seat on the couch in front of her television set, where they had all watched the baseball game a few days before.

Carla picked up the mail. There were two bills, and a news magazine she never had enough time to read. And an envelope, scrawled with her name. And Michael's. She tore the envelope open, noting the postmark. Grand Central Station in New York. The writing was in blue ink:

Dear Michael and Carla,

I tried to do right. Sorry it didn't work. Hope you can understand.
I'll call when I find a place to stay.

You make a fine couple. I'm proud of you.
Try not to think bad of me.

Paul

"He's not going to call," Michael said. "And he won't be back as long as that warrant is active."

He pressed his cheek into his left shoulder, as if he were wiping something away. And he was, Carla realized when she saw the tear streak on the side of his face.

"Michael?"

"There isn't much difference between them," he said. "Hunter Worthington and my father."

Carla moved closer to him. "We all have demons, Michael. Hunter Worthington destroyed his family. But your father is different. Paul really tried to change. That call he made to me . . . he was trying to help. And for all the pain he's caused, he hasn't destroyed you."

They were both silent then, feeling the warmth of the sun coming through the window.

"I need to sleep," Michael said.

She kissed him, gently, on the forehead, and listened while he climbed the stairs to the bedroom. It was late afternoon, and the warmth that had just been comforting now seemed oppressive. She opened the windows to the back porch, then opened a cookbook, looking for something to make for dinner. But the day's events kept creeping onto the horizon of her thoughts.

Carla picked up the phone and dialed.

"Hello." The familiar baritone was a comfort.

"Hi, Dad."

"How's my little girl?" Her father was joyous. She wiped her own tears away, and talked with him for an hour.

EPILOGUE

The following Saturday, an hour before dawn, Michael and Carla drove to Newport, to the rocky shoreline near Brenton Reef. The tide was making its final push before falling slack, the surf boiling with foam and the air filled with the splashing sound of striped bass chasing baitfish. Carla rigged two fly rods with sand eel imitations.

"Remember your timing," she said. "Hold your cast until just as the wave hits." She expertly hauled the line, shooting it into the ebbing surf, then stripping it back in precise, expert strokes. The tip of her rod bent slightly, and she lifted, setting the hook.

The fish, deceived and sensing peril, bolted for the safety of deeper water. The thick, greenish-yellow line spit out of the rod guides until the slack disappeared, and the gears of her reel let out a high, machined, piercing scream. It was a wonderful sound. Carla took eighteen minutes to land the fish, a twenty-nine-inch striper, just large enough to keep.

They released it anyway, Michael helping revive the fish, sliding it back and forth in the surf until it recovered from the battle. The fish thanked them with a flip of its tail.

"Talked to Earl yesterday," Michael said. "He'll be back to work Monday." He tried a cast. The fly line hit the surf a second after the ebb and was washed inshore.

"You're improving," she said. He stripped his line in again and tried another cast. This one was better, and a fish struck the fly, then threw it.

"Damn," Michael said, smiling. He was enjoying himself. After another cast, she told him that Balboni had called.

"What did he want?"

"Still looking for my report. I told him he'd get it this week. He asked me to send him some business cards so he can share them with other lawyers. It's like nothing ever happened."

Michael looked surprised.

"You going to take him up on that?"

Carla smiled. "I think I need to develop another source of referral."

Dawn was spectacular, a blend of yellow and orange and blue, with a string of low, flat white clouds pasting the eastern sky. The breeze began to stiffen. They cast for two more hours, Carla hooking half a dozen stripers, and Michael finally catching one. They released them all, and as they were climbing the rocks the sound of a cannon ripped the air.

"The race got started," Michael said. Sure enough, a line of yachts began to appear, tacking out of Narragansett Bay, toward the open water of Rhode Island Sound and Block Island and, if they steered south and east, toward the pink sands of Bermuda.

Carla traced a finger along his forearm. "Did you ever race?"

"A few times," he said. "But I'd rather cruise. For me, sailing is not being the fastest. It's working with what's natural, holding on to it for a while, and letting it go again. That's a powerful feeling, when you harness the wind. But you can't sail forever. Sooner or later, you have to let the wind blow without you."

Carla smiled. "You mean you don't wish you were with them?"

Michael wrapped an arm around her and slowly shook his head. "The best part of the race is when it's over."

They watched the boats until their sails melted into white chop.